BEYOND BERLIN

Penelope Nelson has worked as a researcher, book reviewer and TAFE teacher, and held jobs in community relations and social policy. She spent nearly five years living near Narrabri, NSW, and a year in New Mexico but has returned to Sydney where she grew up.

Beyond Berlin is her third novel, following *Medium Flyers* (1990) and *Prophesying Backwards* (1991).

BEYOND BERLIN

PENELOPE NELSON

ALLEN & UNWIN

First published in 1995 by
Allen & Unwin Australia Pty Ltd
9 Atchison Street, St Leonards, NSW 2065 Australia

National Library of Australia
Cataloguing-in-Publication entry:

Nelson, Penelope.

  Beyond Berlin.
  ISBN 1 86373 847 9.
  I. Title.

A823.3

Set in 10/13 pt Palatino by DOCUPRO, Sydney
Printed by Australian Print Group, Maryborough, Victoria

10 9 8 7 6 5 4 3 2 1

for Timothy Nelson, who was there

... a melting pot of everything that is evil—prostitutes, drinking houses, cinemas, Marxism, Jews, strippers, Negroes dancing, and all the vile offshoots of so-called 'modern art'.

Adolf Hitler on Berlin,
Volkischer Beobachter, July 1928

PROLOGUE
Australia, 1990

The headlights sliced a yellow path through the darkness. Libby was humming along with the car radio. *Like a bridge over troubled water* . . . Simon and Garfunkel. A seventies song. She remembered bursting into homesick tears in the commune kitchen in Berlin as she listened to it. She'd snapped the radio off when she heard someone coming. In Breisacherstraβe it was a crime to listen to Voice of America. She'd tried explaining to Hannelore, Russell and Guenther that there was no political significance in her listening habits: she just missed hearing English. Russell, who didn't like pop music, refused to come to her defence. 'You can always speak English to me, kiddo,' he'd said. She'd made some crack about his indecipherable Scots accent, but the episode had ended with her sensing, not for the first time, that the other members of the commune considered her frivolous. Perhaps she had been.

By day, it took about nine hours to get to Sydney. At night there was much less traffic on the highways, and none at all on these back roads, so she ought to reach Mascot in about seven and a half hours.

You wouldn't know Berlin, Hannelore had scrawled on her Christmas card. In Breisacherstraβe, Christmas cards had been considered the last word in decadent bourgeois consumerism.

1

Commune members demonstrated outside department stores to protest against the consumer excesses of Christmas. Hannelore had even persuaded a couple of elderly Lutheran nuns to join the students and anarchists waving placards outside Ka-De-We. *Sometimes in my nightmares the Wall is still there, and the past year is just a dream.* Neat, upright handwriting. Hannelore had been the one who drew up the housework rosters and kept the kitchen accounts.

Then, out of the blue, three weeks ago, came the mysterious summons. Just come if you possibly can, Libby, Hannelore had begged on the telephone. The phrases she used sounded like missives from a vanished, cold war world. *Utmost secrecy. Important to all the former members of the commune. Legal ramifications.* 'For God's sake, Hannelore,' Libby demanded, 'what's going on?'

'Just come. Is the money a problem?'

'No, I can afford the ticket, if that's what you mean.'

'We can talk when you get here. You're needed, Libby.'

With a fleshy thwack, a kangaroo collided with the bumper bar. Libby slammed on the brake. The animal was slumped in front of the Landcruiser. She got out, but the lights, on high beam, shone above and beyond her victim. When she adjusted them she could see the crimson gash. 'I didn't mean to, I didn't mean to,' she murmured. Surely the thing was dead; surely it couldn't survive that impact. Please God, please God, she prayed. But life had not yet left the kangaroo: the headlights illuminated an eyeball which was turned towards the source of light and a long ear alert, too late, to danger. Libby's throat constricted.

She could not leave it to die slowly. The question was whether to run right over it, or hit it hard between the eyes. There was no flashlight in the car, so she had to hold the tool box under the headlights while she identified a suitable weapon. Taking the long metal jack in her hand, she walked over to the slumped animal. She was about to take aim when she saw that its head had gone slack and its flanks had stopped quivering. Thankfully she put the heavy piece of metal back.

'I just didn't see it, I truly didn't see it,' she said aloud. But good intentions were no excuse. She ought to know that by now.

Libby drove on cautiously, her right foot never far from the brake pedal.

She'd checked in her baggage and made two tours of the gift shops, tempted by overpriced Aboriginal T-shirts and multicoloured designer jackets when she finally caught sight of Evan. Anyone who saw that walk could pick him as a country boy, she thought, as he strode towards her in his elastic-sided boots, arms swinging, fringe dangling over one eye. He had a friend with him. Should she know his name?

Evan hugged her briefly. 'Mum, this is Ben Overman, I don't think you've met him before. He drove me out here.' Libby greeted Ben, then turned her attention to her son. 'I've parked near the middle lift on the west side, in building B,' she told him, handing over the car keys.

'How long will you be away?' Ben asked.

'I'm not sure,' Libby said. 'Depends how I get on.'

'Isn't it all a bit vague? Shouldn't you be more definite about your plans?' Evan demanded.

'At my age, you mean?'

'No, but it does seem something of a magical mystery tour.'

'I'll send you an address as soon as I can,' Libby said. 'In the meantime you can write to me care of Hannelore in Berlin. I'll keep in touch with her wherever I am.'

'I'm not telling you how to run your life, Mum, it's just that some of us think you're behaving oddly. One moment you're talking about buying a house in Wilga Wilga and divorcing Dad—with God knows what consequences for the future of the property. The next moment you're airily handing the keys to the Landcruiser to me at the airport. You can't just walk out on your life, you know.'

'I know, Evan. I'm not doing that, but do stop pumping me as if some secret was being kept from you. And you'll have to leave Will and me to work things out ourselves, I'm afraid. You're hardly a qualified counsellor, unless psychology I's changed a lot since my day.'

'Jesus, woman, in the last few months I can't have an ordinary conversation with you without you getting all het up. You've convinced yourself that I'm a spy for Dad or something.'

'Evan, I never felt you were a spy or treated you like one. Anyway, we don't want to wash our family linen in front of poor Ben.'

They were interrupted by a voice on the public address system. *Passengers are reminded not to leave any luggage or personal items unattended. Please report any suspicious unclaimed packages to an airport official. Passengers are reminded . . .*

'My father was in a bomb scare at Chicago airport last year,' Ben said. 'They evacuated the whole terminal, but they couldn't find anything.'

'Mum doesn't scare easily though, do you?' Evan half-joked, half-taunted. 'Dad says you were practically a member of the Baader–Meinhof group when you were in Berlin.'

'What a load of garbage you've chosen to believe. He knows that's not true and so do you. And there's no secrecy whatsoever about this trip. I'm simply curious to see Berlin again now that the Wall's down. Apart from that I have an open itinerary.'

'Sounds romantic to me,' Ben said. 'Footloose and fancy free.'

Lufthansa announce that flight 661 to Frankfurt via Bangkok is now boarding. Passengers should proceed to the gate immediately.

'That's me,' Libby said. 'Now don't forget to keep the car registration and insurance up to date, will you?'

4

'No worries, Mother dear, and I'm eating plenty of vitamin C too.'

'Nice to have met you, Ben. Bye, my darling.' Ludicrous how emotional airport farewells make me feel, Libby thought, as her son's hug brought her to the brink of tears. The image which came to her closed eyelids was the gaze of the wounded kangaroo. Almost breaking into a jog, she headed for the security barrier.

CHAPTER 1

Berlin, 1970

'*H*allo.' The emphasis on the first syllable made the word peremptory.

'Good morning,' Libby stammered in her classroom German, 'is it possible to speak with Russell Muir please?'

The female voice replied with a torrent of words. Libby could make out only *Nein, leider* and *nicht hier*.

'What a pity,' she said. It was a textbook phrase. She never said such things in English. 'May I—um—please—excuse me . . .' She abandoned her inadequate German. 'Look, you don't speak English, do you? Perhaps I could leave him a message.'

'Yes, of course. Here I am Hannelore. Russell is away for a day or two. Your message?'

'Could you tell him that Libby Milroy from Australia phoned. I was given his number by Jane Arnold in London. I'm looking for a place to stay for a while. Jane thought Russell might know of somewhere I could get a room for a few months. She even thought I might be able to stay there.'

'More slowly, please. You hope to live here?'

'Well, I hope to rent a room somewhere in Berlin for a few months, and Jane, she knows all these underground types in London, you know, and she suggested Russell might . . .'

'Excuse me, please. This is not Russell's apartment alone. This is a commune. Each resident may invite a friend to stay for two days. For a few months, it is not the decision of Russell or of me. It is a matter for a meeting.'

'Yes, yes, I see. Well, I didn't just expect to barge in. Of course it's up to the whole group. I absolutely understand that.'

'It is a democratic commune. With certain political obligations.'

'Yeah, well, that's fine. I'm quite good at washing up. And other people's political opinions are fine with me.'

'Perhaps I am not clear. It is a matter for the meeting to decide if your politics are fine with the commune.'

'Ah. Yes, there's a difference, of course. I understand. Um, Hannelore, what do you think I should do? Come round and see Russell first or just come to the meeting? When do you get together?'

'We meet at eight on Tuesdays, after dinner. Russell will be here by then. I make no promises about a room, but I invite you to dine with us at seven. You have a map, yes?'

'Yes, I've got a map. Thanks, dinner would be really nice.'

'*Ja.*' Hannelore's monosyllable did not encourage further conversation.

'Well,' Libby said, 'I guess it's *wiederhoren*, or *wiedersehen*, or whatever.' She sat on her hotel bed feeling hot and flustered. It was hard work trying to communicate, even if the other person's command of English turned out to be far better than her German.

The window ledge outside her room was lined with snow. Small scurries of snowflakes fell past the window on to the brick courtyard below. Though situated not far from the Küfürstendamm, the hotel was quiet. It was also warm, comfortable and too expensive for more than a few nights' stay. If I'm not accepted by this commune, Libby thought, I'll either have to move to a youth hostel or go back to London. She'd told her parents she wanted to improve her German. She hadn't studied it since the school certificate. Her determi-

7

nation to come to Berlin was the result of two things: Christopher Isherwood's accounts of the prewar scene; and a conversation at Jane Arnold's London flat in which an English film-maker and a German artist had agreed that Berlin was once again in the vanguard of art, film and ideas.

When she'd mentioned a desire to come here, Jane and the German artist had both come up with the same name: Russell Muir. Now she would have to wait until Tuesday before meeting the photographer whose contacts were said to include the entire Berlin underground. Perhaps they didn't say 'underground' here. That Hannelore woman sounded pretty stitched up. She wondered what political credentials she was supposed to establish. Would it help that she'd thrown a policeman's hat back into the crowd at an anti-war march? Or what about the time that principal had sent her home from a practice teaching assignment because of her moratorium badge? Surely she'd paid her dues for the cause?

She had one other telephone number. Julie Brandon was the former pen-pal of her sister, Sue. She dialled. 'Hello,' she heard again, but this time in a warm southern American accent. Soon she was arranging to visit Julie in a suburb to the south of the city.

Even in the sensible camel-hair coat her mother had advised her to buy at David Jones, and the less sensible high black boots she had bought in London, Libby found it cold in the streets. She looked out the window of the computer train at walls of graffiti, some of it in English. LBJ, STOP THE WAR, NAPALM WASHINGTON. A more perplexing slogan caught her eye. A WAREHOUSE IS BURNING. A warehouse? Maybe they meant department store, *Warenhaus* in German. Hadn't some German radicals set fire to a department store a couple of years ago? Not here, surely. Frankfurt?

The train rushed past a huge wood. Acres of bare white tree trunks standing in white snow. She consulted her map. Grunewald. Not too green at the moment. Next came an icy lake, but there were so many lakes on the map it was hard to be sure which it might be. There was no sense, in this part of the city, of its being the combat zone of her imagination, tense, built-up and dominated by the notorious Wall.

The Brandons lived a few blocks from Nikolassee station. With their picturesque gingerbread architecture, the grocery store, butcher's shop, bakery and shoemaker's cellar looked like illustrations from a children's book. A mother in a fur hat passed, pulling her toddler behind her in a sled. In his red zip-up snow suit and hood, which covered his entire body apart from the cheeks and nose, the child looked like a miniature Santa Claus. Three- and four-storey buildings stood among tall trees and stone walls. They appeared to have escaped the bombing that made it necessary to rebuild much of the inner city. Libby took a newcomer's delight in the bright yellow post-boxes and wrought-iron street signs.

The apartment was on the top floor of a turn-of-the-century villa. 'My, what a surprise,'Julie Brandon greeted her, 'meeting you before I get to meet Sue. And she's the one who wrote to me all those years. Do you look like her? No, not very much, to judge by photographs, do you?'

'Sue's fairer,' Libby agreed. Unsisterly feelings surged through Libby with suddenness and passion. She had spent a lifetime listening to comparisons with her sister. Clever, pretty, successful in areas that ranged from horseriding to chemistry, Sue established herself from an early age as a daughter to be proud of. Libby, three years younger, had been bright and not bad looking, despite stronger features and darker colouring. At school and in the family she felt something of an also-ran when people talked about her sister. Reacting against her sister's knack of delighting parents and teachers, Libby was more of a tearaway in her teens.

Studying in Sydney, hundreds of miles away from her family, Libby had gained confidence in herself and overcome some of her inevitable jealousy. Now, in her twenties, with long ginger hair and a trim figure, she felt as if she had brought the vigour of the outdoors into the overheated, pastel room. Julie Brandon wore black spectacles, and had a great deal of sprayed, bouffant hair around a chubby face. She gestured to Libby to sit on a chintz sofa.

'I don't hear from Sue too often these days since she took up that veterinary—what is it?—artificial something or other. In Brisbane?'

'She does artificial insemination for cattle studs on the Darling Downs, not too far from Brisbane. I don't hear from her much either,' Libby said.

A baby crawled towards them, nudging a wooden roller toy with a bell inside it.

'This is Albert,' Julie said, lifting the child on to her lap. 'Our son and heir. We wanted to give him a name that can be used in Germany as well as America.'

Libby could not remember meeting an Albert before. 'Very nice,' she said. 'Are you expecting to stay a while?'

'Larry's an officer,' Julie said, 'so they'd like him to stay longer than his original term. It depends on a lot of things. We haven't really decided. I'm not real crazy about being stationed here, but when you consider the alternatives . . . '

'Vietnam, you mean?'

'Yeah, compared to that, this isn't too bad, though it's tough being so far from the PX. There's some good things about army life. Everyone's kind of flat out having their families on the army. Babies everywhere. You get your medical treatment free and all.'

'That's great.'

'Before I had Albert I used to get real bored. I baked and I ate, and I baked and I ate, and before I could turn around I'd put on twenty pounds. My O.B.G.Y.N. nearly had a fit. Will you have a slice of cake? I just have to finish the frosting. Maybe you could hold Albert for a moment.'

Libby rattled toys and turned magazine pages for the baby

while Julie whipped brown sugar into a fluffy white mix and slathered caramel frosting over a substantial pound cake.

'I can well believe that it's easy to put on weight, if your baking's as good as this,' Libby said. 'This is an archetypal German thing to do, isn't it, sit around having coffee and torte?'

'I guess so, but I've never dared go into one of those smart restaurants with the tables on the sidewalk.'

'Why ever not?'

'Well, I'd have to speak German, and I don't like that, and I don't want to go into a restaurant on my own. Now I'd have Albert with me, and what if he broke something?'

'He wouldn't, I'm sure. If I'm still here in the warmer weather, we'll go into the Kaffee Krantzler or somewhere like that together. It'll be fun.'

'You think you might still be here in the spring and summer?'

'I'm hoping to get a room in a . . .' Libby hesitated to say 'commune' to her sister's pen-pal. 'An apartment in Dahlem, near the university somewhere. I'm going to see them on Tuesday to see if I'm suitable.'

'German people? Do you speak German?'

'At least two of them speak English. But it would be marvellous to get the chance to improve my German. I did some at high school.'

'I wish I had. It took me almost a year to learn how to ask for a transfer ticket on the bus. We're not allowed to use the S-Bahn, you know, because it's run from the east. If they wanted to, the communists could suddenly cancel all the normal stops and take us right into East Berlin.'

'I came on the S-Bahn. It seemed like a regular suburban rail service.'

'Yeah, well, we have to do what the security people tell us, being army and all. But I hope you stay around for a while. I only ever see other mothers and babies from the base.'

'It will be nice to see a European spring. Our seasons are the other way round, of course.'

'I'll have to do my exercises before spring comes or I'll never dare to get into a swimsuit. I've got some diagrams in one of these magazines.' A tall pile of *Family Circles* stood beside an equally tall pile of *Huntsman and Rifleman*.

'The Wannsee isn't far from here,' Julie went on. 'It's a lake, but it's got a kind of beach—they've carted in sand, I guess—and they have these funny little change sheds. It's embarrassing with the little kids though, they let them run around on the sand as naked as the day they were born.'

'We did too, as kids,' Libby said. 'But we were in the bush.'

'Yes, Sue sent me quite a few photos.' She giggled. 'Not of anybody nekkid, of course.'

'I saw some of yours, too.' Libby remembered a picture of a younger Julie, with even more alarmingly teased hair, in a cheerleader's outfit. She thought she might get to like Julie, bouffant and all. 'I'll have to send Sue some of you with Albert.'

The following Tuesday evening Libby rang a doorbell in a shabby hallway in a villa in Dahlem. The door was flung open by a young woman who wore her brown hair in a waist-length plait. 'Come in. I am Hannelore. You are Libby, *nicht*? We all await you in the living room.' She led the way along a twisted corridor, leading Libby to a high-ceilinged room lined with bookshelves. A stocky man with close-cropped hair and a dark-haired young woman in a tight leather miniskirt were sitting at a long table.

'Now, I present to you, the members of Breisacherstraße commune. Here is Guenther, and beside him Romy.'

Libby gave a tight social smile. She wanted desperately to be accepted. 'Hi, I'm Libby,' she said, moving forward to shake hands.

'Russell must be in the kitchen. He comes momentarily,' Hannelore said.

Libby was standing a couple of feet from the closed kitchen door. Turning towards it she found herself eyeball to eyeball with a bearded man. As she took an involuntary step backwards, he proved to be an optical illusion. With his head turned in half-profile and his beard jutting out at an angle, and badly tailored trousers flapping round his shins, Lenin glared humourlessly from a life-size poster. As Libby stood swaying a little in her fashionable boots, recovering from her double take, Lenin lurched towards her. The door opened, revealing another bearded man, of much the same height but three-dimensional. Russell had reddish colouring, metal-rimmed glasses and a sardonic expression.

'Don't tell me,' he said in a working-class Scots accent. 'Another innocent abroad.'

CHAPTER 2

Dear Jane,

Here I am in Breisacherstraβe, not a guest and not yet an actual member of the commune. Before I could even stay here I had to get through a dinner which was sort of like a job interview. We ate huge servings of soup (the food is not bad here) with Schrippen, the local rolls. All the while these four people stared at me and asked questions, pretending to be casual. How I got to know about them. What I thought of the Vietnam War. Whether I wasn't contaminated by the fascist-imperialist ideology of the Australian government, an ally of America in Vietnam. They really talk like that. Is it my fault Harold Holt wanted to go all the way with LBJ??? Obscene thought! Anyhow I told them about the moratorium marches and having a good crack at the cops that time, but they still looked dubious. Then they got on to the fact that I come from the bush. Suddenly they wanted to know if I knew about putting up tents, reading maps, shooting rabbits and all that. Doesn't everyone, I said, bunging it on a bit. Can't help it—they are so serious about everything. 'Serious' is a term of approval here. I don't remember anyone in Sydney or London using the word that way. Is it just the Germans? No, can't be, because Russell is Scotch. (Scottish?)

Russell acts like he is not so much bored by me as amused by my struggle to get the hang of this very serious commune, where he already knows the rules. They were just more or less deciding in

14

my favour (because of my looks, or my moratorium badge, or whatever) when Russell came up with this scheme that I could stay for a few weeks on probation. They have these Tuesday night meetings, with topics. I am to give a paper in five weeks time on British imperialism in the Middle East, a subject about which I know nothing and care less. I guess I have five weeks to find out. I can give it in English, that's one good thing. After that, I'm either in or out. Hallelujah! Did you have any idea, when you gave me Russell's address, how solemnly political everyone is over here? I keep wondering if Russell's having me on, somehow. Like a boy from Glasgow couldn't be into all this left–right right–wrong shit, could he? He's good-looking—if you like redheads.

Hope all is okay with you. If it gets too hopeless here—or if my paper gets the thumbs down—I'll try to get a cheap ticket back to London. But I don't want to give up too easily. Against my principles. I am picking up a few German phrases, even if they're only political slogans. It's a beaut city. Doesn't feel walled at all. Days go by without any reason to get within sight of the Wall; that could explain it. Haven't been into the East yet or encountered the checkpoints. Cheers, comrade. (Catching, eh?)

Love,
Libby

When Libby pulled back the long amber wool curtain in her high-ceilinged room, she looked out on bare trees, snowy yards, and a street with only suburban traffic. Students went past on bicycles; mothers walked children to school in the early morning and collected them at lunchtime. Impatient with what appeared to be routine, orderly lives, Libby wondered where the artists, musicians and writers were hanging out. Even within the apartment, communal life followed certain routines. Everyone except Russell got up early. Romy, Guenther and Hannelore breakfasted on hot porridge and coffee before setting out, well wrapped, soon after sunrise. Romy wore a lambskin coat with the fleece turned inward;

the outside was decorated with coloured embroidery. Her job involved something to do with children: *Kinder* was the only fraction of her reply Libby could follow when she asked where she worked. Guenther and Hannelore both studied medicine. Russell's working hours were less predictable. He generally stumbled into the kitchen at about ten, talked back at the news headlines on the radio, then took off, saying little more to Libby than '*Tchuss*' or 'See ya, kiddo'.

One roster for household chores was pinned on the door of the refrigerator; there was another in the bathroom. Libby's name was added in neat black script soon after her arrival. She was glad to take turns cleaning the kitchen, cooking dinner and clearing up in the living room. The lavatory was scrubbed daily, by the same mathematical progression through names of commune members as every other task. Even shopping was done to a system. When Libby unthinkingly bought a small jar of instant coffee, Hannelore remonstrated, 'This is not the one we buy, neither the brand nor the amount. You see, this container in the cupboard—better coffee and better value.'

'I'm sorry, I didn't know. Didn't think, I suppose.'

'No matter. But you now understand our system, *nicht*?'

'Yes, I now understand.' Libby smiled wryly. For Hannelore, getting the most out of the communal budget was a moral question.

'You should come with me to eat lunch,' Hannelore offered one day after spending the morning at home studying. 'For the rest of us, that is the main meal of the day. I can get entry to the cafeteria at the hospital for you. It is excellent value, the same food the patients eat. All the medical students and nurses eat there—and some of our friends.'

'Thanks, that'd be good.'

Serious, direct, Libby thought, giving the words a German inflection, as she followed Hannelore along the cobbled pavements. Shoulders forward, her horse-blanket cape held close around her body, Hannelore had a determined stride. Libby, in the camel-hair coat she was coming to view as an archetypal bourgeois garment, followed in her high shiny London boots. 'Many famous paintings,' Hannelore said as they passed the Dahlem Museum. 'In the western tradition, of course,' she added. Libby waited for further labels. Bourgeois? Decadent? But Hannelore had something else on her mind. 'Also many fine ethnographic exhibits,' she added, 'carried far from the region of origin.'

'Egypt?' Libby asked. 'I read something in a guidebook.'

'No, not this museum. Closer to your part of the world. The Asia–Pacific region. You know surely of the German colonial history in Papua New Guinea?'

'Sort of. Now that you mention it.'

'I unfortunately am not an expert,' Hannelore admitted. 'Some fine rooms of things.'

'I'll take a look sometime.'

They took the underground to the teaching hospital. Hannelore guided Libby to a vast basement cafeteria, where white linoleum floors reflected the mauve neon-tube lighting. The smell of boiled cabbage reminded Libby of old country hotels. Hannelore showed her where to pick up a tray, gave her hints on how to pass as an exchange student if challenged, and watched as their plates were piled with stew, potatoes and cabbage. 'You have an international student card, *nicht*?' Hannelore asked.

'Sure.'

'Okay then, you can eat here any weekday you like.'

'Any time I'm starving?'

'Hospital work means long hours and heavy responsibility. It's rather—how do you say?'

'Strenuous. It's fine, Hannelore, I'm just not used to seeing such huge helpings at midday. It's fine, really. Just different. You know, culturally different from what I'm used to. Our students eat sandwiches, fruit and the occasional ice-cream at lunch.'

'How does it go with your topic for the meeting?'

'It doesn't, really, Hannelore. I'm a bit nervous about it. I'm so ignorant. British imperialism, for God's sake!'

'You must know something about it.'

'You mean living in a country that was once a British colony? Perhaps.'

'For example, the economic interests. Oil.'

'Yeah. That's a thought.'

'And the corrupt regimes supported by the British and Americans. The Shah of Iran, for one case. The poverty of his people. The lack of justice in his country. The secret police. Torture. And you know about the demonstration here, the way the fascist police turned on the students?'

'No, I'm afraid I don't.' Libby could only remember stories in the *Women's Weekly* about the Shah's beautiful but infertile second wife, Soraya, who had been replaced by a Paris-educated architecture student who had since borne him an heir. She was about to make some comment about this family saga when she realised that Hannelore had tears in her eyes.

'There was a student demonstration in the middle of 1967, to protest the visit to Berlin by the Shah.' Hannelore's voice was shaking. 'Hundreds of students were there, activists and those just new to politics. The police went crazy. They could have spoken to the student leaders. Everyone would have gone home in peace if we had been permitted to show our placards and have our voice, you know? Instead they turned into fascists. Into animals. They kept us away from the official party completely. They used terrror tactics.'

'Tear gas? Horses?'

'No, my dear, it was shooting, like war. They killed a student. Benno Ohnesorg, he was an innocent young student, he had no gun, it was his first protest march. Dead. From this day the Berlin students formed the Second of June Movement.'

'They killed a student in cold blood? It sounds incredible.'

'Less incredible here. These people, they have an automatic response of violence. The police are led and trained by men who are the generation of Hitler.'

'Even so, you'd think there would be some rules on the right to march. Or a willingness to negotiate.'

'My dear, you speak as if we live in a democracy,' Hannelore said, the confidence returning to her voice. 'It is true, there is the illusion of democracy and freedom. Under those banners the old ways of militarism and repression continue. These are the people who tell their own children that they saw nothing and did nothing during the war. There is a collective forgetfulness, always tricks of the eye and mind. They told us so little in school, and what they did was supposed to convince us that 1945 represented a complete break with the past. Of course, this is just more of the self-delusion of that generation. It is important not to confuse the myth with the reality.'

'My mistake,' Libby said. 'It's all very new to me. This food tastes better than it looks, doesn't it?'

'Even so.'

As the days passed, the warm, filling cafeteria lunches no longer smelt so institutional to Libby; the days were still bitterly cold and by midday she was ready for a big meal. She searched for material on the Middle East in libraries at the Free University near Breisacherstraβe, but there was little in English apart from periodicals. 'You could try the British Council,' a librarian suggested. Libby found the well-stocked library in the city and was soon able to borrow a swag of books and periodicals on British ventures. She would have to add the imperialism herself, but economic exploitation and imperialism were much the same thing, weren't they?

She sat at the kitchen table with the radio on. Half her mind

was singling out references to British capital in the oil industry, British military presence, and suchlike, while half was
picking up military jargon. The PX, squadron numbers, army
ranks, training camps, R&R, 'Nam and the Rose Bowl. She
wondered how many American soldiers were stationed in
Berlin. Several thousand, at least, if the traffic near the PX was
anything to go by. Strange how a few years of this war in
Vietnam had eroded the decades of goodwill towards America
built up by Hollywood, pop music, comic books and bubble-
gum. In the American sector of the city she saw GIs in
uniform every day. The British and French were much less
in evidence. Presumably, they too wore uniforms and carried guns on checkpoint duty, but the entrance to the British
Council was not patrolled by armed guards, as the Amerikahaus was.

A word to the spies is sufficient, Voice of America warned its
listeners. *Your friend may not be a spy, but a chance remark about
your movements, weapons or assignment may be passed on through
apparently friendly networks to the enemy.* The message on vigilance was followed by the upbeat harmonies of the Supremes.

At the sound of footsteps she reached out to turn off the
radio. Russell came into the kitchen, making comedy-routine
faces of mock surprise at finding her there.

'Don't turn off the imperialist crap on my account, babe,'
he said.

Libby was embarrassed. 'It's okay. It's just sort of background music.'

'So how's the great work coming on?'

'I don't know, Russell. I'm worried. How long's it supposed
to be?'

'Oh, depends. Fifteen minutes or so. Enough to start a
discussion.'

'So what kind of topics have you given papers on?'

'Oh, a range of things. Persuasion techniques in the fascist media,'—he looked pointedly at the silent radio—'filmic portrayals of the Third Reich. That sort of thing.'

'They sound a bit easier than my topic.'

'Not a bit of it. All much of a muchness when you put some effort into it.'

'Russell, I've been meaning to ask you . . . "

'Ask, kiddo, I am the fount of all wisdom.' Russell's dark eyes looked directly into Libby's, conveying at once total concentration and a parody of total concentration.

'No, seriously.'

'Seriously?'

'Jane mentioned your photography. You don't do it here. I kind of wonder how you make a living, and whether you've got a studio somewhere.'

'Hmm. Do you now? Precariously, to answer your first question. And yes, a shared studio in Wedding, to answer your second. When desperate, I coach high school kids in English. There's an occasional flush period, when I do the stills for a movie, say. But I'm not raking it in, obviously. I don't do the sell-out stuff I did in London, fashion shots and what have you.'

'You see, I'll have to find some way to earn some money if I'm going to stay here for a few months.'

'Well, in one of my prosperous spells, I might be able to pass a couple of students on to you. Unfortunately this isn't one of them. I doubt if your papers are in order for factory work. You'll have to look for something where your English is an asset. How's your typing?'

'Almost non-existent.'

'Well, there goes any prospect of working for any of the British administrators. What qualifications do you have?'

'I'm trained to teach upper primary school. But in an English-speaking country, of course.'

'There are one or two English-language schools. I suspect they'd be wanting their staff to commit themselves to longer than a few months, but you could ask. Or you could ask Romy about helping out in one of the alternative kindergartens. Younger kids, but less of a hassle dealing with the formalities.'

'I've never quite worked out what Romy does.'

'Romy is a remarkable person. She's from a rich family. Her mother owns this building, in fact. She's so dedicated to a fundamental change in Germany that she's working in the anti-authoritarian kindergarten movement, teaching children some decent revolutionary consciousness before they've hardened into fully fledged little fascist automatons like most products of the school system.'

'She did say something, but I couldn't quite follow. It sounds rather different from the type of school I'm used to.'

'And from the type of school most little residents of West Berlin and the Federal Republic attend. Anyway, they might be able to find a place for you helping out behind the scenes, even if you couldn't take classes.'

'Yeah, thanks, I'll ask.' Libby could see herself cutting carrots into sticks, or damping down the clay. It was hardly an exciting prospect.

'Look, if you're not doing anything at noon on Friday . . .'

'I'm not doing anything at noon any day, unless you count eating at the med. students' canteen.'

'Yeah, well, Hannelore and Guenther will be at the march, not at lunch. There's an antiVietnam march.'

'Should I make some placards?'

'If you like. In English, for preference.'

'By necessity.'

'Yeah, well, the simplest thing would probably be to meet Hannelore up near the hospital. I'll be coming from Wedding myself.'

'Sure.' Libby hesitated. 'Or I could come up to Wedding, help you with some placards at the studio, and go on to the march from there.'

'Nice offer, kiddo, but I think not. No, you go with Guenther and Hannelore and I'll no doubt meet you there.'

'Okay.'

'I'm off then.' Russell buttoned up his heavy brown leather jacket. *'Tchuss!'*

'Tchuss!' Libby echoed. She turned back to her notes about the Middle East.

CHAPTER 3

Libby tugged her quilt a fraction away from her ears. It was pitch dark, but she could hear running water and slamming doors. The hours her flatmates kept! She checked her travelling clock. Six fifteen. She would have to get up if she wanted to speak to Romy.

She rolled out of bed with the quilt wrapped around her, and pulled back the corner of her bedroom curtain. The streetlights still shone outside. There was not so much as a chink of daylight. She yawned. Would spring ever come? How far north was she anyway? The windowsill was lined with new snow; the white-edged streetscape, cold and forlorn-looking, no longer reminded her of English Christmas cards. What had possessed her to come to this wintry city?

In the kitchen she found Romy pouring coffee for a bearded man. 'Akbar, Libby,' Romy said briefly. Her dark hair swung in a geometric curve under her chin; she wore patterned tights with a leather mini. Akbar nodded. Romy poured coffee for herself, then placed the pot in front of Libby.

'I didn't mean to interrupt,' Libby apologised.

'You aren't interrupting,' Romy said. 'We are about to leave the house already.' Her eyes met Akbar's; they exchanged warm sexual smiles.

'Actually, Romy, I was talking to Russell about wanting to

earn some money, and he said it would be worth asking you if there was any chance of working as an assistant at your kindergarten. I've—you know—studied education and everything.' Her voice fell limply. She was conscious of Akbar's foot, rubbing Romy's left leg from ankle to calf.

Romy pointed her toe, stretched and smiled. 'I see. Actually I don't know what is available. I'll ask.'

'You are American?' Akbar asked Libby.

'No, no. Australian.'

'Unusual.'

'Not for me.' Libby watched as the lovers put on their embroidered lambskin coats.

'Where do you get those great outfits?' she asked.

'My friend has a stall at the markets,' Akbar said. 'At Lichterfelde, on Saturdays. It is extremely simple to have such a coat.'

Romy was writing on a slip of paper. 'Why don't you come to the kindergarten this afternoon, and we'll see what are the possibilities? We're just behind the municipal swimming pool. It's not so hard to find us.' She added a diagram. 'One thirty is a good time, when the children have their nap.'

Despite a shabby facade, the kindergarten was a bright, warm place. Two dozen children were stretched out on folding cots. The walls of the open-plan play space were lined with boxes of toys and art materials; cork boards were hung with children's art. Romy, in a checked smock, was hunched over the telephone. She motioned to Libby to wait. When she finished the call, she took Libby to meet a man named Reinhardt, who invited her to sit beside him as he went on folding tea-towels. 'You will have read a great deal of nonsense about these kindergartens in the Springer press,' he suggested.

'Sorry, no, I know almost nothing about them.'

'Perhaps just as well. Our enemies portray us as running a propaganda machine. In fact this is good daycare, with some realistic discussion occasionally.'

'What were you accused of doing?'

'We teach the facts of life, so they say we promote sex contact between the children. We expose the aggression of the Americans in Vietnam, so they accuse us of brainwashing. We cannot have anyone here, even as an assistant, if they wish to enforce order on the children like the old fascist style of education. Everything here is co-operative. Emancipation is the key concept for us. And non-violence, of course.'

'Great.'

'You studied education in Australia?'

'Yes. Some of our lecturers were quite progressive.'

'And what would you consider quite progressive?'

'Well, like you just said, a co-operative atmosphere, and an interest in creativity, and each child being an individual.'

Reinhardt left the linen alone for a moment and looked directly at Libby. He had slightly watery blue eyes and a long nose. 'I must be frank. We have a very small budget. Romy says you need to earn some money. We are not able to offer you anything just now. For the present, we manage with the staff we have, or mothers come as volunteers. So there is nothing, unfortunately.'

'What a pity.' That phrase again.

'Yes, so I thank you for your interest in our work. Perhaps later in the year it will be different. If so, I contact you, yes?'

'Yes. Yes, thanks.' Libby tried not to show her disappointment.

She passed Romy's desk on her way out. Romy looked up. 'Any luck?'

'Not just at the moment, unfortunately.'

Romy made a clown face of chagrin. The hint of insincerity sent a jolt through Libby, a sense that she had been undermined before she arrived.

'Thanks, anyhow,' she said. '*Tchuss*.'

Near the door a collage of photographs and drawings celebrated Ho Chi Minh.

In the cold street Libby stopped to read the many notices outside the swimming pool. It was heated. Costumes and towels could be hired. Perhaps a swim would help. Soon she was exchanging marks for a regulation racing suit, a white towel and a numbered key. She made her way from the lobby into a maze of cubicles and tiled floors. Notices disclaimed responsibility for valuables, reminded patrons to shower before swimming, and outlawed running, shouting, diving and horseplay. It took Libby a while to find the booth that matched the number on her key. The door slammed behind her. She changed into the shapeless suit. When she tried to open the door, it wouldn't budge. After a while she realised that she was supposed to exit by a second door on the opposite side of the booth. She emerged into a steamy pavilion, tiled, with a glass ceiling. She put down her towel and was about to get into the pool when an attendant gestured towards another notice. God help us, Libby muttered to herself, I mustn't forget the compulsory shower. She stood for a minute or two under the running water. Finally she dived into the tepid water and swam a couple of laps. She found herself checking that she was keeping to her lane. No doubt there was a rule about that too.

Libby rolled on to her back and floated in the body-temperature water. Steam clouds hovered between the pool and the glass ceiling. A patch of snow clung to the outside of the glass. She was warm and physically relaxed, but she couldn't get rid of the tension caused by the rebuff at the pre-school and the notices about all the things that were *verboten*.

She quizzed herself about her unease with Romy. Was there any reason to feel Romy did not wish her well? So far as she knew, there had been no one who voted against letting her stay in Breisacherstraße, at least for the time being. Was she giving way to petulance or jealousy over Romy's good looks, money, exotic lover and impeccable politics? She knew herself capable of those feelings. Romy was born the same year as

Sue. Perhaps she was projecting her feelings about her sister on to her.

When she returned to her cubicle, Libby found it locked. She had to seek help from the attendant. Pulling a master key from her belt, the grey-haired woman had the air of a gaoler dealing with a particularly recalcitrant prisoner. '*Schlussel*?' she asked several times, very loudly. Libby explained that the key was probably still inside the cubicle door. The attendant retrieved the key, and with an air of incredulity that anyone could fail to know about such things, demonstrated an attachment like a safety pin. The key should be pinned to the swimsuit, so. Was that clear? Was that all quite clear now?

'*Ja. Danke*,' Libby said, incapable of sounding at all grateful. When the woman left, she sat on the cubicle bench dabbing away her tears of rage with the hired white towel. It would take more than a handful of anti-authoritarian preschools to change this bloody country, she thought. *Ja*. That was all quite clear. Even her supposedly radical commune had rules about approved versus not-approved jars of coffee. She smiled ruefully as she tugged off the wet, chlorine-scented swimsuit. She toyed with the possibility of sabotage, ripping the inside of the seams with the safety pin part of the key. Rejecting the impulse, she handed the wet things back to the attendant. She was not surprised to see a special-purpose waterproof barrel for damp garments, the lid plastered with imperatives.

For the demonstration, Libby and Hannelore made placards reading PEACE NOW. Libby enjoyed the march along boulevards lined with bare trees. The icy wind had dropped. She joined in rhythmic chants denouncing Nixon and Kissinger as warmongers. The march ended with speeches in a large auditorium at the Free University. Hannelore pointed out leading personalities from the student peace movement, while Libby mentally compared proceedings with similar events in Australia. Age was one important difference. In Sydney, the antiwar movement owed a good deal to older women from

Save Our Sons, and to seasoned trade union leaders with decades of social agitation behind them. Here that dimension was missing. Everyone was young.

The speeches dragged on. Speakers moved from the injustice and atrocities of the war to the frustrations of young academics and the authoritiarianism of the German educational system. Libby fidgeted.

'I'm starving,' she complained to Hannelore. They slipped out of the auditorium and bought hot dogs from a nearby stall. Hannelore was due back at the hospital, but Libby wandered into a film club screening of silent movies. She watched as Charlie Chaplin narrowly escaped one peril after another. There was a lot of audience involvement; people yelled advice and wisecracks. When a bumble-footed cop appeared, roars of joy came from the audience as he landed on his behind, recovered, flourished a pair of handcuffs, and accidentally manacled himself to a passing car. He bounced along from one humiliation to the next, to the tune of gleeful catcalls and jeers.

Libby found the footage funny, but she was not doubled up with laughter as the people around her were. She thought of her irritation with all the regulations at the swimming pool: German students had had twenty years of exhaustive instructions, while she had grown up in a country with more laconic, tolerant attitudes. No wonder this audience crowed when a cop was kicked or humiliated: young Germans saw, not the stock in trade of slapstick, but a lesson in turning the tables on authority.

'The generation of Hitler,' Hannelore had said. *What did you do in the war, Daddy?* In most German homes, as her fellow audience members were growing up, that had been a forbidden question. An edgy silence was maintained between parents and children. What did her own father, Philip Stanley Milroy, do in the war? He'd volunteered early, served in the army in Australia and the Middle East. A lucky enough war:

he survived without injuries, and was spared the atrocities of Japanese prison camps. No doubt he'd seen more than he cared to discuss with his family, but he'd been one of the victors. If he and his fellow soldiers kept their war to themselves, the unspoken consensus was that they'd done the right thing. But in Germany, silence had other meanings: buried pain, shame, complicity. Double jeopardy: they'd lost, and they hadn't had right on their side to begin with. To her German contemporaries, the protests of their parents that they were unaware of the extent of genocide and brutality, that they were swept along by social forces that seemed irresistible, their claims not to have known about death camps, were taken as evidence of guilt. But what child could wash away the sins of the fathers? When would the creeks run clean again?

Libby didn't like her father's politics. She didn't like the alliances he'd had to form on the New England shire council where he served three terms. She didn't like the fact that tax accountants in country towns automatically supported the conservative parties. She didn't like the back-slapping bonhomie of the men he cultivated through service clubs. She didn't like the smugness of Uralla, the assumption that only people who'd been there for generations were entitled to an opinion on how things should be run. She didn't like to see a woman as intelligent as her mother deferring to the men when entertaining politicians or graziers. She'd been delighted to leave her home town when she won scholarships to university in Sydney.

On her more recent visits home there had been rows over her insistence on wearing her moratorium badge on occasions that her father found embarrassing, such as the Christmas Eve carol service in the local park. She smiled at the memory of her father holding his hand over the flickering candle in a paper cup, supplied by local Rotarians, as he joined in 'O Little Town of Bethlehem'. Despite the heat, he wore a tweed jacket and a tie. Lambs in a nearby paddock bleated plaintively, as if they'd been persuaded to give the nativity story an authentic background. Philip Milroy's facial expression was not that of a man who felt obliged to believe what he was singing: he had the pained, dutiful look of someone hoping for a cold beer when all this embarrassment was over.

'I don't know what you're trying to prove, wearing that absurd antiwar button,' he complained to Libby afterwards. 'Embarrass me, I suppose. If so, you succeeded.'

'I'm not trying to prove anything,' Libby said. 'I'm expressing a point of view.'

The screen images changed suddenly, banishing Libby's thoughts of home. Scenes from contemporary newsreels had been spliced into the silent comedy. Familiar faces appeared: Nixon, complete with a five o'clock shadow, held a finger outstretched as he emphasised a point. Kissinger frowned as he pushed aside a microphone and followed his president into a meeting. An American general in uniform disappeared behind a well-insulated door at the Pentagon.

The audience went wild. Yells of *fascist, fascist, fascist, shit, shit, shit,* reverberated, bounced, echoed, rose higher. Libby felt a rush of adrenalin. '*Sheiße, sheiße, sheiße,*' she heard herself screaming along with the crowd. She was a woman possessed. The people in the auditorium were united in a collective, animal fury, more contagious than cholera. It was intoxicating.

For Libby, the moment passed. She sat silent among a sea of shouting ideologues. She stayed in her place from a contingent politeness, like her father waiting for the sentimental carols to finish. The yells and catcalls subsided around her; the flickering of the black and white classic comedy resumed. Before long a light-hearted flourish of piano music led to the words The End. The lights came on. She stumbled out of the building, her limbs uncoordinated. She swung her arms and took longer than usual steps as she made her way home, instinctively feeling that physical well-being might restore her equilibrium.

Before she could make coffee with the approved brand of crystals, the telephone rang. She heard the easy, hospitable vowels of Julie Brandon. 'Hi there, Libby,' Julie said. 'How you doin'? Larry and I are having kind of a clam chowder party Sunday. You haven't even met Larry yet, have you? He's real anxious to get to know you. You'll be able to make it, won't you? Round midday? Great. See ya!'

CHAPTER 4

The bus to Lichterfelde left the tree-lined suburban streets behind, travelling past factories, warehouses, and rows of tall apartment buildings. As always on Berlin buses, a high proportion of the passengers were elderly women, widows from two world wars. A sole elderly man climbed unsteadily up the step. He tugged a raffish grey poodle on a leash held in his left hand, while leaning on a walking stick held in his right hand. A large canvas satchel hung round his neck. A couple of the white-haired widows, seated on the parallel bench behind the driver, began giving him advice. Sit there, put your bag down, let me hold your stick for you. The old man ignored them and shuffled along the aisle towards the back of the bus. He sat down opposite Libby. She smiled. The dog bounced across the aisle and sat on the seat beside her.

'*Kuckmal*!' Disapproving exclamations came from the women at the front. '*Sehen Sie?*' Libby could not follow all that was being said, but there was no mistaking the righteous tones of the keepers of public order. She heard the words *Hund*, and *verboten*.

'Good dog,' she said, scratching the dog behind its ear. The dog's owner looked across, apparently pleased. The busybodies were trying, unsuccessfully, to draw the driver's attention

33

to the fact that the dog was sitting on a seat rather than on its owner's lap. What's more it was scratching itself and didn't look particularly clean. How in the name of fortune was the owner supposed to hold the animal when he had a satchel in his lap, Libby wondered.

After a few stops, the old man pressed the button and got to his feet, holding on to the metal grips on the edge of the seat. Meaning to be helpful, Libby held out the poodle's leash, but the old man, who had not yet adjusted his stick, toppled forward a little, spilling the contents of his satchel. Socks wrapped in balls skidded over the floor of the bus like carpet bowls, followed by a shameful parade of soiled underwear and shirts. The keepers of public order were jubilant. One got to her feet to take charge of the poodle, while others kept up a running commentary of 'Da! Da! Und da! Sehen Sie!' Libby, scarlet faced, scrabbled round on the floor helping the old man get his belongings back in the bag. At length he tottered off the bus, dog, stick and satchel once more intact, and hobbled towards the laundromat. The show was over.

Thank God, Libby thought, thank God I come from a society where, by and large, people mind their own business.

At first sight the Lichterfelde market appeared to sell only farm produce. Libby wandered up and down the rows of a canvas township, where stalls displayed fresh oranges from Israel, lettuces from Yugoslavia, rhubarb from Germany, apples from Denmark, cheeses from Switzerland and Norway. Bubbling frankfurts and hot soup smelt enticing in the cold morning air. Stall-holders yelled cheerfully, boasting of the quality of their wares. Libby passed a stall covered with what looked like dead snakes. *Eels, eels, the finest eels*, the man called. '*Ja, meine Dame*,' he said encouragingly to Libby, 'how many will it be this morning?' To her distress, he lifted one of the long, black objects over his head and whirled it around in the air, like a bushman about to snap a snake's head off. Despite

34

his claims about freshness, the eel was frozen stiff. 'Thank you, no. No, thank you,' she repeated, backing away.

'The best in Berlin,' the eel man insisted.

Libby made her way past stalls of cheap vases and photo frames, past socks, stockings and acrylic jumpers, past children's shoes and knitted caps. At a babywear stall she bought a fuzzy blue, zip-up romper suit for Albert. Finally, in a far corner of the market, she found the stall selling Afghan coats, Persian rugs and lambskins. The stall-holder held her camel-hair coat while she tried on embroidered jackets and coats. They felt cosy, but even better, the embroidered, suede exteriors had a marvellously unGermanic air. These were the last garments in the world the busybodies on the bus would choose. Was there a higher recommendation?

She chose a three-quarter-length coat with magenta and turquoise embroidery and metal clasps. 'Do you want to trade this in?' the man asked, fingering her old coat. Libby was tempted, but at length she shook her head. She put the Afghan coat on, stuffing the old one and her present for Albert into a used plastic bag from a pile beside the stall. KaDeWe, the writing on the bag proclaimed.

She kept an eye out for the poodle owner as the bus passed the laundromat, but he was nowhere in sight.

'Ye gods!' Russell was stirring a pot of boiling soup. 'We're all dressed for the revolution, now, are we? There's a kind of unofficial BS Kommune uniform that no one has got around to issuing to me? I'll have to move before the fashion police catch up with me.'

Libby blushed. 'You don't like it?'

'Sweetheart, if you want to dress exactly like Romy and Romy's swarthy swains, in streetwear straight from the kasbah, who am I to criticise?'

'It's warmer round my neck than the other one.'

'Oh, of course. Strictly medicinal purposes.'

'Crumbs, Russell, why do you give me such a hard time?'

'Can't help myself. You leap to such wonderful defences. But do me a favour. Just yesterday I was thinking we get a few points by having people march with us who look straight up and down middle class. Wear the other coat when we do demos, all right? You're less likely to be pinched by the cops, and we might even win a few hearts and minds. Okay?'

'Okay. That smells delicious, Russell, what is it?'

'Cream of chicken. An old family recipe. Never fails. It's for lunch tomorrow.'

'Damn it, I'll be out.'

'Oh, yeah? Our diary just bursting with social events, I suppose?'

'I'm going to lunch with some Americans. My sister's pen-pal and her husband and friends.'

'All military, of course.'

'I guess. Plus wives and families.'

'Well, honest to Christ, Libby, where's your consistency? You're out on the streets trying to stop the war one day, and you're lunching with the aggressors the next.'

'Come off it. It's not as if it's the Pentagon.'

'No, but if their units had been assigned to Asia and not Europe, they'd be pouring napalm on crops and forests and civilians with the rest of the troops.'

'Okay, so they were lucky. Isn't innocence often a matter of luck?'

'Surviving is a matter of luck, if that's what you mean. Especially if you're Vietnamese.'

'For all you know, Russell, they may be as much against the war as you are. Half the information we get about the war comes out of America. The protest movement more or less started there. You can't talk about Americans as if they all think the same way. You think everyone voted for Nixon?'

'Where did you say they live?'

'Nikolassee.'

'Well, if they're trusted to live away from the base, they could be CIA. Has that occurred to you?'

'No, it hasn't. They were called up. They're ordinary conscripts.'

'If you say so. Just be a bit wary, okay?'

'Between you and Voice of America, Russell, I'll be watching my every step.'

Julie was right. Everyone seemed to be having their babies on the army. Janyse Pavich was wearing a waistless corduroy maternity smock.

'When I arrived,' Janyse told Libby, 'I wrote mother, I'm just about the only person here who's not *that way*. And look at me now!' She patted her belly. 'I'm eating for two, I tell Jim. My mom is supposed to be coming over for the birth, but she won't be here until May. Are you married?'

'No, I'm single.'

'Live it up while you can, huh? They say there's quite a night life in Berlin. Nightclubs and naked mud wrestling and all that.'

'I can't say I've encountered it.'

Julie came in from the kitchen, and carried a large tureen to the sideboard. 'Soup's on,' she announced. 'The line starts here. Honey, you haven't met Libby yet, have you?'

Larry Brandon's hair was so short that it looked shaved. He was tall and pale with a light brown moustache. 'So you're the Australian,' he said. 'I wondered who it was, arriving in that way-out coat. Didn't think you'd be American.'

Libby laughed. 'It's not made in America, no.'

'Nup. No Ladies' Garment Makers Union label on that one, I'll bet. But I'm not sure where they do make them.'

'East of wherever you're thinking.'

The speaker was a square-jawed, even-featured man with an accent that reminded Libby of John Kennedy's. He was ladling chowder into bowls. 'Libby,' Larry said, 'this is our friend Dean Adams. Dean, this is Julie's friend from Australia.'

'Australia, how about that? You have chowder in Australia?'

'Out of tins.'

'Not so loud. This may be too. And what are you doing in Berlin, Libby?'

'Sightseeing, so far. And learning a bit of German.'

'Not staying long enough to get a job?'

'I'm a teacher, but my German's not up to teaching here. I might try to get some casual work.'

Dean smiled. 'As you can see from this small cross-section of the English-speaking community, there must be plenty of opportunities for an English-speaking babysitter.'

'That's a thought.'

'And what do you do, Dean?'

'Well, I came over as a conscript, but I kind of took to the place, and now I'm with the education corps.'

'Is that fun?'

'Fun? Well, it's necessary. You see, the average GI has a somewhat limited background. They arrive here thankful as hell they're not stopping bullets in Vietnam, but they know next to nothing about living in another culture. They're here as peacekeepers, but many of them have no idea how to—' he paused while searching for the word—'*comport* themselves. So we play a very necessary role. A divided city like this one calls for a special kind of vigilance.'

'A word to the spies and all that.'

'There's no call to be cynical. Just last week an American couple spent two nights in detention in the East, ostensibly because the wife had dyed her hair since having her passport photo taken. There's a lot of tension here, not just because of the Wall. The reds can stage a go-slow at the checkpoints, holding traffic up for hours, or they take individuals into custody, almost at random. We've got enough genuine problems, without our officials having their time taken up negotiating the release of thrill-seekers. Here, there's a couple of chairs.'

Libby sat beside Dean. The chowder tasted great. Larry Brandon handed round beer and Rhine riesling. Libby took a glass of wine. Looking around, she realised that all the other women were clustered together at the far end of the room, where Julie was now bottlefeeding Albert. She was asking Dean about his background when Larry joined them.

'I've always been kind of attracted to going to Australia,' Larry said. 'I hear you have your coons well under control there.'

Libby felt a flash of anger. 'If you mean the Aborigines, we don't use that term in Australia.'

'You don't? No offence, I hope. What I mean is, they're not so much in evidence.'

'They only make up one or two per cent of the population, if that's what you mean.'

'Sounds good to me. Better than—'

Dean broke in. 'I'm sure Larry is one hundred per cent in favour of integration of all army units and activities,' he said. 'As we all are. No racial distinctions whatsoever.'

'Oh yes,' Larry said sarcastically. 'One hundred per cent. Like every citizen of the United States. Christ! I don't know what that means any more. Bums and radicals are burning their country's flag on every second campus across the States. No pride in being an American left.'

'Surely,' Libby protested, 'students can be against the war without losing their patriotism. Or does it have to be my country right or wrong? I mean, you have to come to terms with other policies you mightn't have chosen, from the sound of it, on race for instance.' She saw Dean watching her intently. Something in his manner warned her to cool it, immediately.

Larry glared over his Heineken, his face red. He mopped a line of beer froth off his moustache with the back of his hand.

'Sounds like we've got one bright lady, here, Larry. She's got your number, any rate,' Dean said.

'If you guys will excuse me, I want to ask Julie something.' Libby made her way to the far end of the room and handed Julie the parcel with the jumpsuit, which was duly admired by the assembled mothers. She waited impatiently for coffee so she could make her farewells. These women are only my age, she reminded herself, as she listened to what seemed endless discussions of paper versus cloth nappies, and the incidence of caesarean sections at the base hospital. She had never felt so grateful to be on the pill.

Many hours of Libby's life were spent trying to work out what made her fellow residents of Breisacherstraße tick. In particular, she wondered about their sex lives, or lack of them. Romy's lover spent the night with her a couple of times a week. Guenther and Hannelore appeared to live celibate lives, their time taken up with lectures, hours at the hospital, and politics. Her curiosity was sharpest when it came to Russell, because she felt attracted to him despite his offhand manner. Somehow his presence put her on full alert, sharpening her sense of smell, her awareness of her body. So far as she could tell, the attraction was not mutual. Explaining the finer points of *Fascismustheorie* on some topic or other, Russell would look at her intently, apparently unaware of her self-consciousness. Russell brought no one to the apartment. Occasionally she took a telephone message for him, but although these gave her a few clues as to what went on in the studio, she learnt nothing from them about his emotional life. *The coated cardboard has arrived. The contact proofs are available. The pamphlets won't be ready until Thursday.*

There were two Tuesday seminars in the weeks leading up to hers. At one, Hannelore spoke in German about the deficiencies of medical education in the Federal Republic. Hannelore had a nervous habit of circling her left thumb and forefinger round the strands of her plait. She rattled through her paper in a state of indignation, pointing out that rich and middle-class people fared better than the poor. The health of migrant workers was neglected: Turkish guest workers, despite their mental health problems, seldom received psychiatric care. She quoted statistics on industrial accidents, on suicides, on nervous breakdowns. After she had finished, there were few questions. Guenther said that he supported the points Hannelore had made. 'I may move into the East after I graduate,' he said. 'There's more social responsibility there.'

Libby suggested that it would be a good thing if more Turkish interpreters were trained. Russell broke in. 'That's a bandaid idea. Bourgeois tokenism. What's the point of having people to give you some fuck-awful diagnosis in two languages, when the real problems are poverty, separation from your own community, exploitation and racial discrimination? Wouldn't those be enough to make anyone depressed? To make any halfway sensitive person feel suicidal? Isn't it typical of this two-faced society, where the fat hogs stuff themselves and the underdogs fight over scraps?'

'Underhogs?' Libby challenged, in an innocent tone of voice.

'That kind of flippancy is an insult to all Hannelore's hard work. I suppose it's only to be expected from someone who comes from a land of surfing and barbecues which applauds anything American.'

'Any worse than a land of bagpipes and haggis which derides anything English? I'm not just the result of my nationality any more than you are.'

'I'm not sure what you two are disagreeing about, but I thank Guenther for agreeing with me,' Hannelore said. 'And Libby is right—interpreters are needed. But so is more fundamental reform. So perhaps Russell is right also. And now, we adjourn together to the pub, *nicht*?'

A fortnight later, when Romy talked about the history

syllabus in German schools, Libby kept quiet, in part because she didn't want Russell to pounce on her for flippancy again. The task of facing the facts of the Holocaust and the Third Reich, crucial for her German contemporaries, would gain nothing from the glib comments of outsiders. 'Even now, we cannot trust German parents to overcome the mistakes of the past. Antifascist education must begin in daycare centres and kindergartens,' Romy concluded. 'By the time students reach high school, their moral attitudes are already formed.' She talked about the philosophy of emancipation and the *Kinderladen* movement: the challenge to produce children who were free from aggression and competitiveness.

Russell pressed his knuckles together on the edge of the table, and looked up through his sandy-red eyebrows. 'Does it ever strike you, though, Romy, that all of us are products of our education? And that education was not at all progressive. Indeed, I may safely say, the nuns of Glasgow, fond of wielding the tawse so that great stripes of stinging flesh came up on our palms, were probably more reactionary in their approach to education than most German teachers. To the extent that they formed our attitudes, we united against them. We grew up convinced of the need for change. What if the anti-authoritarian *Kinderladen* end up producing not revolutionaries but arch-conservatives, people who hark back to their grandparents' values? Do we really know how social consciousness evolves? What if, like you, those children grow up wanting to find the gaps—the things they weren't taught? What if they despise us the way we despise the ruling class now?'

'These are difficult questions,' Romy admitted.

'I truly believe,' Hannelore said, 'that children who grow up in freedom and tolerance will fight against racism and oppression, just as we do.'

'We have to work on that assumption, true,' Russell replied. 'But it worries me that we simply take it on faith.'

'The revolution is not only kindergarten,' Romy's boy-friend, Akbar, suggested. 'Also guns. Also grenades. Also attacking the centres of the old values.'

'But Romy speaks of peaceful things,' Hannelore said. 'I do not want to use guns. There can be change without violence.' She paused, fidgeting with her plait. 'Can't there?'

'I certainly hope so,' Guenther said.

'Me too,' said Libby.

'Och,' Russell shrugged, 'it was just a thought. Someone has to play the devil's advocate.'

'You do it to the manner born,' Libby told him.

At the next seminar, she shuffled her index cards and cleared her throat before plunging into her talk on British imperialism in the Middle East. She'd found more material than she expected. She began with the size of the British diplomatic presence in Iran after the Second World War; the huge profits from oil; the growing discontent at the compar-atively small return to Iran. She described the conflicts that had arisen with the governmet of Mohammed Mossadeq, and his replacement by the Shah of Iran in a coup that received tacit support from the Americans. She went on to the Suez crisis of 1956, the effects of that debacle on British prestige, and the spin-off effects on trade. She made brief mention of the plight of Palestinians left homeless with the creation of Israel. Winding up, she felt that having to research this obscure topic had not been such an ordeal after all.

There was a pause. She looked at Russell, confident that if some oblique attack was to come, it would be from him. To her relief, Akbar led off the discussion. 'You say the Shah had tacit support from the Americans. He had open support, always. Who pays for our weapons and military training? The Americans, of course. Do they do it because they care about democracy and the free world? Of course not. The CIA replaced a democratic government with a dictatorship. There cannot be peace in my country while imperialist tanks roll through our streets to intimidate us, or while the secret police, with money from foreign countries, terrorises any effective opposition. I am forced to live outside my country if I wish to speak my political views. Libby tells us about the British, but I see a partnership of the several western industrialised countries exploiting the resources of the weaker ones.'

Libby relaxed as the others followed up these points, addressing all their remarks to Akbar, who had the air of a man who could keep up a tirade against the west until dawn if he had listeners. 'One moment, Akbar, please,' Hannelore said, getting to her feet. 'Russell, Romy and I have something to discuss in the kitchen.' The door closed behind them, the paper Lenin standing guard while they conferred.

'I'm glad you were here, Akbar,' Libby said. 'It would have been too much for me otherwise.'

'It's okay. God, I wish Hannelore would let me smoke in here.'

'No, it's one of the commune rules, I'm afraid. No smoking in the shared rooms. It's for medical reasons, she says. She's going to make a very good doctor.'

Russell, Hannelore and Romy returned from the kitchen with a bottle of cognac and an assortment of glasses. 'Congratulations, Libby,' Romy said. 'You are now a member of the BS Kommune.'

'I am so happy, Libby,' Hannelore said, putting her arms around her.

'Good on ya, love,' Russell teased. 'Isn't that what they say on your side of the equator?'

'This is so sweet of you all!' Libby was somewhere between laughter and tears.

'A toast!' Hannelore said. 'To the future! To the commune! To the revolution!'

'The revolution,' everyone repeated, as the cheap liqueur singed their throats.

Glasses were refilled. The toasts got rowdier. Romy put on

some music. She and Akbar rolled up the old woollen rug and shimmied on the floorboards. With their contrasting looks, Romy with her lithe, tall figure and Snow White colouring, pale skin and neatly trimmed black hair; Akbar olive-skinned, compactly built, with shaggy dark curls, they made a striking couple. Hannelore clapped and drummed her feet; soon Libby and Guenther were also keeping time for the dancers. Only Russell, looking as though his thoughts were far away, sat nursing his drink without any response to the music.

Libby moved across the room to sit beside him. 'Something's worrying you,' she said, 'just when the rest of us are having fun.'

Russell grimaced. 'I've been expecting to hear from someone, that's all. I don't mean to cast a pall on everyone's party spirits. Just a bit preoccupied.'

'I'm so relieved that I've passed the test or whatever, for staying here. I was terrified before I gave my talk.'

'You needn't have been. It was obvious it would be at least fair average quality once you started getting all those books.'

'Yeah, well I felt sort of on trial, so I'm grateful that you all had enough faith in me to get in brandy and everything.'

'We could have drunk it without you, if you'd been too dreadful. We could have sent you out on some errand and then polished it off in your absence. Sent you off with a letter to the British ambassador about his foreign policy.' A brief flicker of humour in Russell's eyes belied his deadpan expression.

'Anyway, I'm grateful to you all, and to you in particular, for not picking holes in everything I said. It means a lot to me. Actually, Russell—' she took a breath—'you mean a lot to me.'

Russell's movement was almost imperceptible, but it was not towards her. 'That's foolish talk, girl. That's the brandy.'

He drained his own glass and looked across the room towards the dancers.

At length he looked back at Libby. 'If we mean a lot to each other, it's because we all share similar goals. We're political allies, if you like. Comrades. Let's not get into this awful sentimental stuff about what we mean to one another as individuals. It's either bourgeois crap, or it's the sure road to heartbreak. Believe me, I know what I'm talking about.'

'You're taking it too seriously. I just mean I like you.'

'Fine, well, we'll leave it at that, will we? I've been meaning to ask you a bit of a favour, Libby. I've got clashing commitments tomorrow week. Do you think you could take on my English classes for the afternoon? A schoolboy, fourteen years old, his English isn't too bad really.'

'Just the one day?'

'Yes, that's it.'

'Where would it be?'

'Zehlendorf. I'll give you the address. Not too far from the station. It's not difficult, he just does conversation and some translation and stuff like that. I'll give you the text.'

'Fine, no problem.'

'Good, I'll let them know tomorrow that I'm sending a substitute. And there's another thing, Libby. Didn't you say you're pretty well up on camping and surviving in the woods and all that?'

'I would have said in the bush, but yes.'

'Well, whenever spring comes, and let us have faith despite these freezing nights, when spring comes, we must all have a bit of a safari in the Grunewald.'

'Sounds like fun.'

'Well, welcome aboard.'

'Thanks, Russell. This commune isn't a bit what I expected, but I'm glad I found you all.'

Hannelore's voice interrupted them. 'I'm sorry, Romy, but unless your guest confines his smoking to your room, he'll just have to leave. These are the communally agreed rules. Are they not? Guenther? Russell? Any change to our charter must be made in a meeting. We do not make reproaches, Akbar, we are simply frank about our standards.'

'Forget it, I'm going.' Akbar retrieved his coat from the rack. The fumes of his recently extinguished Gaulois lingered in the room.

'Akbar, wait! Wait!' Grabbing her identical coat, Romy hurried down the corridor after him. The front door slammed behind them.

'That's a bit peculiar, isn't it,' Libby asked Russell, 'when you told me Romy's family owns the building?'

'Come off it, kiddo. Romy would be the first to insist that the resolutions of commune meetings apply equally to all of us.'

'Even so,' Hannelore said.

'You look as if you disagree, Libby,' Russell said.

'Me? No, actually I'm just very tired.' Libby mimed a yawn; then yawned genuinely. She scurried off to her room.

CHAPTER 5

Russell was assembling his breakfast—a banana cut into a bowl of cereal, topped with dates and dried milk. Libby wrinkled her nose as he held this concoction under the cold tap, then carried it back to the bench, stirring all the while. 'I thought you Scots ate porridge,' she said.

'Aye, lass, that's what ye heard?' Russell teased, in a parody of his own accent. Lumps of undiluted milk powder were visible on his spoon.

'Yeah, well I suppose people think we eat steak and eggs,' Libby said, eyes averted from the white globs.

Russell switched on the radio. Libby's comprehension had improved, but she could still only get the gist of most of the news items. Russell's expression grew fierce as he listened. 'The bastards. The absolute bastards. Those goddamned fucking infernal bastards.'

'The Americans again?' Libby asked.

'Those unforgivable murdering swine. Not only are they bombing Laos and Cambodia, supposedly neutral countries, but now the Sihanouk government in Phnom Penh has been replaced in a coup by an army type named Lon Nol.'

'And you blame the Americans?'

'Use your skull, girl, who does it sound like? It's got CIA written all over it.'

'Yeah, but that's just what you'd expect an East Berlin radio station to say.'

'Oh, I'm sorry, I'd forgotten you prefer the niceties of the American propaganda machine. *Body count. Vietnamisation. Free fire zone.* Is that more to your liking?'

'Of course not. You know I hate the war and Nixon's bombs as much as anyone. I'm just suggesting that both the east and the west give the news a certain slant. There's communist propaganda too. It's not a one-way street.'

'You know what I sometimes suspect, Libby? I sometimes think you're not a revolutionary at all, you're just a sweet little sit-on-the-fence middle-of-the-road wishy-washy liberal.'

'Thanks a lot, but where I come from we don't have fences in the middle of our roads. And Liberals are conservatives.'

A child's voice cut in. They fell silent and looked at the radio. In pious tones the boy proclaimed that he was very proud of his *Mutti*. Not only did she have a full-time job, but she also collected money for the brave people of North Vietnam, locked in a struggle with the imperialists. He was happy, because the Democratic Republic provided its children with such excellent kindergartens.

'See what I mean?' Libby gloated. 'What five year old ever talks like that? The poor little bugger's probably been learning the script for days.'

Russell seemed momentarily quelled. 'You're a hard woman, Libby. What if he's genuinely pleased and proud?'

'Lucky little him then, that the tape recorder was there just at the right moment.'

'I was very proud of my mother.' Like many of Russell's statements, this was said as a challenge.

'Yes, but you didn't get on the radio proclaiming the fact.'

'No, I didn't. In capitalist countries, reporters don't often ask the children of the working class how they feel about their parents.'

'What did your mother do?'

'She worked in a dye factory, finishing cloth. Fumes everywhere. She used to get appalling migraines.'

'And now?'

'She died. Died too young. She's been dead for three years.'

'What about your father?'

'Aye, he's still in Glasgow. He's moved to some council flat in Dumbarton. He gets by.'

'You don't sound as if you like him much.'

'Oh well, my mother was a grand woman, she'd do anything for people, she worked bloody hard all her life, and she was good for a joke. The old man's more—well—let's just say she was more of a giver and he's more of a taker.'

'That's what women of her generation were supposed to do—put themselves last.'

'There's a bit of that in it, but my mother was nobody's doormat. No, she just did what she thought was the best.'

'You must miss her.'

'It could be one reason why it's all the same to me if I'm in Berlin or Glasgow, aye.'

'But Berlin's more interesting, surely. I've heard Glasgow's rather a—'

'An ugly city? Dangerous? Too industrial? Full of horrible working-class people?'

'Well, not quite in those words, but something along those lines.'

'They used to say even the Alsatian dogs had to go out in pairs. It's not a dull city, if that's what you mean, and in its way it's beautiful. It doesn't have a ruddy great wall running down its middle to symbolise the political divisions of the cold war, if that's what makes Berlin interesting.'

'You know, I haven't been over the Wall yet. I thought I'd go into the East practically the day after I arrived, but I still haven't made it. I was wondering if you'd go across with me, on Saturday, say?'

'Nice idea, but I'm not too keen to go over just at the moment.'

'But as a foreigner you're free to come and go as you like.'

'In theory. In practice I don't want to get too many stamps on my passport in case I strike the authorities as an interesting person. It's no good asking any of the commune members, because West Germans can't go. Why don't you get one of your American pals to go with you?'

'They're not allowed to. Security, Julie says.'

'And you say these people aren't in intelligence? It all adds up, Libby, when you think about it. But you'll be perfectly all right on your own. Tell me when you're going, and if you're not back by midnight I'll alert the British ambassador. There— can I say fairer than that?'

Libby shook her head. 'I have no intention of being part of a diplomatic incident. I dare say you're right. I'll be fine on my own.'

'Just take the train to Friedrickstraße. It's easy. And by the way, I've got the notes for you for my student in Zehlendorf. You haven't forgotten you're helping me out?'

'I certainly haven't. I'm delighted to be earning a bit of money.'

There was an unwritten rule in the commune about staying out of each others' bedrooms. Russell fetched a folder of newspaper clippings, a comprehension book and a BBC tuition book. 'I'd have expected you to choose more radical teaching materials,' Libby commented.

'My motto is, say anything you like but don't leave any inflammatory stuff for the paying customers—parents—to get their hands on,' Russell said. 'The thing they really want is improved school results for the kid. With Erich, I usually ask to see his English homework and go over that with him before we do anything else. Then I do the grammar that he's having trouble with at school, or we do exercises from one of these books, or we just make conversation in English.'

'Okay. It doesn't sound too difficult. What are your plans, while I'm tutoring this kid?'

'Oh, nothing much. Kind of a sit-in. The others will be there too.'

Zehlendorf was to the south of the American sector, not far from Nikolassee, so Libby arranged to meet Julie Brandon for coffee the same afternoon. As she walked along the streets to the U-Bahn station, she noticed shoots of green on the trees, and a few stalks of some bulb poking up through the hard earth, beside the remaining patches of snow. Responding to the calendar rather than any distinct change in the weather, householders had greeted spring by placing plaster gnomes in their gardens. Red-capped and grotesque, they had the bent-spine and bent-elbow postures of old rustic men in sentimental paintings.

The quiet was broken by roars and cracks from the blue sky, as jets flew overhead. The military posturing of the cold war, Libby thought, is as kitschy as garden gnomes. All parades, visible threats, uniforms and stand-offs. Boys' games. *My army's bigger'n yours, yah-de-yah-yah! My dad can lick yours, any day. Washington's stronger'n Moscow. Is not. Is too. I can break the sound barrier, so there. So what? So can I. CRACK! BOOM!*

Was her peaceful stroll along these back streets really made possible by the thundercracks in the sky? Better the show than the substance, when it came to military might, of course. Berlin was luckier than Cambodia: no bombs, no napalm, a certain order. She wondered what Berliners thought about years of occupation by foreign powers. Her flatmates were from other parts of West Germany, so their attitudes were hardly typical. Not even Romy had spent her childhood here.

Outside the Dahlem underground, she bought a paper from a long-haired student. She flipped through it as the train swayed south. The same old issues. Authoritarian professors. Lack of consultation with students. Exploitation of junior academics. Vietnam. Nuclear weapons. Finally her eye fell

52

upon something more entertaining, an article about sexual freedom and communal life. They don't know about Breisacherstraße, she thought. We live like Dominicans up there. Life was obviously different in Kommune Number One, better known as K1. She read about the antics of Fritz Teufel a few years earlier. Snatching the regalia of a university official, he paraded around half-naked on a bicycle, mocking the solemnity of formal convocation. The accompanying cartoon featured a slogan, *Wer zweimal mit dem gleichem pennt gehört schon zum Establishment.* Screw the same person twice and you're already a member of the Establishment? How exhausting, how impersonal. Perhaps the austerity of Breisacherstraße was preferable.

Erich Keilmann, a reserved boy of fourteen, was alone in his family's apartment. He was anxious for Libby to help with a composition on the subject of ice hockey. Libby suggested some changes to word order and the removal of some surplus capital letters, but the weakness of the piece did not lie in its grammatical mistakes. 'The trouble with this,' Libby suggested, 'is it doesn't give any idea of how exciting the game is. Can you try describing the atmosphere at a match, the cheering, the cold wind, the thrill of winning?'

'That is good. Will you write it, please?'

'No, Erich, this is your essay. You write it.'

'Mr Muir helps me always.' The boy leant on his left elbow, his petulant expression conveying frustration.

Bloody Russell, he probably wrote the kid's assignments word for word. 'Does he now? Well, I don't think I'm really here to write your work for you, but if you give me some suggestions in English I'll help you add them.' Sentence by painful sentence they worked on, until at last Erich managed to describe the crowd leaving the stadium, club scarves wound around their necks.

The hour was nearly up. 'Do you listen to English on the radio at all, Erich?'

The boy's waxy skin grew pink. 'Pop,' he said. 'Voice of America.' It was the first time she had heard any trace of enthusiasm in his voice.

'Well, maybe I can help you write down the words of your favourite songs if I come again.'

'But Mr Muir comes next time?'

'Yes, Mr Muir's coming next time.'

'Thank you for the lesson. I learn much.'

'I've learnt a lot.'

'Yes, I learn a lot.'

'Fine, I've enjoyed it too. Give my regards to your parents. Bye!'

Half an hour later she was talking to Julie Brandon in a cafe not far from Woolworths. 'This is a bizarre city,' she said. 'On one side of the Wall kids are parroting this stuff about *Mutti* collecting for the Vietcong, while on the other, spoilt kids are soaking up American pop culture and expecting their tutors to do their homework for them.'

Julie laughed. 'You can't judge a whole city on one or two kids.'

'I guess not,' Libby admitted. 'Of course it's Russell's fault. He must have let him get away with that kind of laziness.'

'Did it occur to you, Libby, that you did teacher training and Russell didn't? He's a photographer, right? So he's probably doing the best he can, and all. You said he just does it as a sideline to make a bit of money?'

'Yes, only he's busy today.'

'A commission?'

'No, I gather they're busy with something in the city. A kind of sit-in or something.'

'You like this guy, Libby? He sounds pretty weird.'

'He's all right. Sure I like him, but just as a flatmate. You know.'

'Flatmate! I'll never get used to how you talk. So where is this sit-in supposed to be? Maybe at the Free U? I hear that the sit-ins are getting real rowdy in the States. They set fire to the admin. office in some of them. It's right out of hand. Larry thinks that the radicals on campus are going crazy. They're manipulated, of course, by communist agitators.'

'So Larry doesn't consider the possibility that the protesters are sincere, that they're idealists?'

'Sure, they can be idealists, and still be manipulated.'

'But Julie, it's a mass movement. There are huge, deep divisions in the community, between the generations especially.'

Albert, squirming in his mother's arms, tugged at his right shoe and hurled it across the table. Libby reached out to catch it, missed, and bent down to pick it up from the floor. Julie, flustered, tried to pin the child closer to her; he wriggled angrily, and began kicking his heels. A waitress came with their order. 'We could ask for a highchair,' Libby said.

'No, he'll settle down in a minute.' Julie addressed her child. 'Behave yourself. You want to grow up to be a trouble-maker, is that it?'

Albert tossed his second shoe after the first. Libby laughed. 'Don't laugh, it only encourages him,' Julie said.

'Sorry.' Libby retrieved the shoe. 'It's awful for them, isn't it, all the layers of clothes children have to wear in this climate?'

'Yeah, I guess it is a lot warmer in here than outside. Hey, this torte is delicious. Here, Albert, try a bit of this. It tastes good.'

The next ten minutes bore witness to the fact that a good Berlin chocolate cake can create harmony between generations and nationalities, temporarily at least.

That night the Breisacherstraße commune members clustered around the television set. They watched impatiently as Brandt was interviewed on the need for good relations with Russia, and Kissinger refused to comment on the extent of the bombing in Cambodia. Then came the Berlin news. A huge demonstration outside the Amerikahaus had turned violent as protesters hurled cobblestones and paint-filled missiles. Libby looked furiously at Russell. She'd been excluded from the major political event of her time in Berlin, fobbed off with an offhand reference to a sit-in. 'God, Russell, you send me to fill in for you in the suburbs, while the real action's in the city,' she complained. *Shhh!* Hannelore and Romy hissed in unison. Russell signalled that something important was about to happen. They all stared at the screen. A reporter began giving an account of the confrontation between students and police. For a second the soundtrack sounded scrambled. Then it became clear that the reporter was trying to make himself heard above a megaphone chorus of *One, two, three, four, stop the fucking Vietnam War*. The police and the Amerikahaus guards were looking around in bewilderment, unable to detect where the voice was coming from.

One, two, three, four, stop . . .

The voice had a Scottish accent.

'You bastard, Russell, you absolute bastard,' Libby said.

'But it was a great success,' Hannelore said.

'That's not the point. The point is, I was sent off to tutor for Russell without anyone having the courtesy to tell me what was going on.'

'Naturally we assumed that Russell told you he had to be somewhere else,' Romy said. 'He could not be sure the electronics would work.'

'Absolutely,' Russell said. 'Rather than call me a bastard, you might congratulate me on the success of our tactics.'

'You played an important part, Libby,' said Hannelore, 'allowing Russell to be at the demonstration instead of working.'

'But hell, you could have told me.'

'I told you I was going to a sit-in. Am I supposed to be a fortune teller? Did I know anyone would throw cobblestones? Did I know the police would arrest anyone?'

'You knew you'd be trying to use the mikes.'

'Yes, but as Romy just told you, I didn't know it would be so effective.'

'It was really marvellous, Libby,' Hannelore said.

'Yeah, well, congratulations. And you might all treat me more like a member of the commune next time. I've had it up to here with being made to feel an outsider,' Libby said.

'Sure, Libby,' Romy promised.

'Where's Guenther anyway?'

'Guenther went to the emergency room. Many students went to receive first aid. It got very rough. You were much safer down in Zehlendorf,' Hannelore said.

'Yeah, and I'd be safer still if I'd never left home. But I didn't come to Berlin to be shunted off to the suburbs.'

'My mistake,' Russell said caustically. 'I keep forgetting that you came as a client of Radical Tourism.'

'Shut up, Russell!' Libby felt like rushing out of the room, but she forced herself to stay for the rest of the news, including the weather forecast. A thaw was expected.

'You can come in the May Day parade, Libby,' Hannelore offered.

'Okay.'

Libby had a sudden vision of another group of people sitting near a television set: Julie, Larry, and a shoeless Albert. She wished that she had said nothing to Julie about Russell's plans for the afternoon.

CHAPTER 6

The year's last snow fell early in the morning on the first of May. Carrying May Day placards out to Romy's small Renault, Libby cursed the slush underfoot. 'When does spring come in this bloody country?' she demanded.

'Usually before this,' Romy said.

'Next week for sure, we go swimming,' Hannelore promised.

'And in a week or two we'll be camping in the woods.' Russell put his bundle of wires, loudspeakers and microphones into the boot.

By the time they joined the other marchers, the snow had vanished. Libby felt exhilarated as she held her PEACE NOW placard high in the air. These boulevards were made for marching, she reflected. It was great to be part of a throng, to take over the streets in the name of peace and international brotherhood. Marchers beat drums, played South American flutes and shook maracas. There was no opposition from the police on this occasion: it was a legal demonstration. Shoppers on the footpaths paid little attention as the carnival troop went by.

They swung on to the Kürfürstendamm, passing the bombed-out shell of the Gedächniskirche and parading along past the fashion shops and department stores of the city centre. 'Last Christmas, here, and just outside the Ka-De-We, we had a tremendous demonstration against consumer excess,' Hannelore told Libby. 'I persuaded some of the Lutheran nuns who work at our hospital to join us. They were quite happy about it, because to them Christmas is something spiritual, not just ever more enormous parcels of presents. So—the police and the storekeepers—they had to be nice to us, with so many dear silver-haired nuns there.'

'They're not here today, though.'

'Unfortunately not. But there are some older people again. The traditional workers' craft unions, and so forth.'

'Yes. Makes you feel safer than when it's just students.'

'Even these bourgeois with their shopping bags, perhaps many of them remember that May Day has a history,' Hannelore said.

'The whole city has a history,' Libby said, reminded of pictures of Berlin lying in rubble that she'd seen in the Gedächniskirche. Doubled over with hunger and resignation, old people and children had made their way aimlessly through the ruins of Hitler's capital.

'History is not our strong point,' Hannelore sighed.

Even Russell seemed buoyed by jubilant spirits. *What do we want? World peace. When do we want it? Now!* blared forth from his megaphone. The crowd took up the chant, marching unimpeded through the commercial heart of West Berlin.

That night, they expected to see themselves on television, but the news coverage was restricted to the military theatrics of the Russian occupying forces in East Berlin, as tanks rolled in their dozens and Russian generals took the salute.

Days later, Libby could hardly make out what Julie Brandon was saying on the telephone. Her voice was choked with tears.

'Could you repeat that?' Libby asked. 'Kent what?'

Julie sobbed. 'Libby, half the time I believe Larry when he

says that college radicals are bums and all that, but you must be right, some of them just want peace. And now the National Guard have been into one of the colleges, shooting people.'

'Firing over their heads, I guess.'

'No. That's just it. They shot to kill. Students are dead. It's just awful.' Her voice was becoming inaudible again. 'Look, I'm too upset just now. Listen to the radio headlines, okay.'

'Fine, Julie. I'll talk to you later.'

Libby was the only commune member at home. She turned on Voice of America. *Where have you gone, Joe DiMaggio*, Simon and Garfunkel sang, *a nation turns its lonely eyes* . . . She switched to the British station and waited impatiently for the next news bulletin. She did not have long to wait. Even the usually impassive, upper-class voice of the BBC announcer seemed to betray a trace of emotion as he read the details of the military occupation of Kent State University in Ohio. A student sit-in had led authorities to call in the National Guard. Armed soldiers rushed on to the campus, where amid general confusion it was not clear whether the order to fire had been given. Four students, two of them girls, had been shot dead. Some eye-witnesses doubted that all the victims had been part of the sit-in. Students who were simply making their way from one classroom to another had been caught up in the melee as the entrances were blocked off by armed soldiers.

Libby waited for further bulletins. An announcement was expected from the president. Surely he would denounce the National Guard for exceeding their authority? At least he should have the decency to express his grief at the deaths of four unarmed young people. Now would be the time to take back his previous references to half-educated bums.

Hours later, a statement was issued through a spokesman. Violence led to violence, the president believed. Libby listened through tears of rage. Everything's changed, she thought. From today, everything's changed. And just days ago I was thinking how much common ground we had with other

60

groups, how the peace movement was gaining allies with every march. Now there's an unbridgeable gulf between us and the people in power. Gun-toting bastards.

Succeeding bulletins confirmed her sense of outrage. Across the United States, universities were closed to commemorate the deaths at Kent State. The father of one of the victims, Allison Krause, announced, 'My child was not a bum.'

Libby dialled Julie Brandon's number, but no one answered. Anxious for company, she walked to the campus of the Free University, imagining that she would find sit-ins in progress there. Even a film club meeting with some cut-in newsreels would have been welcome. But the place seemed deserted; the action was elsewhere.

She felt very much an outsider.

On her way home, she detoured through the Pacific galleries of the Dahlem Museum. At first it seemed a better than average collection of objects from what the labels called primitive cultures, but when she got past the first couple of galleries she heard music. Following the sound of jungle flutes and drums, she sauntered past dugout canoes and cases full of masks, baskets and pots. All at once she found herself in a village straight from the New Guinea highlands: a long house stood on poles, fringes of dried grass hanging from its thatched roof. Canoes decorated with pigs' tusks were propped beside real-looking trees; there were groups of grass huts, bark artefacts, ceremonial spears and masks of carved wood. The haunting, high-pitched notes of reed instruments marked the boundaries of a timeless world. Libby stood spellbound. For long minutes she had the sensation of having blundered into an undiscovered village. The air smelt of dried mud and sunshine. She knew that the display was an illusion, that she was responding to the clever use of space: these objects were the spoils of colonialism. At the same time she felt suspended in a sunny afternoon in a place where war and dissent did not intrude.

Back in the apartment she felt impatient for Hannelore or Russell to come home, so she could share her rage and disbelief. It was dark before they arrived. She felt let down when Russell merely shrugged and said, 'It's all a part of the whole, isn't it?'

'We felt the way you feel now a few years ago,' Hannelore explained, 'the day Benno Ohnesorg was shot. It's the same pattern, peaceful demonstrators up against armed agents of fascism.'

'Maybe.' Libby was always saying maybe these days. *Vielleicht, vielleicht, vielleicht, perhaps, perhaps, perhaps* . . .

Romy came into the room still in her coat and scarf, carrying a scrolled piece of paper. 'Look, Russell, at this picture by one of the children. We can make a poster, *nicht?*'

In a child's clear-edged style, in reds and browns, the picture showed a figure lying on the ground in a pool of blood. A hail of bullets made a pattern between the victim and a line of soldiers. The horizon was in flames.

'Yes, it's deadset poster material,' Russell agreed.

'Things have reached a new stage, I believe,' Romy said. 'Akbar and his friends are right. At a certain point we must fight back. We must arm ourselves.'

'Surely being without arms gives us our moral strength,' Hannelore said.

'I agree,' said Libby. 'But what do you think, Russell?'

Russell tilted the child's fingerpaint poster back and forth. 'I'm thinking, lass, I'm thinking,' he muttered.

It was true, as Russell said, that it was easy to get to East Berlin: you just stayed on the S-Bahn as far as it went. Looking at the bricked-up tunnels which corresponded with the Wall above, Libby smiled as she remembered Julie's fear of being carried beyond the checkpoint. As she queued to show her passport to the two sets of border guards, Libby found herself among a crowd of old people with cardboard suitcases and shabby rolled bedspreads. Pensioners from the east had a freedom of movement that was denied to people of working age.

There were no queries or delays. The spruce-looking Russian guards were even younger than their British counterparts. Within minutes of leaving the train, Libby was finding her bearings east of the Wall. From this side, the no-man's-land strip of bombed out buildings and prime city blocks covered with rubble had an even more desolate air. She wandered along Unter den Linden, but there was not a lime tree to be seen. Had they been cut down for firewood in the war, or removed since then so that Russian tanks could roll grandly along to the square? Thousands of waxy little plants stood in neat rows in concrete flower beds. Libby felt an urgent need for a cup of coffee, but could find no cafes or street stalls. At last she found a restaurant on the ground floor of a hotel that looked like a bunker. A huge party of tourists from eastern Europe was assembling near a coach. The tour guide was making an announcement on the public address system: Libby caught references to the war cemetery and a people's housing project. It did not sound like a fun tour. At length she managed to get a cup of coffee.

She set off for the antiquities museum. A man in a wine-coloured tracksuit approached her, wanting to know if she could trade any western currency. Libby shook her head. For all she knew he could be a police agent. At a party in London a Melbourne man had told a terrifying story about being taken to prison after selling a Bic biro in Red Square. She scurried towards the ancient pillars and gates which marked the entrance to the museum. How did those nineteenth-century adventurers get all this stuff here, she wondered.

Riches from Egypt and the Mediterranean filled room after room, but the displays lacked the verve of the New Guinea setting she'd seen in Dahlem. A few people were finding their own way about, but by far the majority were with organised parties. Libby dodged several tours, German speaking and

Russian speaking, but their guides left her with an overriding impression of life in East Berlin: a didactic female voice reciting a memorised script.

Back at the checkpoint, she had to remove her scarf and comb her hair in order to resemble her passport photograph more closely. 'Smile, please,' the Russian guard insisted. She flashed an insincere grin, thinking wryly of the Armidale photographer who'd taken those shots, a year and a half ago. 'All in order,' the guard snapped at length, returning her stamped documents.

After changing from the S-Bahn to the U-Bahn at the Zoo, she walked home from the little thatched Dahlem station in the near dusk. The gnomes in the neighbourhood gardens had been joined by crocuses and snowdrops. The trees were coming into leaf. Something green and growing made the air fragrant. An old man with an unkempt grey poodle on a leash nodded at Libby. *'Guten Tag,'* she said, realising only a few paces further on that he was the man she'd met in the bus the day she'd bought her coat. Compared to the no-man's-land of the city centre in the east, this area felt like home.

At Breisacherstraße, a communal meeting was in progress. Romy, Akbar, Russell, Guenther and Hannelore had piles of pamphlets and some fabric banners. Russell handed Libby a glass of wine. 'Well, kiddo, you felt left out last time we went to the Amerikahaus. We're going again tomorrow, and this time we mean business. Every opposition group in town will be there. We're expecting thousands. I take it you'll be with us?'

'Yeah, sure.'

Guenther shook his head. 'Not I. I'll be in the emergency room again.'

Libby took a swig of beaujolais. She picked up one of the pamphlets. It was strange. Days ago she'd wanted to find people who shared her outrage over Cambodia. Why did she not quite share the passion behind the event being planned?

Even when her flatmates were going out of their way to make her feel part of the action for once, she retained some sense of being an onlooker.

'It all seems very sudden,' she said.

'Things are moving quickly, yes,' Hannelore said. 'Russell just got these flyers run off, in a big rush. And I have been at co-ordination meetings with other commune members at the Free U.'

'Wear hats, hard construction-site hats if you can get them,' Akbar advised. 'And carry something you can use as a weapon if you have to, even if it's just a small knife to dig up stones from the road.'

'Gosh,' Libby said, 'I knew that Swiss army knives had a gadget for taking stones out of horses' hooves, but I hadn't thought of them as tools for ripping up cobblestones. Sorry, Akbar, you're not joking, of course.'

'Not at all. In fact, Romy and I go now to another meeting. We pick you up, Hannelore and Libby, in the morning in the car, yes?'

'What about Russell?'

'I'll come from the studio. Might meet you there. We've built a new security set-up for our sound gear.'

Romy and Akbar departed. Hannelore turned on the radio. A Mozart piano concerto filled the room while Libby tried to describe how crestfallen she felt after her brief visit to East Berlin. 'I don't know how Guenther can think of living over there,' she said. 'I presume that once he became a citizen he couldn't just come and go.'

'Actually not,' Russell drawled. 'There's some kind of—did I hear something about a wall?'

'Come off it, Russell, you know what I mean. If he went there of his own accord, would they let him come back and forth more often than ordinary people?'

'I do not think,' Hannelore chided, 'that in socialist countries you find a distinction between doctors and ordinary people.'

'So he'd be stuck,' Libby insisted.

'That is not how he thinks.'

'Just as well.'

Romy parked the Renault in a side street a few blocks from the assembly point in Hardenbergstraße. Hannelore and Libby held a fabric banner stretched between two wooden poles, STOP BOMBING CAMBODIA. Romy had an armful of pamphlets to hand to passers by. She and Akbar both wore hard hats. Like their coats, they matched: yellow plastic.

A huge throng advanced towards the Amerikahaus with arms linked, shouting slogans and waving banners. As the crowd surged forward over the cobblestones, Libby had the sense of being adrift in a sea of people, unable to guide her own course. The babel of unfamiliar slogans—Russell was nowhere to be heard—and the hostile mood of the crowd added to her sense of foreboding. A ring of police, in helmets and carrying shields, stood guard around the glass-fronted building. The sound of shattering glass brought an end to the noisy stand-off. Suddenly there were sirens: fire alarms, police reinforcements. Students, knocked sideways by full-blast jets of water from fire hoses, staggered back on the rows of demonstrators behind them. The screams of the wounded joined with the wail of sirens, creating high-pitched waves of panic. Libby and Hannelore were thrown against one another and had to drop their banner. They were trapped by the press of bodies from behind them and in front of them. 'Try for the side of the road at least,' Hannelore suggested. They turned back and moved to the footpath where they found themselves in a surge of people near the entrance to the Renaissance Theatre.

A new note of terror entered the screams of the crowd. It failed to muffle a sound that until now Libby had known only in films, the echo of horses' hooves on cobblestones. This was no cheerful clip-clop, it was more like the drum roll of war. Mounted police! The coats of the bay horses shone as if for a parade. A double line of armed men on horseback bore down on the demonstrators in a slow-motion cavalry charge. Their shields gave them the look of medieval warriors. People scattered before them, terrified of being trampled underfoot, while those at more of a distance began to retaliate. The clash of stones on shields, batons on skulls, and the intermittent showers of breaking glass mingled with shouts and screams. Pandemonium, Libby thought, wondering where she might find safety.

'Barricade, barricade, barricade.' The word flew through the section of the crowd where Libby and Hannelore were wedged near an advertising pillar. Without words, without time to think, they joined some young men near them who were lifting either end of a silver Porsche coupé. The crowd bulged and made way as they turned the car at an angle, blocking one lane of the road. Other groups were pulling more cars into position, forming a metal barrier against the mounted police. A horse whinnied and tossed its head upwards in panic, showing the yellow of one eye, as access was cut off and missiles flew. The poor horses, was Libby's automatic response: those large, vulnerable eyes on the corners of their faces. Poor us, she corrected herself. Poor everyone.

Kristallnacht. She had heard panes of glass breaking in Berlin before, on the soundtracks of documentaries about Nazi attacks on Jewish businesses. Now there was something gleeful in the sound, a primitive percussion instrument. But as flagpoles were used to break the upper windows of business houses, and sharp shards of glass flew through the air, she felt a new fear. To stumble now would mean cutting one's hands and knees. The shrill pitch of noise and panic jarred her ears and made her pant in fear. She wanted to escape from the whole scene.

But how? The sway and push of a directionless and fevered throng kept her wedged with a group of people in the partial shelter of the advertising pillar.

'We're not achieving anything here,' Libby told Hannelore. 'Let's try and get out.'

'Hold on to me, I will find the street where we parked the car.' Heads down, they shoved their way along, moving sideways and taking advantage of every small break in the waves of demonstrators. As they stumbled towards Savignyplatz, they were hailed by a familiar voice.

'Hannelore, Libby, thank God. Can you help me?'

Romy was attempting to guide an injured person along the far side of the footpath. The embroidered coat was blood-stained, and a huge bump over his left eyebrow made Akbar all but unrecognisable under his yellow hat.

'The bastards, they especially beat anyone who looks foreign to them,' Romy said. 'Is he all right to walk, Hannelore, do you think?'

'Yes, probably, but anyway it is not safe to stop. We're not far from the car.'

Libby put Akbar's other arm over her shoulders, while Hannelore dabbed at his cuts with tissues. Before long they had reached the Renault. 'Libby, you get in the back while Romy drives. We need something better to put over his wound. Yes, your scarf will do. Keep it pressed down, like that. I don't know if his eye is damaged: he will need tests. Hold him steady, like that. Me? No, I think I make my way to the Technical University at a distance from the crowd. They will be needing first aid up there too. *Tchuss!*'

'See you, Hannelore. Good luck.'

As Romy sped towards the emergency centre, Libby sat with Akbar's head on her lap, pressing the scarf over his split eyebrow. She wouldn't be able to wear that scarf again. 'At least you were wearing the hard hat,' she said.

His reply was a moan, or perhaps an attempted prayer.

CHAPTER 7

Romy telephoned. She had been with Akbar all night at the hospital. The corridors were crammed with emergency cases waiting for x-rays and other tests. 'As a favour to me, Libby, perhaps you could take my place at the preschool for a week or two?'

'Sure, Romy.'

Guenther staggered home groggy with fatigue. 'Akbar will be okay, I think, but some of the others are in worse shape. Many police are injured too. They tell me also that two horses had to be destroyed.'

Libby was glad to have work to do. Her stomach was still churning from the demonstration. She hadn't known she was capable of such strong feelings. Such rage, such terror. She felt vaguely guilty at having escaped unscathed. A work routine might calm her down; besides, she wanted to show that she could make herself useful.

Reinhardt rearranged the schedule so that he did most of the group work, leaving Libby to act as a backup, arranging materials, talking to children about their paintings and craft, comforting the ones who cried, distracting the ones who quarrelled. Once she got down on the floor and communicated with the children at eye level, they seemed quite willing to accept her, despite her accent and the fact that she wasn't

Romy. It was demanding work, paying close attention to a roomful of children, but it was not at all dull. She wondered whether she should have trained to work with younger children rather than upper primary. No, those piano-playing elocution freaks from the Kindergarten Union would have driven her barmy. The days she spent with Gisela, Horst, Johnny, Konrad, Regine, Michael, Petra, Magnus and the others were dense with mundane tasks. She tied aprons, set out lunches and organised trips to the bathroom. The anti-authoritarian propaganda seemed less obtrusive from her new perspective than it had on her first visit.

She thought about survivor guilt. She had heard the phrase first from Harry Stonebridge, a professor of politics who she knew in Sydney. They met at either the Alternative University or the Shed, a radical discussion group that met in an old iron barn on the perimeter of the campus. A dozen academics and fifty or sixty students met there to discuss moratorium tactics; some of the inner circle worked on a radical syllabus for philosophy and other humanities courses. Harry, with his hair turning photogenically silver at the temples, his intelligent, deep-set eyes and deep voice, was one of the glamour figures of the Shed. An invitation from Harry to have lunch at the pub or to spend an afternoon in bed conferred high status on the student singled out. Evacuated from Germany with a small group of other Jewish children a few months after *Kristallnacht*, Harry had been one of the few members of his family to survive. After a gap of about ten years, he discovered that his only sister was living in Québec. His parents, grandparents and elder brother had died.

'Are you close to your sister?' Libby asked, on the first occasion that she was taken to lunch.

'Not really. She's into all the family history, tracing what became of everyone, copying our few photographs, contributing to Holocaust histories and museums. All that.'

'And you're not?'

'Not overmuch, no. Of course Karla says it's neurotic avoidance. She thinks I have survivor guilt.'

'What does she mean by that?'

'She wants to believe I'm as obsessed as she is, but just don't want to show it. She finds plenty of evidence. Doesn't like me anglicising our name—though that idea was given to me by people at a Jewish welfare agency the week I arrived. She's appalled that I haven't married a Jew, that I never go to the synagogue. She's been out here a couple of times but we quarrel so much that Annabel—my wife—finds it exhausting.'

'I think personal history is important. Recording the stories of people who lived through extraordinary times. Including you.' She smiled.

'I long ago ceased to believe I would do the world a favour and write the great novel of the migration experience. In fact, I think there should be special grants awarded to all those of us who have made a conscious decision not to inflict yet another volume of memoirs or soulful little monographs or series of articles on the world.'

'That's a bit cynical. Aren't academics supposed to publish?'

'Precisely my point. Let the ones who want to publish, publish, and reward those of us who would rather set a few young minds on fire through the spoken word with special grants on condition that we don't publish.'

'Good luck with it.'

'I'm serious.'

Libby smiled to herself, remembering that conversation. Serious Harry wasn't, not in the sense that Hannelore was serious. His every utterance was laced with irony; his green suede jacket was a caricature of an academic's green suede jacket; his lectures (Libby was not enrolled in his subject) were spiced with limericks and double entendres. Libby spent many memorable afternoons in bed with Harry in his house

71

in Annandale. His wife, who worked at an art gallery nearby, was not home. As a lover, Harry was versatile and proficient, if silent. His air of observing himself wryly from a distance no matter how intimate their actions prompted Libby to keep her emotions in check also.

One Friday in winter Harry suggested that they spend the night at his beach house. He drove his old Simca through Frenchs Forest and past Avalon, coming to a halt in a fern-laden carport in front of a small bungalow at Bilgola Beach. They collected driftwood to burn in the fire, played old 78 records, ate hamburgers and made love with more abandon than before. It was their first night together. Libby was not used to sharing a bed: it took her some time to fall asleep with Harry's hand on her breast and his knees behind hers. Eventually she fell into a deep sleep. At seven forty-five the next morning she was jolted awake by sunlight, the sound of doors opening, and crockery clinking. Harry was talking to someone, and that person was not her. His exact words were, 'How lovely, darling, scrambled eggs and bacon.' Annabel Stonebridge, a fair-haired woman in her thirties who was smiling like a well-trained room service maid, was standing at the foot of the bed with a breakfast tray set for two.

In a fluster of embarrassment and rage, Libby grabbed her clothes from the floor and dressed in the bathroom. 'Don't go, darling, let's be adults about this,' she heard Harry say. She heard Annabel's laughter. Grabbing her bag from the living room—it was still on the hearth where they had made love the night before—she left the house, slamming the door on the complicities and mysteries of marriage. She knew she could hitch a lift to the city from the main road.

When Libby looked back on that humiliating affair, she wondered if she had been drawn into it in the first place through the younger-sister jealousy that had motivated much of her behaviour in her teens. It was hard to know. It was not a chapter of her life she'd felt free to discuss with her sister, at any rate.

One afternoon as Libby walked home from the *Kinderladen*, the streets of Dahlem were jammed with police cars. Some had been barricaded off with metal barriers. Police were redirecting traffic to Clay-Allee and other major roads. 'What in the world's going on?' Libby asked Russell, who was sitting with the telephone in his hand.

'I'm just trying to find out. Something's happened up in Miquelstraβe.'

'They're waving cars away from the Free U just near here.'

'Och, well, you know you can't trust students.'

'Would you, this week? It's terrible publicity, Russell, horses being put down.'

'What a terribly British response. Hundreds of students are injured, but you weep for the horses. You rode a pony as a little girl, no doubt?'

'Yes, I did win some gymkhana ribbons as it happens, but I'm talking about how we look in the media. How are we going to form a mass movement if we make ourselves such easy targets for the right-wing press?'

'You don't imagine we could win over the Springer press and the American news agencies by being *nice*, do you? Being reasonable?'

'Being non-violent might work in the end. Like Gandhi.'

Russell dialled again. From his whoops of disbelief and glee, it was clear that he'd found someone who could fill him in on the nearby drama.

'Get this, Libby, get this!' he announced when he'd hung up. 'Andreas Baader has been sprung from prison, from a bloody library. It's bloody brilliant! They went into the Institute for Social Questions in plain daylight, doing some damned research thing, Baader as a prisoner and the others as his co-workers. It's a bit hazy what happened next, but he's out and free and the authorities have egg on their faces that they'll never live down. It's the most audacious escape in the world, and it worked!'

'The guy who set fire to the department store? That Baader?'

'Yes, of course that Baader.'

'And he was just up the road? In a *library*?'

'That's what I'm trying to tell you, girl.'

Libby exhaled. 'This is a very peculiar town,' she said at length.

Russell was capering about in a bumblefooted dance that bore some relation to a Scottish reel. 'It's the centre of the bloody universe, Elizabeth. It is, as they say in the vernacular, where it's at. It's the Mecca of revolutionary thought and praxis. *Berliner Luft!* It's another world from half-dead old so-called Great Britain.'

'It's not at all what I expected.'

'It's not what anyone expected, because we here in this commune, and others like us all over the city, are at the absolute frontier. The brink of revolution.'

Libby assumed a country-hick accent. 'Gee, eh?' she said.

Russell laughed.

Before long, the facts of the escape were widely known. Ulrike Meinhof, a well-regarded journalist, had posed as a researcher. Baader was brought to the research institute's library to consult her about a joint project. Armed accomplices dashed into the room with masks on. Guards closed in on Baader, but he and Meinhof escaped after breaking a plate-glass window. The masked rescuers also got away. A day later a bank was robbed, with suspicion falling on the same gang that had sprung Baader.

Libby's enthusiasm was dampened by the fact that a security officer from the insitute was left wounded and later died.

'He was an innocent bystander,' she said, after she, Russell and Hannelore watched the news.

'Libby's so tender-hearted she weeps for horses and little grey men,' Russell scoffed.

'Libby is right. Violence compromises our social critique,' Hannelore said. 'I am surprised at these tactics by Ulrike Meinhof. She has a name already as a journalist, and I have heard an interview with her. She talked about a play she's written. She's intelligent; she has a conscience. This cops and robbers stuff seems out of character.'

'What you two don't seem to realise is that this is Berlin,' Russell told them.

'*Na und*?' Hannelore challenged.

'Well, it's not London during the suffragette movement or India in Gandhi's day. Baader could have gone on a hunger strike and starved to death, and there's no guarantee the outside world would ever have known. We need new ways of drawing attention to the cause. These people have been very creative.'

'Their actions create danger for other radicals, even for us,' Hannelore said. 'These people, Meinhof, Baader, whoever the others are, have glamour as fugitives, for now. Almost like Bonnie and Clyde. That enrages the authoritarians. Police raids are being made on communes all over the city. They could knock on our door any moment. We have to be very careful what we have here—anything could be confiscated. So far as I know, none of us has drugs. They are not above planting them if they are desperate. We all need to be ready with what we are prepared to tell the police, and what we aren't. You, Libby, for instance, should not tell them you are filling in for Romy at the kindergarten.'

'Why not?'

'You don't want to draw official attention to your work-place or to Romy. More than likely the paperwork has not been done with the authorities, *nicht*? So, it is better not to make them too curious, it only creates problems. And as for you, Russell, I trust you have security at the studio, and that

75

anything compromising is in a safe place. They can charge you with sedition and take everything. They can send you back to Scotland.'

'Hannelore, I'm the invisible man. No one sends me anywhere.'

'But what she says makes sense,' Libby said. 'I aim to keep well clear of the authorities, full stop.'

'Did you ever register it with the police that you are sharing this apartment with us?' Hannelore asked.

'Should I have?'

'Actually yes, but this is not the month to do it. Better to leave it now, if you did not fill in the forms when you came.'

'You tell the police where you're living?'

'Yes, it is normal here. You do not do that in Australia?'

'Of course not.'

Hannelore smiled. 'They say that we Germans like order. This is an example, perhaps. But I don't think you need to worry. The other people in this building are long-term tenants, we've always been on good terms with them. They want to keep in our good books, of course, because of Romy. Besides, we're a quiet lot. No one is going to make any complaints about us, or to notify you as an unregistered resident.'

'I should hope not.'

The following night Romy brought Akbar home from the hospital. His forehead was still bruised, and one eyebrow had been shaved off, replaced by a prominent scar and a line of stitches. He appeared to be in good health generally: he walked with a swagger, leading with his scar. Romy announced that she wanted to call a commune meeting to discuss allowing Akbar to stay in Breisacherstraße indefinitely. She was worried that he might be victimised if he stayed at the student hostel. A meeting was scheduled for the earliest they could all meet together, soon after Guenther's return from late shift. While his fate was being decided, Akbar stayed in Romy's room with the door shut.

'Until now, we've each had our own rooms, but my room's really very big, and I'd rather share it with Akbar than have him go back to the hostel. The guy in charge really has it in for anyone who's active politically. Not only does this guy pass information on to the police, but he interferes with the privacy of any student he doesn't like. While Akbar was in hospital, someone went through all his things—obviously the supervisor gave them the key. We know Akbar's one of us, politically. You've heard him at our meetings. Well, now I ask that you consider him a member of BS Kommune.'

Libby remembered Akbar's support the night she gave her talk. 'I'm in favour,' she said.

'Obviously, I am too,' Russell said.

'And I,' said Hannelore.

'I speak as a minority here, it seems,' Guenther said. 'We are acting in too much haste. There has been no discussion of the ordinary household rules the rest of us had to agree to when we joined—the rent we pay, and the rosters for cleaning and cooking. Akbar's smoking has been an issue in the past. Can we be sure it will not be a problem again? And would someone mind telling me exactly what he was doing when he got that crack across the face?'

'He was pushing a flagpole,' Romy said.

'To tear down an American flag?' Guenther asked.

'Not really. Some people wanted to use the flagpole to smash windows. He was helping them lever it out of the ground.'

'So it could be said he was asking for trouble.'

'Guenther, you're the only one of us who wasn't there,' Libby said. 'It was extraordinary, honestly it was. You just can't apply normal rules of conduct to what we did. I helped move some businessman's Porsche into the middle of the road as part of a barricade. I just grabbed on to the nearest bit I could get hold of. It felt like moving the teachers' Morris Minors on April Fools' Day, the way we used to do at school,

77

except for the terror all around us. The other side had horses, fire hoses, batons, shields, everything you can think of. Why wouldn't people try to prise out the nearest flagpole in self-defence?'

'Libby's right. Everyone flipped out, but only in response to the terror tactics of the police,' Russell said.

'Both sides had their injuries,' Guenther reminded them.

'We need a decision on Akbar's membership,' Hannelore said, 'not a post mortem of last week.'

'I do not oppose him,' Guenther said, 'if the same rules apply to him as the rest of us.'

'That makes it unanimous,' Hannelore said.

Romy smiled. 'I thought you would all agree, but I'm so happy now that you have. I'll go and get Akbar. We should all have a drink to celebrate.'

'He shouldn't drink for another week or two, in my professional opinion,' Guenther said.

Libby was looking out her bedroom window one morning when a small red creature skidded down the trunk of one of the trees. She opened the window and leaned out to get a better look. The squirrel was scampering around at the base of the tree. A few seconds later it vanished up a different, leafier tree. Her first instinct was to rush out and announce to Hannelore or Russell that she'd seen a squirrel. For fear of seeming too naive a recent arrival from the southern hemisphere, she decided not to. But the squirrel's speed was astonishing. It didn't swing like a possum or claw the trunk like a koala. It skimmed; it briefly touched base; it jumped; it all but flew.

Warm weather had come at last. The residents of BS Kommune scoured the disposal stores and pantry shelves, getting together the groundsheets, backpacks, tents, matches, torches, dried food, metal pots and compass they needed for their long-awaited survival weekend in the woods. Libby found a topographical map at the Technical University bookstore. The woods looked tame by her standards; although they stretched for miles, they were crisscrossed by neat trails at right angles. 'I suppose even the deer run in straight lines,' she commented to Hannelore.

'Of course. They are German deer.' But for once Hannelore was joking.

Romy arranged to take campers and gear to the Grunewald in two trips. Everyone was going except Guenther, who had spent many nights at the clinic since Akbar joined the commune. 'I think he arranged weekend duty just to distance himself from us,' Romy said. 'He is sulking like a petulant little boy.'

'Well, he's working such long hours,' Libby said.

Romy tugged at the leather straps of her backpack. 'Nonsense. Like most things, this is sexual in origin.'

Libby was astonished. 'You and Guenther?'

'Why not? I am a female, he is a male. Such things are not unknown.'

'Of course not. It's just that I'd never have guessed. You know, you two.' Blushing, Libby bent down to lift an armful of equipment.

They had chosen a drop-off point just west of the autobahn, on Fischerhutten-Weg. Russell, Libby and Hannelore humped their gear away from the noisy highway and walked a few paces into the woods. The two Europeans gave Libby a crash course in the difference between alders, elms and birches. 'You can tell the silver birch by the silver trunk, see?' Hannelore explained.

'I still get muddled up. I can tell a fir tree from something that loses its leaves, but that's about as much as I know.' Last year's pine needles were underfoot: in a surprisingly short time they were away from the fumes of traffic and able to breathe in the scent of pine, earth and new growth.

'If it gets hot,' Hannelore said, 'the Wannsee is in walking distance.'

They consulted their map. 'Yes, and several small lakes as well,' Libby said.

'We'd better not go too far, or the others won't be able to find us,' Russell said.

In half an hour or so, the Renault was back. Romy parked off the road in a little clearing. When she joined the others, they saw that she had another man with her besides Akbar. The newcomer was dragging a heavy suitcase.

'Hannelore, Libby, Russell, this is Akbar's friend Bahman, from the hostel,' she explained. Without much enthusiasm, everyone said hullo to the small man with the unsuitable luggage.

'There's a problem here,' Libby said. 'The rest of us have got backpacks so we can do some hiking and orienteering. You won't get half a mile with that bag.'

Bahman gave a winsome smile. He had long, wavy, light brown hair and a certain boyish charm. 'It's okay, really. I'll carry it, no problems.'

'After a mile or two, it'll obviously be a problem.'

'How about a compromise?' Russell suggested. 'We can set up a base camp not too far into the woods, leave our tent and heavy gear there, and continue on foot.'

'You don't think our things will get stolen?' Hannelore asked.

'Unlikely,' Russell said.

'I don't suppose we have much choice,' Libby admitted.

They tramped into the woods single file, Libby leading, followed by Russell, Hannelore, Romy and the two Iranians, who took turns with the suitcase. When Libby called back to ask whether they were exhausted yet, they insisted that they were fine. She plunged on until they found a place she thought they could use as a camp site. It was dry and secluded, and two trees, one of them half-hollow, made a natural hiding place for their gear.

'Okay,' she said, 'we'll leave the stuff here, mark the place on our map, and go and find the water. It's hot enough to swim.'

'Actually,' Romy said, 'these guys and I might just stay here and think about dinner.'

'What's the point of coming at all, if you're not interested in bushwalking or map-reading?'

'Oh, we're fascinated,' Romy said. 'Tomorrow we'll give it our full attention.'

'Have it your own way. I supppose this means the rest of us only need to take our towels. We might as well have gone straight to the beach, for all the bushcraft anyone's going to need. Coming, Russell? Hannelore?'

Birds darted from tree to tree as they walked through the woods. For the most part the path was shady, but filtered sunlight fell on the occasional patch of wildflowers. It was exhilarating, after the long city winter, to be in the open, surrounded by beauty.

'We ought to sing some German hunting song,' Russell said facetiously.

'I am a happy wanderer?' Libby suggested ironically. To their surprise, Hannelore took up the tune in earnest. She had a small, clear soprano voice. The others joined in the chorus.

By the time they reached the shore of the lake, their fore-heads were moist with sweat. There was no one in sight. Hannelore and Libby raced each other to take their clothes off, then dived into the water. More slowly, and with unex-pected self-consciousness, Russell took off everything but his underpants and waded waist deep into the water. Although the water was clear, the mud underfoot was dark slime. 'Come and join us,' Hannelore called. Russell swam a few metres in a feeble stroke somewhere between a dogpaddle and a crawl. Libby and Hannelore grinned at one another. 'They don't have any real summer in Glasgow, I guess,' Libby said. 'He's never had much of a chance to learn.'

Stocky Hannelore and slim Libby floated on their backs,

swam out into the lake, dived underwater, skylarked about and finally made their way back towards the shore. Russell was already sitting on the bank with a towel over his shoulders.

'Sunscreen,' Libby reminded him. 'Very important with your redhead's complexion.'

'Afraid I left it back at the camp site.'

'Then put your T-shirt back on.'

'Certainly, Fraulein Kommandant.'

'Fair go, Russell, you were the one who wanted to learn about the outdoors.'

'Yes, it's a foreign country to me.'

'The midges, too, can bite you something awful,' warned Hannelore.

'Well, I guess we'd all better get dressed,' Libby said.

They stretched out on the bank in the partial shade. A small sailing boat came into view on the far side of the lake.

'This is the kind of setting where German poets always think about suicide,' Russell said, 'but it beats me why they can't just lie back and enjoy themselves.'

'There was a cult of romanticism,' Hannelore said. 'It became very fashionable to be always pale and hopelessly in love and contemplating the end of life.'

'Yeah, a sensitivity contest. What pains in the arse.'

'How about that, Guenther and Romy being lovers?' Libby said. 'I was astonished.'

'Yes, obviously. We could see that,' Hannelore said. 'But it's no big deal. I, also, have spent the night with Guenther from time to time.'

Libby laughed. 'Really? Well, you astonish me even more than Romy did.'

'Guenther is not one of our pale, romantic heroes, however,' Russell said. 'He is entirely a practical man.'

'He is already an excellent physician,' Hannelore said.

'Yes, no doubt he is, but not a man to write love poems, do you think?'

'Not a man to say much at all. But that does not make his emotions something to joke about.'

Libby and Russell made eye contact.

'No, of course not,' Libby said.

An hour or so later, they made their way back to the camp site. Romy and the Iranians had lit a fire and put up one of the tents. Libby, Russell and Hannelore hammered in the tent pegs of the second one, then joined the others for a meal of soup, tea, kebabs, bread rolls and cheese. They passed around bottles of beer. Afterwards, they sat in a circle around the fire, singing the few songs—mostly Beatles and Elvis numbers— that had crossed all international boundaries. 'I have something special for us all,' Akbar announced, producing a pipe. They passed the joint around, everyone inhaling except Hannelore, who said that as a non-smoker she was not about to take up pot.

'Fabulous,' Libby said. 'That's really good stuff, Akbar.'

'The best,' Akbar agreed.

Libby lay back, looking at the sky through the branches of trees. Usually she had trouble identifying the stars in this hemisphere, but tonight she was sure she could make out the Big Dipper and Sagittarius. It had grown cooler. The night air had a pleasant tang of animal fat and marijuana. She felt happy. She interrogated herself about this rare feeling. Is it because I've submerged my own concerns in the activities of a collective, she wondered, or is it just that we're young and in the woods and it's springtime? Or simply the pot?

Before midnight they climbed into their sleeping bags and settled down in the tents. Libby wriggled around for a while, trying to find a position where her hip bone did not feel uncomfortable. In the end she pulled the zip up tight and stretched out flat on her back. In that position she slept until well after dawn.

In her dream, she was in an old jeep on a pig-shooting jaunt in the wild hills behind her uncle's property near Boggabri. Dogs ran beside the jeep barking; all the men had their rifles ready to fire. Her aunt was driving. Suddenly a small boar shot out of the undergrowth, across the bows of the jeep. The men jumped off, firing the rifles as they went. Libby clung on to the sides of the jeep as her aunt turned sharply. The gunfire continued sporadically.

Suddenly she was awake. She hurried out through the tent flaps. Hannelore, alone at the embers of the fire, was patting at some damper on an iron sheet. 'They're all out shooting,' Libby said.

'Yes, and you haven't heard the worst of it yet,' Hannelore replied.

'Meaning?'

'Listen.'

The sound of a semi-automatic replaced the single shots.

'Jesus, I should have been more suspicious of that fucking bag.'

'As you say, we should have been more suspicious of that fucking bag,' Hannelore echoed.

'What are you going to do?'

'Well, I'm not staying here, if this is their idea of a nice weekend in the woods. I don't like being taken places on false pretenses. Now that you're awake and can pass a message on for me, I'll leave my sleeping bag in Romy's car, and I'll hitch down to the train station with just my backpack.'

In less than a minute, Hannelore had departed, leaving Libby alone. Gunfire spattered nearby. The damper had blackened; the smoke smelt like burnt toast.

CHAPTER 8

Libby threw some dried wood on the remains of the fire and made billy tea. The sound of shooting continued. Before long she heard the snap of twigs as someone approached along the forest trail.

'Hi, you're up,' Russell greeted her.

'Yes, I'm up. What an inanely inadequate thing to say. What do you and Romy think you're doing? Who is that guy? What kind of a gun has he got? You must have known what was in that bag all along.'

'I could guess, yeah.'

'How stupid do you think I am, telling me you want to learn about bushcraft, when you really want to have target practice with a couple of crazies from Iran?'

'One, they're not crazies. Two, I am interested in bushcraft. I'm interested in everything to do with survival. We're moving into a new era, Libby. The soft bourgeois days of peaceful protest are behind us. This is the time of the urban guerrilla.'

'By which you mean . . . ?'

'That it's time to risk our lives for our cause. We've been mouthing off for long enough. We need direct, physical action against the forces of fascism. We're going to need every type of survival skill. We have to be able to change our appearance, to forge papers, to live off the land, to sleep in the open, to outwit and outlast the enemy, the way the Vietcong do.'

'Russell, this isn't Vietnam. It's a city. We might have hundreds or even thousands of students who agree with us on some issues—the war, for instance. But what's the point of pretending that a city dissident is really a revolutionary soldier? I don't want to go round shooting people.'

'But you can use guns.'

'Sure, I can use a rifle. We used to go rabbit shooting as kids. Until I was about fifteen, and suddenly felt physically sick about it, I used to hold the spotlight when the guys went out kangaroo shooting, too. But Bahman's got a semi-automatic over there. It's just so stupid, Russell. It can be heard for miles. Foresters will be zeroing in on him in no time.'

'They'll stop in a few minutes. Not all of us have had your privileges, Libby. Horseriding, camping, shooting—these are run of the mill experiences for you. If you grew up in the slums of Glasgow, those things belonged to another world, I can tell you. I couldn't even join the Boy Scouts, because my mother thought they were too Protestant. So it's a new thing for me to hold a gun or to put up a tent. One of these days my life could depend on that kind of competence.'

'Jesus, you're not going to leap in a hired Mercedes and dash round holding up banks and throwing barbed wire tyre rippers out the window like a gangster movie, I hope, like these lunatic Baader people.'

'No, I'm not. But I'm not going to prison over free speech, either. Don't you care that these two Iranian guys have been persecuted by immigration and the student authorities, probably on tip-offs from security agents? Is that acceptable in a democracy ? Do you think it's right that I have to worry about raids on the studio?'

'No, but it doesn't mean we should arm ourselves with semi-automatics. Hannelore's already left in disgust, and if I hadn't been still half-asleep I'd have gone with her.'

'If you hadn't been waiting to be alone with me, you'd have gone with her.'

Libby looked up. Russell squatted down beside her, the sun glinting on his metal-rimmed glasses and making his hair and beard coppery. His nearness added to her confusion.

'Yes, I did want to talk to you. Is that such a joke?'

'Far from it. I wanted to be with you, too. Why do you think I left the other three and came back here?'

'You might have wanted a mug of tea.' Tea leaves made patterns in the liquid as she poured it into mugs.

'Yeah, great. That too. Look, Libby, the absolute last thing I want to do is spoil your weekend. Why don't you and I go off somewhere quiet by ourselves, and leave this lot?'

'You don't think they'd mind?'

'Who gives a twoppeny cuss whether they mind or not?' Russell clasped her tightly and pressed his face to hers. Arguments and misgivings vanished as tongue met tongue and Libby inhaled the scent of Russell's body. There was a faint taste of tea in his mouth. His arms and shoulders were surprisingly muscular. Desire surged through her like sap moving up a tree trunk.

The rifle shots and automatic rounds stopped. In the sudden calm, Russell and Libby broke apart, dusted dust and pine needles off their jeans, and blinked in the bright sun. Russell put an arm round Libby's shoulders. 'It'll all be fine, lass. Don't worry so much.'

'You'll have to make our excuses to the others.'

'No problem.'

Libby busied herself making fresh damper as they waited for them to reappear. She smeared cranberry jam over the first slice, and split it with Russell. It tasted good, the slightly tart flavour of the jam contrasting with the thick dough. 'At home we have this wonderful stuff called cocky's joy,' Libby said.

'Cocky's joy?'

'Yes. Golden syrup. I guess it was always more popular in the bush than in town. In the Country Women's Association cookbook, which is something of a bible in the kitchen at my parents' place, you put golden syrup in every damned thing. Pies, slices, cakes, you name it.' I'm babbling, Libby thought. My brain is completely addled. Hormones.

'This is a bit like a scone,' Russell said.

'Here they come.'

Romy advanced along the forest trail, looking more like the radiant star of a soft drink commercial than a would-be guerilla. Akbar followed her, and Bahman, with suitcase, came last.

'Morning all,' Romy said. 'Are we in time for breakfast?'

Libby frowned. 'Hannelore's left, and I'm very unhappy about this secret gun business. What happened to collective decisions? When did any meeting discuss this?'

'You have a right to be cross,' Romy said. 'But things are not the same in the rest of the world as they are in quiet Australia. Bahman and Akbar live in a police state. They must learn armed resistance; it is not enough to be passive.'

'But you all agreed the other day that it's not safe to have anything in the house—including guns, I presume—in case of police raids.'

'Fine, we won't keep guns in the house then.'

'It's a genuine problem, Romy,' Russell said. 'I think we should discuss the whole issue of armed and unarmed resistance tactics at our next meeting.'

'It is fine with me,' Akbar said.

'Okay. Meanwhile I get the impression we're not very popular around here. The guys and I might just head back to town. I presume you two won't want to cut short the weekend's camping. Can you make it to the train from here? Do you want me to take any of your gear in the car?'

'Where does that semi-automatic come from anyway, Bahman?' Libby asked.

Bahman gave his ingenuous smile. 'You are asking about my gun?'

'Precisely.'

'Oh, who knows?' he shrugged. 'Kazakhstan, perhaps.'

'Where the bloody hell is that then?'

'Oh, for Christ's sake, Libby,' Russell interrupted. 'You know those things are Russian.'

'No, I don't actually. My expertise stops at a .22.'

Save your breath, Libby told herself. She helped fold rugs, stow sleeping bags and make decisions on which cooking things she and Russell should keep. Soon the Renault was neatly packed. Bahman got into the back seat, Akbar sat in the front. Romy sprang into the driver's seat and turned the key. Libby felt irritated and resentful, and somewhat baffled about the origin of these emotions.

'She's so elegant, Romy, isn't she?' she complained to Russell. 'So studied? Even in the woods. She thinks she's gearing up for the revolution, but she walks about with a little Middle Eastern admirer on either side, like some nineteenth-century countess flanked by two wolfhounds. It gives me the shits.'

'She is a bit on the *schili* side, I guess.'

'*Schili*?'

'Schick links. Just what you said, elegant leftie. Or armchair revolutionary, perhaps.'

'We say Bollinger socialist at home.'

'Romy's pretty genuine though. She doesn't have to work in an unglamorous place like that preschool: she could sail into film or television or modelling if she was so inclined. She doesn't have to live in Berlin or turn her apartment into a commune, but she chooses to.'

'You'll be telling me she collects money for orphans next.'

'Very possibly she does.' Russell gave a sidelong smile. 'What are we going to do in the woods, now that we're alone at last?'

Libby grabbed a towel. 'Let's swim again,' she suggested, running ahead. Alarmed at how she had all but swooned in Russell's arms, she was consciously keeping her distance. She grinned at a sudden vision of physical disintegration—her legs buckling, her head sailing away into the clouds like the buoyant Russian wife in a Chagall painting.

This all reminds me of those boundary riding jaunts with Gavin, she thought. Five years ago, her first lover, Gavin Seager, had smuggled her into remote shepherds' huts while he was out boundary riding on his family property, checking for gaps in the fences. Perhaps that was why the smell of just-cooked damper had such erotic power: it reminded her of nights of love on splintery floors and rugs by the banks of creeks. She remembered the sound of wind wuthering through the cracks of bent wooden doors, windows with taped-up panes, the smell of eggs fried in bacon fat, and the inevitable bottles of rich red Fountain tomato sauce.

She'd liked Gavin, she really had, but whenever they discussed anything political, they'd wound up on opposite sides. Gavin was worried about South Africa, he said, but his concern turned out to be for the safety of the whites. He was a tall, good-humoured young man with blue eyes, brown hair and a fair complexion which time and sun would turn ruddy like his father's. It was a fair bet that he would follow his father into politics.

Mr Seager was the local National Party federal member, and in that part of Australia seats were often passed from father to son. Libby could not see herself wearing gloves and declaring the local primary school fete open, regretting that her husband had been held up in Canberra. The affair had come to an end not long after she'd moved to Sydney to study. Gavin, she'd heard, had married a Catholic girl called Maria. That must have given the district something to talk about. They had a baby already and lived in a cottage on the family property. The Seagers raised beef cattle; their heavy Hereford bulls won prizes at the Brisbane and Sydney shows.

Russell followed without much enthusiasm. 'You and Hannelore are so much better at this,' he complained.

'Nobody's giving marks. It's not a competition.'

'No, of course not, but I don't want to make a prize idiot of myself.'

'You won't, don't worry.'

When they were within sight of the lake, a uniformed man hailed at them from a side path. Russell stopped. 'I've had a report of unlawful gunfire not far from here,' the official said. He wore high tan boots, more like flying boots than hiking ones. 'Did you hear anything, by any chance?'

'Yes, we did, as a matter of fact, about half an hour ago,' Russell replied. 'It seemed to be coming from just south of here, somewhere over that rise.' He gestured into the distance.

'Many thanks.' The man hurried on.

Bamboozling authority did Russell's spirits good. He hummed cheerfully as they made their way to the shore. The ground was twiggy underfoot; they hopped about after taking off their shoes, until Libby waded into the soft mud of the lake. She swam strongly out, then turned and joined Russell nearer the shore. They had the water to themselves: it seemed a little warmer than the previous day. She turned on her back and floated, gazing at some distant puffs of cloud. She remembered the puffs of steam on the room of the heated baths, and her rage that day with what had seemed an endless succession of German imperatives.

'You look like some pale lily, lying there naked on the top of the water.'

'Lily white, I suppose.' She stood up. The water just covered her breasts. 'In Australia it would be thought a disgrace not to have a bit of a tan by this stage of the season.'

'What nonsense. It's just another consumer craze. Conspicuous consumption.' They waded to the shore and sat in the shade of a nearby shrub. Libby pulled on her jeans and T-shirt.

'How come?'

'Proving you've got the leisure to lie around getting a suntan while your social inferiors do the world's work.'

'I think that's putting it a bit strongly.'

'Not at all. That's the social message of the suntan: I've just been to the Riviera or the ski fields and you haven't, you inferior clod.'

'It could mean the opposite, that you've been working outside.'

'It could, but not when it comes with luxury clothes and chauffeured cars.'

'I don't think I'm as strong as the rest of you on the link between consumerism and fascism.'

'Well, it's there. Follow the money and the oil interests and you find the CIA.'

'Follow the semi-automatics and you find the corrupt elements of the Russian military.'

'Libby, you're far too worked up about a couple of little bits of hardware.'

'Am I? I don't think so. Anyway, we're going to sort it out at meeting.' She looked across the lake. A light haze was forming above the water. A pair of white swans swam around the nearest inlet and paddled straight towards them. 'Aren't they beautiful!' she exclaimed.

'Swans? Oh, aye.'

'Don't be so bloody nonchalant, Russell, they're incredibly beautiful,' she insisted.

'Aye, I said so.'

The nearest swan edged closer to the bank, neck outstretched. 'Look, they're coming to talk to us.'

'Talk to us my foot, they're begging for food.'

'Really? What a shame we didn't bring any with us.'

The swan scouted round the bank hopefully, then turned its long neck back to its partner and paddled out again. The second swan raised its neck to full stretch and hooted and honked, simultaneously beating its wings, remaining stationary all the while. 'God, they're so much stronger looking than I thought,' Libby said. 'Leda and the swan doesn't seem such an impossibility after all.'

Russell laughed. 'I suppose you had wild black swans, along with the gymkhanas and rabbit shooting of your childhood.' With glances of contempt, the swans resumed their paddling towards the northern end of the lake.

'Yes, as a matter of fact, but not right near home. Further south and west. I always saw them when I went to visit my grandparents in western Victoria.'

'A man along the road had homing pigeons,' Russell said, 'but I can't say they had as much—is class what I want to say?—as these. Yeah, a working-class pastime, homing pigeons. But I found it remarkable when they started arriving back from miles and miles away.'

'It is extraordinary. Pretty mysterious the way they do it. Like bird migration, across the continents. These swans probably feed here every summer: the last thing that would occur to them are cold war checkpoints or national boundaries.'

'Birds have their own territoriality, just as fierce.'

'Let's move the camp somewhere a bit more pleasant. We really just dumped stuff near the track because of that stupid suitcase.'

'Good idea.'

They rolled their belongings up, stuffed them into backpacks, and pored over the map. At Russell's suggestion, they made their way over the highway towards a smaller lake just to the east, the Schlactensee. It looked no distance at all on the map, but they walked for a couple of hours. Eventually they chose a secluded patch of ground, sheltered by alder and birch trees, not too far from the water. 'We'll need insect repellent,' Libby said, getting a roll-on stick from the pocket of her pack.

'You think of everything, my dear.'

'You're the one who told me this was for real. Outdoor survival skills.'

'You're still a trace cross, Libby, but weapons come high on the list of survival techniques.'

'Shut up and roll some of this on, or the midges will be the death of us.'

'Aye, we couldn't have that.' Russell smiled. For a moment Libby thought that he blushed. The inevitability of their love-making was creating a shyness between them.

'What brought you to Berlin in the first place, Russell?'

'Oh, a girl, you could say.'

'Where is she now?'

'She's in Leipzig. At the conservatorium.'

'In the east.'

'Aye.'

'But you didn't want to go over there?'

'Well, there's work for me in West Berlin. There's politics. Contacts. I've got a share in a studio. And I'm not cut out for being a civil servant, whatever the complexion of the government. The idea was that Gretta would only go for a year.'

'But she hasn't come back?'

'No. It's eighteen months now.'

'Maybe she wants to stay.'

'Aye. She says so. But I can't be sure she's not being leaned on.'

'That's terrible.'

'Well, if she's been coerced in any way it's terrible. If she's happy, I guess it's a good thing.'

'But you miss her?'

'Well, I worry about her. It's weeks since I last heard anything from her. But you know how it is with something like music. She's a pianist. You get patrons who promise you concerts, or tuition, and you fall in with other people who enjoy the same musical styles that you do. She's part of a quartet now. She'd probably think twice about leaving that.'

'Are you in love with her?'

'What a question! That kind of talk went out with high-wheeled bikes.'

'But you really like her.'

'Aye, I do. But she's . . . "

'On the other side of the Wall.'

'If you like. Yes. That's one of the problems. And what about you, Libby, are you "in love" with anyone?'

'I had a very serious affair a few years ago. Might have married the guy if I'd stayed in the country, but he was impossible politically. Far too conservative for me. I liked him a lot in all kinds of other ways. In the last couple of years my relationships have been more casual, I guess. I got involved with a married man who was big in the moratorium movement. Really interesting man, despite his huge ego. But in the end I felt he and his wife were playing some sort of game and I was just the latest casual player who'd happened along. It was very disconcerting. The strangest of my relationships to date, I guess. Not that there's been so many. I'm not into one night stands.'

'No, you'd put any poor contender through the third degree about the gun laws and his views on the third world.'

Libby laughed. 'Yes, I'd interrogate him about British imperialism in the Middle East. What sort of initiation do you think that was?'

'You did great. We had to make sure you weren't just some flibberty-gibberty little tourist.'

'Or at least a little flibberty-gibbert who could use a library.'

'At the very least. We have our standards. As it happens, Libby, you're a bit of a dazzler. I didn't want to look as if I was just taken with you physically.'

'Of course not. Your sole interest is in my mind.'

Libby leant towards Russell, who kissed her again. 'I love the feel of your beard,' she said.

'That's good. Let's get on to the rug.' Russell spread the rug behind a screen of trees. Libby blinked as she stumbled out of the sunshine into the cooler shade. As Russell caressed her neck and lifted the hem of her T-shirt, she felt her nipples tense in anticipation. She sighed and ran her hands down his spine. They undressed quickly and lay with their naked bodies close, losing themselves in a world of touch. The lovemaking that followed was urgent and fast, almost frenzied. They made themselves a picnic meal, then made love again with more languor. Dusk led at last to darkness, and under a starry sky they continued exploring each other until exhaustion overtook them. The temperature fell rapidly, and as the sleeping bags proved too narrow for two bodies, they cuddled close in their separate zippered cocoons.

CHAPTER 9

In the morning Libby and Russell walked to the Krumme Lanke station. Again the distance seemed much longer than it looked on the map. At a small bakery they bought *Pfannkuchen*—plump, sugar-dusted jam doughnuts—instead of the usual breakfast rolls. They were still licking sugar off their fingers and dusting it off their faces when the train came in.

Near the Dahlem station, an unsmiling, intelligent face gazed from a police poster. Citizens were alerted to the fact that the police were searching urgently for Ulrike Meinhof. The wanted woman had dark hair with a straight fringe, and good features. It was a face to be expected on the inside cover of a hardback book, or on a billboard advertising a film noir. The police were also looking out for a recent jail escapee, Andreas Baader, and a number of accomplices, in connection with robbery with violence.

'She's better looking than I thought,' Libby said.

'Aye, and they're driving the police to distraction. There are rumours that they're in East Berlin, that they're in Jordan, that they're in West Germany somewhere, that they're in Libya. They've vamoosed. Vanished into the blue.'

'Yeah, but they must believe that they're somewhere here, or there wouldn't be all these raids on communes.'

'Come off it, lass. You think they need a legitimate reason to raid communes? Give a German in uniform a chance to curtail someone else's civil liberties, it's like jam doughnuts in front of famished hikers. They can't help themselves.'

'It's mysterious, though, about her twins. You can't just make two little girls disappear.'

'Not so difficult, especially if they're not together. You could hide them each in a different household.'

'Yeah, but would you, with twins? They're often very close.'

'I couldn't say.' Russell put a hand on her arm. 'Do me a favour, hey, Lib? That boy Erich—d'you suppose you could tutor him again for me tomorrow? I'm a bit tied up.'

'Sure. Will you let him know to expect me instead?'

'Of course.'

'Actually, Russell, I'm going to see the principal of a private college about some more permanent tutoring.'

'Oh, aye?'

'Yes, the Ivy League Institute. In Breitenbachplatz, near the Max Planck Institute.'

'They're usually slavedrivers at these places. I haven't heard of that one, but I'd blacklist most of the so-called institutes and colleges I've worked for.'

'Beggars can't be choosers. I've got to find some work if I'm going to stay here.'

'Fair enough.'

Libby's face and hands were sticky; her back ached from the weight of her pack. 'I don't think I've ever been so desperate for a hot shower.'

Yet when they reached Breisacherstraße, they did not go into the bathroom together: the protocol of the commune, with its emphasis on privacy and political commitment, made itself felt even when they had the place to themselves. Libby showered, shampooed, and mopped surplus water off the floor before leaving the bathroom, as required by one of the communal reminder notices. Russell took his turn after her, then left the apartment, whistling. She collapsed on her bed to rest her aching muscles and to puzzle over how quickly lovers could revert to colleagues. Or comrades? It was exasperating. The intimacy of last night was left behind the second they crossed the threshold.

After dozing for a couple of hours, Libby dressed in her most conservative outfit, a fawn skirt with a cream blouse. She had to see the bank about transferring some cash from her Sydney account: nearly all that remained of the money left by her grandfather. Berlin was not a cheap city, and she'd had only the most casual of jobs. She tried to work out how long she could afford to stay here before making use of her return ticket.

There was an aerogram in the letterbox in her elder sister's unmistakable forehand.

Dear Libby,

I have had a very worrying letter from Julie. She and Larry were just thrilled to see you at first. She was lonely there with the baby, and you had news of me etc. But she tells me you are being influenced by a very unsuitable group of flatmates—dangerous radicals, Julie says, who attack American buildings so viciously that all the windows shatter and the police have no choice but to use fire hoses. I know you were involved in the moratorium here—fair enough—but this sounds like way-out. So far I haven't said anything to Mum and Dad, you know what they're like, anyway we are getting too old to keep running to them.

We are adults now but I wonder if you are behaving like one. I don't mean you should be 'settling down' in Mum's sense of the word, marrying some Gavin Seager type, but making a start on a career. You're wasting your potential. Julie thinks you are just floating around museums etc. most of the time. What is the attraction of that city? It would be the first target in Europe in case of war. Your postcards have told me next to nothing, unless you count the fact that there are whole rooms of Rembrandts. That's fine, Libby, but Julie thinks you are getting out of your depth, and as she's the one on the spot, I have to respect her point of view, and you know she wants what's best for you.

It is calving season now, and the losses in the IV program have been almost nil. Very gratifying to see healthy little calves after all the hard work! It's a rather dry season, and many of the graziers are trucking in hay to feed the stock. It is months since I went to a film or bought a dress, but the rural life suits me, and I don't miss those things. Mum and Dad were always a bit dubious about this line of work, but even they can see I'm happy. Are you? That's what worries me. Do write soon.

Love,
Sue

Libby's teeth clenched; her jaw moved slightly. I'm literally grinding my teeth, she thought. Blast Julie! Damn Sue! What right did these conventional bitches have to tell her what was in her best interests? Snippets of commune jargon bounced into her mind: *Reactionary bourgeois elements! Accomplices of fascism!* She would ignore Sue's letter. She would give Julie a piece of her mind. She wouldn't buckle under this kind of pressure.

Sue had always tended to use an imperious older-sister tone. Athletically gifted and extroverted, was the kind of girl who was voted class captain every three or four terms. She was the district champion junior rider at eleven, then, at fourteen, lady's equestrienne runner-up. The rider who beat her, Evelyn Rhys-Johns, went on to train with the Olympic team. Sue was pleased for her rival's success but said she had no desire to compete in England or Europe. Libby found Sue's self-effacement unforgivable. If she'd had half Sue's talent, she would have done almost anything to get the better of Evelyn. As it was, she had to be content with a few ribbons for the barrel race and other novelty events.

She hoped that Sue would keep her panic to herself. Even

in their childhood disputes, Libby had never enjoyed as much credibility with their parents as Sue. She folded the letter into a tight square and put it in her wallet.

As she neared the station, Libby saw that a tall black GI was standing near the Wanted poster, frowning at the text. Seeing Libby, he looked up. 'Excuse me, ma'am, do you speak English? I'm tryin' to figure out what she done.'

Libby smiled. 'No one's exactly sure what she's done, but among other things she's supposed to have helped her lover escape from prison, and they and their friends have been robbing banks. There's a kind of left-wing gang. Or so they say.' She shrugged.

'She sure don't look like your usual criminal. I thought maybe she'd murdered her husband or something.'

'A man did die, when they all escaped from the library, but I'm not sure who shot him.'

'Wait on. You tol' me he escaped from prison.'

'Oh, they persuaded the prison superintendent that the guy who escaped had to work on some research thing in a library.'

The black soldier laughed. 'They fell for that? You tellin' me a German prison chief bought that?'

'He wishes he hadn't, I guess.'

In the train, Libby and the black soldier sat next to one another. 'Your English sure is good, ma'am.'

'Please don't call me that. I'm Libby. Libby Milroy. And I'm Australian.'

'Oh, right. I'm Kirkland Cartwright. A pleasure to meet you, Libby.'

'Have you just arrived in Berlin?'

'Been here just four days. My wife and my baby son are due to come next week.'

'That's nice. How old's your son?'

'Kirkland junior is exactly six days old now. I ain't never seen him. The day he was born, I got my transfer from camp to Europe.'

'Better than Southeast Asia, anyway.'

'Sure, we all say that. This doesn't seem a bad town. Pretty trees. But my wife will be real pleased to meet someone who knows English who's been here for a while. You live near here?'

'Just up the road.'

'How about that? Us too.' Libby tore some unused deposit forms out of her chequebook for scrap paper, and they wrote down their addresses.

'Where do you come from in the States?'

'Atlanta, Georgia. My family moved there from the Sea Islands. You ever hear of them?'

'In the Caribbean somewhere?'

'No, ma'am—Libby—they right off the coast of Georgia, right by Brunswick. Real pretty coastline. Lots of people from Atlanta go there for their vacations.'

'What do you do when you're not in the army?'

'Mechanic. Service station. And Ardena, she's a beautician and hairdresser.'

'When did you say she's coming?'

'Wednesday. She'll be real pleased when I tell her I met you.'

'I'll give her a call on Thursday or Friday.'

After arranging for a transfer of funds which would allow her to stay in Europe another two months or so, regardless of whether she got more work, Libby strolled along the main shopping streets, gazing at the window displays of summer clothes. The fashionable Berlin woman would be wearing a mid-length raincoat over cream linen trousers and matching vest. This was a Berlin that she'd seldom encountered: international finance, high wages, designer clothes, and expensive restaurants. Just a few stops away in the U-Bahn, she was inhabiting a world of student protest, Afghan coats and cheap pub meals of lentil soup, hot dogs or moussaka.

She went into the biggest department store, Ka-De-We, and

fell into an almost mesmerised state among dozens of mir-
rored display cases under soft neon lighting. The sturdy old
escalators took her up floor after floor, passing coats, shoes,
manchester, menswear, toys and haberdashery. At the top she
found herself in a food hall the size of a sprawling outdoor
market. The top note of the mingled odours smelt like salted
herrings, but she could also identify cheese, smoked meats
and fresh baked bread. At the game counter, the feathered
carcases of many birds, grouse and peahens and wild turkeys,
dangled from hooks, swaying in a parody of flight. She passed
the fish counter: smoked haddock, sardines, whitebait, pinky-
white fillets of something. Some large, dark grey fish were
swimming in a small tropical tank. As Libby watched, a
customer pointed to one, the fishmonger reached into the
shallow water with a gloved hand, spread the squirming fish
on his wooden counter, and cracked its head loudly, once,
with a large mallet. The sound reverberated like a gunshot,
ending Libby's trance and prompting her to dash away to the
escalators.

'*Meine Dame*?'

Libby realised that a ground floor sales assistant was speaking to her. The woman's eyelids drooped under two rows of
false eyelashes.

'Excuse me, I wonder if you could repeat that?'

'I was offering you a free demonstration of our new per-
fume.' The woman brandished a bottle.

'Thanks, but no.' Libby headed for the door. Russell would
disapprove of the mere thought of her being here, without
Parisian scents advertising the fact.

She took the U-Bahn to Breitenbachplatz. The Ivy League
International Linguistic Institute was up two narrow flights
of steps in a building without an elevator. A small entrance
foyer was decorated like a suburban travel agency, with airline
posters and a large wall map with a banner reading ILILI
draped above it. Libby pressed a buzzer and waited. She could

hear voices in an adjoining room, a distressed woman and a man. From further along the corridor came the sounds of a student repeating sentences from an elementary tape. *Would you mind taking my suitcase? Would you mind opening the door?* Still nobody came. Would you mind answering the damned bell, Libby thought. She pressed the buzzer again, longer this time.

The door nearest to her opened. A woman with greying hair and red eyelids dashed past her, floral skirt kicking out as she made her furious way to the door, zipping documents into a canvas carry bag as she went. It was not a good omen.

A stocky man with curly, greying hair stood in the doorway appraising her. 'My apologies for the delay, dear lady. You would be Miss . . . ah . . .'

'I'm Libby Milroy.' She reached out to shake his hand. They were about the same height.

'Jeremy Moulder. Professor of modern languages.' His accent was hard to place. Welsh? American? Dutch?

'How do you do?'

'Now, my dear Miss Milroy, let me explain a little about the Ivy League Institute. We have the facilities here to tutor anyone from beginners to postgraduate research scientists. Some very distinguished people indeed are alumni of ILILI. Oh, yes.'

'Yes?' Libby asked.

'Absolutely. Very distinguished. But this is not the time of year for that, actually. It is more your September or January student who is apt to be here on a scientific sabbatical. Right now, our typical client is a young office worker who wants to holiday in Miami or London. Someone who wants to party or shop without language difficulties.'

'So we're talking about conversational skills? Tourist phrases?'

'Precisely, Miss Milroy. Precisely. You have your university transcript with you, I trust? Ah, teacher training. We like to see that, though it's not essential. There's a bit of a problem with your—ah—nationality, though.'

'A problem?'

'Yes, not that some of my best friends haven't been Australians, some very fine people come from your part of the world. It's not so much a question of accent—yours is unobjectionable—as of people's silly prejudices. People who learn Russian like to learn from someone from Moscow. With French students, it's Paris. If anyone brings it up, I'd prefer it if you could say you're from London. Are you with me?'

'I suppose so.'

'Fine, fine. Now at ILILI we have a certain amount of—ah—staff turnover at this time of year. People will go off on holiday, not that I blame them, far from it. But we get sudden gaps in our timetable. We need a certain reservoir of substitute tutors. Are you with me?'

'You're saying you can't offer me regular classes but you'd like me to fill in for someone who's away?'

'In a nutshell, yes. We'd be talking about Thursday and Friday evenings, six to eight, for the next few weeks, with the possibility of extra hours if other vacancies occur. How does that strike you?'

'You pay by the hour?'

'Ah, remuneration. While our rates may not strike you as high, they are the industry standard.' He named a figure. It was less than Russell had paid her to teach Erich, but at least she had the hope of two nights' work a week.

'That's fine, Mr Moulder.'

'Professor.'

'Sorry, Professor Moulder. You'll show me the teaching materials you use, won't you?'

'Delighted, delighted.' He gave her a brief tour of the premises—a bleak classroom, a small laboratory with booths and headsets, some individual sound consoles, and a meagre resource centre. There was no staffroom, and only one student was in evidence, a frowning Chinese teenage girl who was still making her way through phrases starting with *Would you mind . . .*

'So I'll see you on Thursday, at five thirty?'

'Fine, Professor Moulder. See you then.'

Jeremy Moulder gestured at the map of the world and the ILILI banner. 'Welcome to the Ivy League Institute,' he said, with a small bow.

Libby grinned, said goodbye and managed not to laugh until she was safely out in the street.

At a tobacconist's stall she bought a postcard of the Kaiser Wilhelm tower and Gedächniskirche, and scrawled a message to Sue. *Letter received. Julie's worries greatly exaggerated. Not just hanging about museums, but hiking, swimming, improving my German and tutoring for an international language institute. Don't work too hard. Love, Libby.*

She stamped the card and dropped it in a yellow postbox. She's lucky I restrained myself from writing *Running dog of the fucking capitalists*, she thought.

Back in Breisacherstraβe, she called Julie, doing her best to sound spontaneous and natural. 'Hi, there,' she said. 'Guess what? I'll be tutoring in Zehlendorf again tomorrow. How about meeting me at the coffee shop for some more of that terrific torte?'

'I'm a bit tied up tomorrow, Libby. The paediatrician and all.'

'Albert's sick?'

'No, no, just a checkup.'

'Well, we talked about meeting in an outdoor place on the Ku'Damm when spring came. It's pretty warm out now. How about making a time for next week?'

A high, strained note came into Julie's voice. 'Face it, Libby, it's best for us not to see each other just now. Your current associates are a definite security risk. You seem a good enough person, and I hope to meet your sister one day, so I don't want to close your family out of my life forever. Perhaps we can take up our friendship when you've acquired a little maturity.'

Libby's restraint vanished in a flash of rage. 'Maturity! We're talking about maturity? Let me tell you this, you wouldn't be a bad person yourself if you had the maturity to sift through all that CIA crap you get from the army. They've got you mouthing pure cold war propaganda, Julie, and it's a pity, because you're basically quite intelligent.'

'You ought to face a thing or two about the army, since you bring up that subject. Without the US armed forces, this town wouldn't last two minutes. The whole of West Berlin could be swallowed up by the east in less than a day. So let's not talk about propaganda, because if you think those crazy Trotskyites or whoever they are in your so-called commune could protect you, you're out of your mind. My advice to you is to go home to Australia now, before you find yourself in real trouble.'

'I'll obviously know who to thank, won't I, if we're reported to the authorities? When you see Larry, you can tell him from me to go to hell!'

'I don't think we have anything more to say to each other.'

'No? Well, I have a thing or two to say to you . . . "

The telephone began giving a monotonous beep. Julie had rung off. Libby sat for a minute with the receiver in her hand, her heart pounding. She could not think straight. She re-ran the conversation in her head. The word *Trotskyite* stood out: she'd never used it, so Julie must have picked it up from someone else, presumably Larry. *Current associates* sounded like security jargon too. Bugger it, the bastards had been running a check on them.

This time Erich's mother was at home. She wore a flowered housecoat over her dress, a garment reminiscent of the Donna Reed Show. '*Guten Tag, Frau Keilmann*,' Libby said, as the woman pumped her hand up and down in a demonstrative handshake.

'He has improved his results so much since the start of the lessons, Erich,' Frau Keilmann said. Libby nodded and smiled.

'English is such a universal language,' she said, feeling that she sounded ludicrous.

'Even so. My husband says the same thing exactly.'

Erich had his composition topic ready: *A day in Ancient Egypt.*

'Well, this is fun,' Libby told him. 'Who are you going to be, one of the pharaohs, or a slave building a pyramid, or what?'

'You tell me.'

'Come on, I'm not here to produce the ideas as well as the words. And don't give me that shit about what Mr Muir does.'

Erich looked at her with a little more respect. 'You sound just like him, sometimes,' he said. He flipped open an encyclopaedia. 'What if I'm a cotton farmer on the Nile, and then I get eaten by a crocodile, and there's only about half a body left to turn into a mummy?'

'Sounds very promising.' They worked through the essay in high spirits. When Erich's mother came in with a tray of fruit cake and pear juice, they were deciding on the grave objects for the limbless corpse: crutches, a wooden wheelchair embossed with ibis, and an urn filled with cotton seeds. Frau Keilman cocked her head to one side with pleasure at the sight of her son and his tutor laughing together.

CHAPTER 10

It was Libby's turn to cook. She cut up spring onions and green capsicums from the outdoor market, and scalded tomatoes in a steel bowl. 'That looks good,' Hannelore said.

'Gazpacho. It all has to go in the blender and then be kept cool before it's served.'

'Good vitamin C and good texture,' Hannelore said.

'Glad you approve.' Libby ladled the ripe tomatoes from the hot water to cold, then slipped off the puckered skins.

'I'm worried about the meeting,' Hannelore said.

'Me too.'

'Yes. I have been reading the underground newsletters. These Baader gang people are calling themselves the Red Army Faction. There's a statement from them, "Did any pig imagine we'd speak about the spread of the class struggle and reorganising the proletariat, without arming ourselves at the same time?" Apparently I am, in their terms, a pig. I don't want to arm myself. It was bad enough on the day of the cavalry charge, treating students who'd been beaten with batons and crushed by the crowd, without asking for gunshot wounds. I sometimes think that I have a more conservative attitude because I study medicine. The hardliners seem to come from the humanities.'

'I don't want to carry Russian light automatics around either,' Libby said. 'Or whatever craziness those Iranian guys have in mind. We've just got to hold our ground—make everyone stick to the rule of not having weapons here.'

'Sure,' Hannelore agreed, 'and Guenther will vote with us. Romy and Akbar, probably not. That makes the vote of Russell most important. We must persuade him that non-violence is the answer.'

'You know Russell. He likes to oppose people's arguments just to be provocative.'

'But Libby, you have influence with him, *nicht*?'

Libby blushed. 'Less than you might imagine, Hannelore.' It was embarrassing how transparent her emotions were. Since her first meal in Breisacherstraβe she had been alert to Russell's movements. Russell's voice, Russell's face, Russell's views on everything from chicken soup to Marcuse were woven into the fabric of her Berlin experience. 'He's sort of elusive and hard to fathom, isn't he? He says he likes playing the devil's advocate, but often I feel it just amuses him to confuse me.'

'Perhaps it doesn't pay to take him too seriously.'

'If only I knew any more how to be flip and cool. I'm not very good at it. I get obsessed or something.'

'Don't apologise. Human beings are emotional. They are not born to be flip and cool.'

'But it's decadent and bourgeois to want love, isn't it? Russell is into all this stuff about urban guerillas hanging loose and being able to vanish or flee across the borders at a moment's notice.'

'Russell may laugh at the romantic poets, but he shares some of their delusions. He confuses the non-conformist with the revolutionary.'

'I'll have to think about that,' Libby said. She filled the blender with the chopped peppers and squishy tomatoes, and for a couple of minutes the mechanical whine made conversation impossible.

'What brought you to Berlin?' she asked, sampling the puree and adding a little salt.

'I started off my university studies in Schwäbisch-Gmund,' Hannelore said. 'I thought once I might study theology. Then it seemed to me the 1960s were not the decade for reflection or introspection. I became active in socialist student groups; I began to hold political views that upset my parents. My father is an industrial chemist, quite a high-up executive now with a Swiss pharmaceutical company. When my parents moved to Zurich I had the opportunity to go there, but Zurich is not for me, politically, you understand. Besides, it made sense to finish my studies in Germany. I applied to study medicine here, and I got in. Simple, really.

'My parents send me money. It is no more expensive for them to keep me here than anywhere else. For my father, perhaps, there is a kind of patriotism in helping keep some young people in West Berlin, so the city doesn't just die on its feet. It suits me from a medical viewpoint: there are so many old people here. Gerontology is an important specialty, and I like the old. They're really tough, many of them. Survivors. One patient told me she would have died of starvation in 1944 if it hadn't been a good year for mushrooms. Berliners were so hungry that year that they used to steal the grain from the university's wheat research centre. The city was a shambles. People lived in cellars with no heating. Public transport didn't run, the black market was incredible, and all the women, even the old ones, were terrified of being raped by the Russians. So many of the German men never returned. It's a city of ageing widows. So I make a career perhaps among them.'

'You don't wonder which of them voted for Hitler?'

'Yes, I do from time to time, and I'm angry sometimes about that. There's plenty to be angry about. But with the people at the clinic, no, I'm not often conscious of their past. I think about more practical things, whether they are eating well enough, whether they can manage the stairs, and that kind of thing.'

Libby felt a stab of envy. 'You sound so sure of yourself, as if you've mapped out your life. I haven't a clue what I'll be doing in ten years' time.'

'You'll be teaching in Australia, naturally.'

'I won't be making films somewhere with Russell? Or filling in for Romy at a Berlin preschool?'

'Of course not. You will make delicious soup, you will marry some nice man, you will teach.'

'How dull. It doesn't sound possible, after Berlin. Hannelore, what I really want to know is, who's this Gretta of Russell's?'

'I haven't met her. She plays the piano, I believe. I think her parents are Latvian, but they live in West Germany somewhere. Gretta was offered a scholarship to Moscow, but her family thought it was—you know—the tentacles of the communist octopus grabbing their baby. Then she got the chance to go to Leipzig, and still her family was against it, but she went there before anyone could stop her.'

'So what about Russell?'

'Oh, Russell did photographs for some youth quartet that she was in. They met in London, then they came here. I am not sure it is a big deal.'

'Hannelore, you're always saying sex is no big deal. What about passion? Don't you believe in meeting the one perfect love?'

'Passion! Passion is for the great symphonies, not for the sexual escapades of students. There is no one perfect love. Great friendship or great physical attraction can lead to loving. It is something you do, not someone you meet.'

Libby considered. 'Not sure I get you,' she admitted.

'Russell is a nice-looking man, Libby. He has lovely fiery

hair and beard and sometimes a special smile. But he is not the one for a lifelong passion. Truly.'

'You just don't want me to get hurt.'

'Everyone gets hurt. But yes, I prefer you not to be hurt. Also, the great passion would not suit you. You came dancing into our commune, a very light-hearted girl. No idea about our politics.'

'No idea? I was the only one in my year who'd heard of Marcuse.' She blushed as she remembered she had first heard of him through Harry Stonebridge.

'Yes, okay, but compared to us, you were not political. But we go through a lot together, the police come at us on horseback. So you change. Fine. But don't change too much.' Hannelore gave a quizzical grin and left the kitchen.

Libby poured the soup into the metal bowl and placed it in the back of the refrigerator. She reflected that she must have changed. In the beginning she had found Hannelore very hard to take, a bustling little terrier, always ready with a reminder about the commune rules.

The soup, served with ice cubes, black rye bread and unsalted butter, was a success. The group was cheerful for the start of the meeting, which began with routine items about the household budget. Romy announced that she would be away for three weeks in August. She would pay her share of rent as usual; she did not want the room occupied in her absence.

'I also have an announcement to make,' Guenther said. 'After my graduation I plan to go to Cuba, where my work will help the people of the revolution. So from September my room will be available.'

'Cuba?' Hannelore asked. 'But you never mentioned this. Will you go there on a contract, or how does it work?'

'A three-year contract. After that my fares home are met. The salary is not huge, but who needs much money when there is papaya to eat?' Guenther seemed to be blushing even on his scalp, visible through the close-cut tufts of hair.

'Well,' Russell said, 'I'm sure we all wish our comrade bon voyage, and we'll make sure you have a decent send-off before you go.'

'Yes, good idea. But it is some weeks away. Tonight we must deal with the issue of arms,' Hannelore said. 'I do not believe that arming ourselves is the right revolutionary tactic. The fact that some splinter groups are engaging in robbery and violence does not signal to me that the contradictions in our society are at a flashpoint. We are outnumbered, and we lack the support of the proletariat. Violence only leads to more violence. Our moral strength comes from non-violent protest, and from rational criticism of what we do not like. Look at the sit-ins in Mississippi and Alabama: the students there achieved integration without resorting to violence.'

'I agree,' Libby said.

Russell's metal spectacles caught the light as he looked around the table. 'God,' he groaned, 'the self-defeat of these pacifist attitudes, I've had a gutful of them, I tell you. Under all these high-minded statements about rationality and non-violence, what I hear are the voices of respectable middle-class girls who wants to be nice all the time. Of course the corrupt consumer society is about to crack open. You can smell it in the very air of this city. What better emblem do you want of capitalism than all those bloated old fat bitches gorging themselves on Black Forest torte in the Ku-Damm? A society that can turn horses on its own students is on its last legs. These people are desperate. The Red Army faction has put the very fear of God into them. If we're on the side of revolution, now's the time to show a bit of backbone. Guns, why not? A well-aimed bullet can silence a fascist forever. A few well-directed acts of terrorism could have the whole continent of Europe on its knees.'

'Russell is right. Guns demand guns.' Everyone turned towards Akbar, but he had no more to say.

'I have no intention of arming myself or of sheltering terrorists,' Guenther said.

'The two things must be distinguished, surely,' Romy said. 'We may decide that it is inappropriate for a commune of students in a quiet suburb to keep guns here, yet our duty to our comrades may require us to offer sanctuary to people on the run, or to victims of fascism from other countries. Our parents were the experts at not seeing what was going on around them. We don't have that luxury. We don't want to be deluded. We know what our political police are like, and how the authorities treat civil disobedience. There has to be a more effective stand against that than wringing our hands like Lutheran theologians and talking wistfully about peace. We have to be ready to show our solidarity with dissidents, even at some risk to ourselves.'

'We can't do anything if we're not honest with one another,' Libby said. 'Probably everyone except Hannelore and myself knew that the main aim of the wilderness weekend was target practice. Why the hell weren't we told? I object to being taken for a sucker by people who then use terms like comradeship and solidarity.'

'For that you have the right to criticise,' Romy admitted.

'Romy has brought up a good point,' Russell said. 'There may be no need at present to arm ourselves, though I for one don't want to rule out the possibility for the future. But I don't believe we should refuse sanctuary to fugitives, just because the right-wing press is having a field day demonising them. Our commune should be able to function as a safe house, if the need arises.'

'But for how long, and at what risk to us?' Hannelore asked.

'That's the excuse people used when refusing to hide Jews,' Romy said. Tears of shame filled Hannelore's eyes.

'Surely we're not talking about something as long and drawn out as the Second World War,' Libby said. 'I don't mind giving a fugitive a bed in a good cause, but I agree with Hannelore, not forever.'

'Can we trust each other after last weekend?' Hannelore demanded.

Romy looked at Akbar and Russell before speaking. 'We must apologise for keeping some people in the dark about Bahman's weapons. Let us agree it was wrong. The weapons are not here—you can search my room or the loft or the cellar if you like—and we won't engage in the next stage of revolutionary protest without consulting others. But I want us to resolve that, given proper consultation with the group, we can offer the commune as a safe house to comrades on the run.'

'We'd be consulted?' Libby asked.

'On those terms, perhaps yes,' Hannelore agreed.

'Not without a meeting,' Guenther insisted.

'No trouble at all,' Russell said. 'Ulrike Meinhof arrives on the front doorstep one morning, just before sunrise, begging to be let in. We hand over our bureaucratic request forms and demand that she fill them out in triplicate and have them witnessed by a public notary. Then, at the next available Tuesday meeting, we put the matter to the vote. Meanwhile she hangs around on the landing waiting for us to make up our minds. Have I got it right?'

'You're exaggerating, Russell,' Libby said. 'Guenther just meant that secret arrangements like last weekend are quite unacceptable.'

'Can I be assured also that Guenther's room will not be let to someone from the armed revolution camp?' Hannelore asked. 'Otherwise I must also arrange to go somewhere else.' She looked hopefully towards Libby, who said nothing. Russell also glanced at Libby, who turned crimson with self-consciousness.

'No hasty decisions of any kind,' Romy said, with the air

of bringing the meeting to a conclusion. 'Total consultation at every step. No guns on the premises. Worthy fugitives to be given shelter if the group agrees. Thank you, comrades.'

There was a feeling of relief as the meeting broke up. Libby doubted that the differences within the group had been resolved; postponed was nearer the mark. But no one wanted the pain of a big bust-up, she least of all. She was grateful to Romy for plastering over the cracks. Romy stood up from the table and gestured theatrically towards the Lenin-covered door, as Akbar walked in with a tray of Arabian coffee and Middle Eastern pastries. The tray wobbled slightly, but Akbar managed to deposit it safely on the table. Everyone applauded. Libby inhaled appreciatively as the sweet thick aroma of the coffee filled the room. Surely the sense of affection that she felt for everyone here would be lifelong. She tried to catch Russell's eye to establish that the feeling was mutual, but he was intent on his paperback copy of *One Dimensional Man*.

Libby fetched a book from her room, a Doris Lessing novel that she'd borrowed from the British Council, and sprawled on a leather stool underneath the standard lamp, doing her best to seem as preoccupied by her reading as Russell did. In fact she was distracted by what she told herself was an unworthily bourgeois scenario, in which everyone would creep off to bed except Russell, who would throw himself at her feet, remove her boots, kiss her toes, and sweep her off to bed. Guenther settled himself at the table with a pile of medical texts, notebooks and pencils, putting an end to Libby's fantasy. Hannelore went off to her room, Akbar and Romy to theirs. Russell continued to read, Guenther to scratch away at his notes. At length Libby gave up.

"Night, guys, I'm off to bed,' she said.

Both grunted cordially without looking up.

She left her door open just enough to be able to see whether the living-room light was on. Unable to concentrate on her book, she decided to write to Jane Arnold.

Dear Jane,

This continues to be an amazing town. We went camping in the woods at the weekend. Woods, you ask—isn't it a walled city? Yes, but they stretch on for miles, with lakes and swans and all, rather lovely. I like the people in this commune, but life has had its dramas. We were lucky to escape uninjured at the demonstration against the invasion of Cambodia. Would you believe horses? Mounted police! There is also a lot of tension caused by the fact that Baader and Meinhof and co. are on the run, no one knows where, possibly hiding in Berlin somewhere, but rumours have them everywhere. My sister's American penfriend wrote to her that I am living with dangerous Trotskyites! With Lenin on the wall, I ask you . . . Hope Sue doesn't tell the oldies though.

Have a casual job teaching tourist English at a grandly named but shabby-looking college, the Ivy League Insitute. The money will be useful.

You were right about Russell. He is interesting. Interpret that any way you like. Write soon.

Love,
Libby

At long last the bedroom door was pushed open. Russell peered in. 'Can I come in?'

'I thought you'd never ask,' Libby said.

'Well, Jesus, girl, you were making it a bit bloody obvious. Poor old Guenther probably thought you were trying to vamp him.'

'You're joking.'

'You have quite a way of stretching out in those god-damned boots.'

'I was reading my book, just as you were.'

118

'If you say so.' Russell peeled off his clothes and wriggled under Libby's quilt. 'You're still dressed,' he complained.

'Not for long.' Libby tossed her nightshirt towards the foot of the bed and snapped off the bedside lamp. She snuggled against Russell's naked body, tracing the line of his leg with the sole of her foot.

Libby's first group at the Ivy League Institute consisted of five people, a good-natured married couple, the Hoffmans, and three office workers, Eva, Susi and Maria, all in their twenties. Together they plunged into useful phrases about meals, shopping, and travel timetables. Libby hoped she would not be asked too many questions about her London childhood, but she need not have worried. It was easy to keep the focus on the students themselves, where they lived and worked, and when and where they planned to travel. Towards the end of the session, Professor Moulder appeared, pushing a film projector. 'A special treat, exclusive to our college,' he announced, as he switched off the light and started the film. The five-minute tourist promotional film was available, Libby knew, to anyone who cared to apply to the British travel board, but she sat back to share her students' enjoyment of the changing of the guard at Buckingham Palace and mountaineering on the Isle of Skye.

At the end the students applauded politely. Professor Moulder gave a small concertmaster's bow.

CHAPTER 11

'**W**ould this be Libby Milroy?'

'Yes?'

'Well, my husband wants me—told me—well, he said he met you.'

'You're Kirkland's wife?'

'I'm Ardena.'

'Oh, good. Welcome to Berlin. When can we get together?'

'Well, I've got Kirkland junior, but he's real easygoing. Whenever you say. Kirk says you really know your way round. He doesn't want me hanging round in the apartment playing babies all day. He thought you could show me how to use the subway.'

'Yes, of course.' Libby arranged to call for Ardena early in the afternoon. She smiled to herself as she walked along the leafy side streets: she'd never been commandeered into friendship by someone's husband before. She and Ardena might hate the sight of each other.

The ground-floor flat was in a plain brick box of a building. She beat out four notes in a Fifth Symphony rhythm with the iron knocker. When the door opened she saw a thin black woman, about her age, tall, with very dark skin, straightened hair, and an alert expression. Ardena carried her small baby in a webbed sling between her breasts.

120

'Hi, I'm Ardena, this is Kirkland junior. It's Libby? That's kind of unusual, isn't it?'

'No one's said Elizabeth since I was his age. Libby's fine. You can say it in German, even.'

'You speak German? I hear it's real difficult.'

'All languages are difficult if you get upset about making mistakes. If you plunge on you eventually pick some of it up.'

Ardena laughed. 'I can say *Auf wiedersehen*, but it's too soon for that. Come in! You want a coke or something? Or some coffee?'

'Coke's fine.'

'We've got all this stuff Kirk bought at the PX, but you know what men are. Some very elementary things he didn't buy. I know I should just go into a local store, but I don't know what to say.'

'You can go into a supermarket, just like in the States, and not have to say anything.'

'You're sure?'

'Yes, I'll show you.'

'Oh, I'm real glad Kirk found you. He got me a map, but it's all these real strange names.'

'They'll get less strange. It's a good city. If you have to be posted overseas, you could do a lot worse.'

'You're not kiddin'. I used to pray and pray, *Don't let Kirk be sent to the war, don't let Kirk be sent to the war.* I guess my prayers were answered.'

'Looks like it.'

'What are you in Berlin for, Libby?'

'Good question. I tell my parents I'm improving my German. I'm—checking out the scene, you could say. I've got a part-time job, two nights a week, teaching English. Like every second foreigner you meet.'

'You got a boyfriend?'

Libby laughed. 'There's a man, yes, but I don't know that

121

"boyfriend" is the word. Russell's always talking about hanging loose, travelling light, that kind of thing.'

'You won't marry him?'

'I guess not. But I'm only twenty-two.'

'*Shee-it*, I'll be twenty-one next week, and I've been married more than a year.'

'Well, that's great, if you meet the right person. And if you want kids.'

'But you'll want babies, Libby.' Ardena glanced down at the face of her sleeping son, nestled so close to her body that even his breathing could keep time with hers.

'When I look at Kirkland junior, yes, babies look nice, but I can't say I give them a thought most of the time.'

'You don't think when you're with this guy of yours that you want to give him a son?'

'Never.'

'Well, Libby, he may not be your one and only. You have to face that.'

'I guess I'm not into one-and-onlys, then. Not really.'

'Okay, so you're not ready for marriage and commitment yet. What about him?'

'Russell? He's a Not Yet man from way back. He should have it stencilled on his T-shirts.'

Ardena smiled. She had a winning smile: her nose crinkled up and a small gap between her front teeth showed under her top lip. Libby laughed. She felt tension evaporating from her neck and shoulders. It was refreshing to be able to talk to someone without the undertow of sexual tension and wariness that she felt when she was with Russell. With him, mutual attraction seemed matched by an instinctive hostility which, despite her hopes, had failed to evaporate since they became lovers.

'Well, then,' Ardena asked, 'when do I get to see this famous Wall?'

'As soon as you like.'

There was a brief delay while Ardena changed the baby. Then she and Libby set off on an orientation tour that included taking the subway to Checkpoint Charlie to marvel at the wasteland of concrete, tank traps and barbed wire of the Wall; shopping for small items in a supermart without uttering a word; and walking through the grounds of the palace at Charlottenburg while eating soft ices. 'It's all so—' Ardena groped for the word and produced it with a flourish—'palatial!' She and Libby both choked with laughter. 'Oh, Lord,' Ardena said, licking strategically, 'I'm nearly dripping ice-cream on poor Kirkland junior. Imagine being drowned in Dairy Queen by your own mother.'

Secure in his papoose, the baby looked serene. 'He's a little cherub,' Libby said. 'We'll have to look at the Botticelli paintings in the Dahlem Museum, his babies are nearly as beautiful as Kirkland is. Not today though. Maybe next time.' The outing with Ardena had been a distinct success. There would certainly be a next time.

'Kirk may give you a call,' Ardena said when they were back in sight of her apartment. 'I think he's planning something for my birthday.'

'Great.'

The door of the Breisacherstraße apartment was open. Libby put her key back in her bag. 'Russell?' she called. 'Hannelore?'

No one answered. But there were voices ahead, gruff and unfamiliar. Burglars! She must dash downstairs and ask the neighbours to telephone the police.

'One moment!' A man with insignia on his shoulders yelled at her from the far end of the corridor. 'Come back at once, please. This is an official inspection.'

'Is that what you call it?' Libby advanced into the living room. Three men were sitting amidst a jumble of papers, boxes, bags and folders. Two were in uniform; the third wore a black leather jacket and flying boots. 'What right have you got to be here?' she demanded.

The senior man picked up a small booklet from the commune table. Libby felt queasy at the sight of the navy vinyl cover and the gold embossed lettering. Her passport. 'Indeed, Miss Elizabeth Frances Eva Milroy, ' he said, looking from her photograph to her and back again, 'I might ask you the same question. You are not registered officially as a resident of this borough.'

'I've only been here a little while. I haven't got round to it,' Libby said.

'Registration is required by anyone occupying a private residence for more than six days. You are in breach of the civil code. You must report to the police immediately.'

'I'm astonished. We have no such requirement in Australia.'

'You are not in Australia.'

'No, obviously not.'

'You can help us, perhaps, Fraulein. Officially we have only four persons registered as living here. With you here, there are five. Is that the total?'

'Um, yes, I think it is.' Anything to get rid of these guys, fast, Libby thought. With any luck, they don't know about Akbar.

'You think?'

'Yes, definitely.'

'And we have another question. Have you had any visitors in the apartment recently? Anyone at all? Even overnight? I must warn you that we interview the neighbours, so there is no point trying to deceive us.'

'No one.'

'You're sure about that?'

'Positive.'

'We have a few documents here that we will remove for further investigation. You may tell your associates, if they're worried, to inquire at the political police urban security unit.'

'Will they ask for you?'

'The name is Pillensbarger,' the officer replied. 'Yes, they

124

may ask for me. Come, colleagues, I think we have all we need. We have one or two things to send elsewhere, to the British authorities, for example.'

'Don't try blackmail with me,' Libby said.

'Oh, just a friendly letter from your sister,' Pillensbarger said, with a look.

'How dare you? That's private property.'

'Indeed yes. I'm sure you'll receive it back, along with your passport, all in good time. You may enquire from the British Embassy. Well, Fraulein, we take our leave of you. *Auf wiedersehen.*'

Libby did not reply. She walked into the kitchen and slammed the door behind her, letting Lenin stand sentinel until the intruders had filed out of the flat, taking her passport and other private papers with them. She leaned on the kitchen bench with her eyes closed. Her pulse was beating fast and she felt slightly dizzy. She poured herself a glass of water and went to check that the front door had been shut and the apartment was empty. Then she went back to the dishevelled living room to call Romy.

'*Ja*? Hallo?'

'Romy, it's Libby. Look, I think you ought to come home at once. We've had visitors. Strangers. They've just left.'

'Better to say nothing more on the telephone. I'll be there in fifteen minutes. Are you okay?'

'Yeah, fine.'

'I'll be right there. *Tchuss.*'

'Bye.'

Waiting for Romy, she gave way to tears. Within minutes, Romy strode in, crisp, elegant and purposeful as ever. 'My God, the bastards have been through everything. I feel invaded. It's sickening. Now, let's try to work out what they might have taken with them. Did they say who they were?'

'Urban political police, or something like that. There were three of them. The guy in charge was called Pillensbarger. I was too taken aback to get a good look at the others. They were younger; in uniform. The senior guy was plain clothes. Black leather.'

'We'll have to make an inventory of everything that's missing.'

'They took my passport, and a letter from my sister.'

'It's Akbar's things I'm worried about.' She went into her bedroom for a minute. 'Check your room very carefully too,' she told Libby.

Libby did not have the heart for systematic list-making. She checked her cupboard and suitcase: her clothes and shoes all seemed to be there. She checked the drawer of the small dresser: her passport was gone, Sue's letter, and perhaps another couple of letters from Australia. A health card with her vaccination record and warnings about yellow fever and smallpox had also been taken. Her address book was safe; she'd had it with her in her bag, along with her bank book. She felt an absurd sense of relief that her eye make-up had not been confiscated.

Romy was sitting at the dining table. 'Tell me exactly what they asked you, Libby,' she said. 'We have to work out if the raid was part of a general sweep of left-wing households, or whether they have us in their sights for any definite reason.'

'I didn't get the impression they were after anyone in particular. They were very pleased with themselves for finding my passport and being able to identify me from it. They didn't ask about anyone else by name.'

'Just tell me word for word what they said and what you said.'

'It was only Pillensbarger. The others just sat around like zombies.'

'Well, him and you. Word for word.'

Libby did her best to reproduce the conversation.

Romy was silent for a moment, then tossed her head with a slight smile. The word *cool* was invented for this woman,

Libby thought. 'I don't think it's too bad,' Romy said. 'They didn't ask any questions about drugs, or make any move to plant any, so far as we know. They didn't mention guns. Of course, there were none here—you and Hannelore were right to insist on that. I'll check with Akbar, but so far as I know he didn't have any personal papers here. So what have they made off with? Your passport, which they'll have to give back. A few books and papers. No doubt Guenther had a few seditious volumes—Marx, Engels or whatever. They'll have to give those back too. It's not as if the idiots are going to educate themselves by reading anything.'

'My health card.' A pause. 'And a letter from my sister,' Libby said.

'Oh yes?'

'Yes. She said she was worried I'd fallen in with dangerous radicals, or something along those lines.'

'Well, they can try making big fellows of themselves, but I don't think there's anything much they can do with that. Anyway, what cheek! It's a private letter.'

'Exactly.'

When Akbar returned, he confirmed that he hadn't been keeping anything in the flat that would identify him. Hannelore reported nothing missing. Guenther was unable to find a couple of political pamphlets or a book on sexually transmitted diseases. 'Maybe the pigs have the pox,' Romy speculated.

Russell was the last to return. He took the news of the raid far less calmly than everyone else. Enraged, he rushed from room to room, with cries of 'Jesus H. Christ!' and 'Fucking hell!' In his room, he tossed books and papers off shelves and emptied the contents of drawers on to the floor.

Libby stood in his doorway as objects and curses flew. 'You'll never work out what's missing if you toss everything around like this,' she protested. 'Just calm down, and I'll help you look systematically.'

'I don't need your advice on sorting through my own possessions.' Russell's coppery hair and beard seemed to emit electricity; his arms flailed and there was no trace of friendliness in his eyes.

'Okay, there's no need to snap. I was trying to help.'

'Well, since you're so interested, I'm missing a photograph of Gretta, a picture of my mother, and a letter from my father. And that's just for starters. I haven't had a chance to look properly yet.'

'All right, I'll get out of your hair.'

Libby slunk away to the kitchen, where Hannelore was preparing dinner, and flicked on the radio. 'Now here's a special request for Norm and Sarah,' a British voice said. 'This one comes with all love and best wishes from Pop, Nanna, Sam and Lulu in Hull.'

'You'd think the bloody BBC would give you the bloody news,' Libby complained, changing stations.

'Russell's upset you,' Hannelore said.

'Guess so.'

'You mustn't allow him to. You must decide not to give him so much power.'

'It's not a matter of just deciding.'

'No? But that could be a good beginning, I believe.'

'It's all right for you. They didn't take anything of yours.'

'No. You're cross about that too?'

'Oh, I'm being ridiculous. Sorry. I guess you're right. I shouldn't let Russell get me down.'

Russell did not come to dinner, but stayed in his room. They could hear him shifting his things about. When they were having coffee he came out and confronted Libby.

'Where were you when these guys arrived, just as a matter of interest?'

'I was at Charlottenburg with Ardena Cartwright.'

'The wife of that GI you met?'

'Yes. And her baby, Kirkland junior.'

'Well, God help us, Libby, don't you ever think? Don't you see the connection? The fucking CIA gets interested in you, gets some poor soldier to send you off on an afternoon jaunt with his wife, and while you're out, thank you ma'am, the Popo raid the place.'

'Don't be paranoid Russell, there's no connection whatsoever.'

'No? Well, the timing seems pretty suspicious to me.'

'So I'm supposed to spend all my days at home just to discourage the political police from searching the flat? Give me a break. There are five or six ways they could keep an eye on us. The neighbours could be spying. The cops could have a vantage point of their own somewhere nearby. They could just telephone, for God's sake. The Cartwrights are innocent people from Georgia, just arrived. They couldn't possibly have anything to do with this.'

'No? And what if your other American friends, the ones who told your sister what a threat we are, put them up to it?'

'Kirkland's a mechanic. He's repairing jeeps and tanks in some workshop. He's the last person you'd ask to do intelligence work. He's black, he doesn't know any German—he couldn't possibly pass unnoticed. You've got such a set against Americans that you just can't handle the fact that some of them have nothing to do with your conspiracy theories.'

'Don't give me any more crap about innocence. They're all contaminated by consumerism and jingoism.'

'Oh, get lost.'

Romy spoke up. 'It's not Libby's job to be a housekeeper, Russell, any more than it's yours or mine. You know that.'

'But the timing's so fucking suspicious, and she plain refuses to see it!' Russell slouched off to his room. Libby sat under the lamp trying to read, but could not concentrate. A strong visual image came to her of Ardena laughing in the palace gardens as she licked frantically at her ice-cream while sheltering her baby. She would have some memories of Berlin that were not bound up with Russell.

She went into the bathroom and sat contemplating a patch of grey tiles she could not recall seeing before. Of course.

'The rosters have gone,' she told Romy. 'They mightn't have found Akbar's documents, but sure as fate they've got a list with six names on it.'

'Oh no,' Hannelore moaned. 'I feel so terrible.'

'It's not your fault, Hannelore,' Romy and Libby hastened to reassure her.

'There must be fifty Akbars in Berlin,' Akbar said, 'and whoever this one is, he evidently lives with some very clean people.'

Everyone laughed, but with the almost unhinged laughter of anxiety.

CHAPTER 12

Libby went to her room, but she could not settle down. Even with her door shut, she was conscious of the muffled sounds of Russell heaving things about in his room. She started a letter to her parents, then abandoned it, tearing it into small fragments. Reading was not much help either: she leafed through Bertrand Russell's letters, which she'd borrowed from the British Council library, but the indiscretion of his love letters failed to amuse her for long, and his arguments with Wittgenstein were too mathematical for her. Footsteps, voices, a closing door: her flatmates were moving about. Libby pulled her camel-hair coat over her nightshirt and went into the living room. Romy was sitting under the reading lamp; Akbar was speaking on the telephone, in urgent-sounding Persian. At Libby's approach he finished his conversation and put down the receiver.

Romy looked up. The artificial light showed up a furrow above her eyebrows, the first sign of wear on her finely etched face. 'Russell's gone out,' she told Libby. 'He's in a frenzy about all this.'

'It's just crazy, what he's saying about Ardena and the CIA. She's a beautician, for God's sake. I don't know what's wrong with him: he's desperate for it to be all my fault somehow.'

'So that the blame shifts from him. I believe the Popo may have had their eyes on Russell himself for some time.'

'Oh, why?'

'Any number of reasons. His megaphone. His posters. His photographs. Or they may have identified him as one of the people breaking windows at the demonstration.'

'I got so caught up with Akbar's injuries that I didn't even know Russell was breaking windows. Didn't he go out with a megaphone?'

'Yes, but that doesn't mean he didn't get involved with anything else.'

Libby sighed. 'There are people in this movement who'd shove flagpoles through windows just for the sound effects.'

Romy shook her head. 'No. That's not it at all. It's a real beginning. If we choose the right targets, we can really destabilise this complacent heap of shit.'

'Romy, if you'd come strolling home and found those goons here, you'd be upset too.'

'I am upset, but I see these reactions as a small sign of progress. They worry about bystanders like us, and meanwhile the Red Army gets a free ride. The left is too strong and wily to be intimidated by such obvious scare tactics. Heavy-handedness by the pigs only radicalises us further.'

'Could be.'

'Don't let it get to you. That's the effect they want to have.'

'I suppose you're right,' Libby said.

'I've got a great idea,' Romy announced. 'Why don't I make cocoa for us all? What could be more soothing?'

Akbar laughed. 'If our visitors planted listening devices, they must be having a great time listening to us. The cocoa conspiracy!'

'It could be code, of course,' Libby said, smiling at last.

'Two or three sugars?' Romy asked from the kitchen.

'Three,' Akbar and Libby replied in unison. They sat on the

floor in the circle of light, their mugs held in two hands, inhaling the aroma of hot chocolate.

'This is like something out of Enid Blyton,' Libby said.

'Who is this person?' Romy asked.

'She wrote stories for children. Englishwoman, very popular.'

'I read her books myself,' Akbar said, 'as a boy in Teheran. I liked the Famous Five best.'

'How amazing,' Libby said. 'Me too.'

'Why amazing? The English dominated our oil industry—why not the books we read?'

'So,' Romy said, 'she makes a bond between you two, this Blyton.'

'She's easier reading than Marx,' Libby said.

They sipped in silence. If I count to five, Libby thought, Romy will discover some other political agenda in a cup of cocoa. You don't mention Marx in the same breath as Enid Blyton in this company.

Romy obliged. 'Of course cocoa itself was a product of colonialism and the slave trade,' she said.

Next morning it was hot and humid. Soon after nine o'clock, Libby telephoned the British headquarters in the north of the city. 'That's an Australian accent, isn't it?' a junior official asked after she outlined her problem.

'Yes.' She resisted the temptation to lengthen and nasalise this reply.

'Well, you should really be contacting the Australian military attaché: he handles everything to do with Australian passports.'

'And where do I contact him?' She wrote down the number.

'*Guten Morgen*,' a female voice greeted her. Libby asked in English to speak to the Australian official.

'Mr Mackenzie is not available at present.'

'Is there someone else I could speak to about a confiscated passport?'

'Not really, no. Mr Mackenzie is in Geneva for a couple of days. He'll be here first thing Monday morning. Do you want to make an appointment?'

'I guess so.'

'Shall we say ten fifteen?'

'Thanks. Could you tell me how to get there?'

A few minutes later the telephone rang. 'Hi, Libby, it's Ardena. I have a favour to ask. I was wondering if you'd be able to come over and keep an eye on Kirkland junior while I fix a couple of people's hair?'

'Yes, why not? When would it be?'

'Tomorrow afternoon. About two?'

'Yes, no problem. But, hey, Ardena, they're forecasting blazing hot temperatures today. What have you got planned?'

'Nothing at all. Just sitting around with Kirkland junior.'

'Why don't we go to the beach?'

'The *beach*?'

'Well, the Wannsee. There's a beach there. It should only take us about half an hour to get there. An hour at the most.'

'Sounds good to me. Will you come by? Kirkland will be waking up in about half an hour.'

'In an hour then?'

'Great.'

They took the U-bahn to Zehlendorf and the bus to Nikolassee. During the trip Ardena learned to ask for transfer tickets in German, a task that had taken Julie Brandon a year. From the station they took a forest pathway towards the lake, Ardena carrying her baby in his sling while Libby carried the beach bags. Libby wiped a line of sweat from her forehead. 'This is as hot as northern New South Wales in February,' she said.

'Yup. Or summertime in Georgia.'

'You don't expect it here somehow, do you?'

'The army mentioned swimming costumes in the information package.'

'They're very thorough, your information people. But I guess no Australian boards a plane without a swimsuit either.'

The trees along the walkway, tall firs, lent a welcome shade. Libby fought against memories of her night in the woods with Russell, evoked by the smell of pine needles. It took about twenty minutes to reach the beach, a strip of white sand on the lake shore, dotted with small canvas cubicles. Libby bought lemonades and hired a beach umbrella. She and Ardena took turns minding the baby and changing into their swimsuits. 'You swim first,' Libby offered.

Ardena dipped her long toes in the water and squealed. 'It's freezing!'

'Not once you're in, I'll bet.'

'Okay.' Ardena ran into the water, then swam strongly towards a pontoon about fifty metres from shore.

A dripping wet pregnant woman paused near the beach umbrella. 'Oh! Don't you think little black babies are just darling?' she asked.

Libby looked up. It was Janyse Pavich, the woman she'd met at the Brandons'. 'Mmm hmm,' she said. 'How are you?'

'Don't know when my friend is ever going to put in an appearance,' Janyse said, patting her bulging abdomen through the billowing floral fabric.

'Let's hope it's not too long. I thought you'd have had it by now. Do you want to join us?'

'No, no. Jane-Jo and I are just leaving. You're a friend of the mother, then, are you?'

Something in Janyse's tone invited defiance. 'Yes, I am.'

'Well, that's fine. Have a nice visit.' With a flutter of her wet fingers, Janyse moved away up the sand. Libby sat up with Kirkland junior on her lap.

'Look at your clever mother way over there,' she told him, wondering whether babies his age could focus on distant objects. Ardena waved from the floating platform, then sprang into the water in a textbook dive, her long lean legs neatly

135

together. 'You'll probably grow up to be an athlete,' she added. The baby responded as best he could, gripping her finger in a strong pink-palmed fist.

'That was good,' Ardena said, reaching for her towel. 'But my hair!'

'Tomorrow's the day for worrying about hair.'

'No, I'll have to fix mine tonight so I'm looking good when my ladies come.'

'You could try an Afro.'

'Me? You're kidding. I've spent a fortune, girl, getting rid of that curl.'

'Just a thought. It suits some people.'

'For my birthday, Kirk's taking me to a theatre restaurant place near the Ku-Damm on Saturday night. You want to come, and bring Russell?'

'Oh. Saturday's kind of a problem. I don't think we'll be able to make it.'

'Well, that's a disappointment. This was a neat idea anyway, coming here. I never thought we'd be close to a beach. Hand Kirkland back to me now. You must be dying for a swim yourself.'

'Thanks.'

Libby dashed into the chilly water, lifting her feet as the sand gave way to weeds and squelchy mud. She swam out into the lake in an unhurried breast stroke. From the water, the beach with its striped cabins and colourful umbrellas looked like a Dufy painting, or a film set awaiting the antics of Monsieur Hulot. Artificial charm, she thought. Nothing like a brush with the political police for stripping away glamour. She trod water and took some deep breaths before heading back to the shore. By the time she lay down on her towel beside Ardena, she was panting.

'That was quite a swim.'

'Mmm hmm.'

'You seem to have something on your mind, Libby.'

'I am worried, yes.'

'Anything you want to talk about?'

'Oh, I don't know. I had a kind of quarrel with a guy at the commune. Russell.'

'What did you quarrel about?'

Now was her chance to say *He thinks you're a spy, he says the CIA put you up to calling me. He blames me for things I had nothing to do with.*

'Oh, he's got a neurotic side, I suppose. He slammed out of the flat last night without telling me he was going, and earlier on he flung some remarks at me about his former girlfriend.'

'Is he still in love with her?'

'You don't know Russell. He thinks that's a meaningless bourgeois cliche. He's the unconventional type.'

'Yes, but he upsets you, Libby.'

'Yes, he does.' Libby sighed and tugged a comb through her matted, wet hair. 'He blames me for things.'

'What kind of things?'

Libby shrugged. 'Oh, hard to say.'

'He's jealous?'

'No, it's a different kind of suspicion. Oh, I can't bear even to talk about him.'

'If he picks fights with you, and he's still hung up on this other girl, and he don't even tell you where he's going, he's not worth it, Libby.'

'I tell myself those things, but I don't feel very convinced.'

'I have to go and change Kirk. Shall I buy us a sandwich?'

'That'd be nice.'

'With sign language,' Ardena said with a laugh.

'Great.' Libby closed her eyes and stretched out, head in the shade and legs in the sun. She repeated Ardena's formulas to herself. He picks fights, he don't even tell me where he's going, he's hung up on this other girl, and he's not worth it. Light danced in yellow patterns on her closed eyelids. It was

137

not easy to put Russell out of her mind. By some mysterious process, he and Berlin had become indistinguishable.

That night there was still no word from Russell. Libby chopped vegetables for Guenther, who was making a risotto with brown rice. Red and green peppers, parsley, onion. 'What's the matter?' Guenther demanded.

'It's the onions, they make my eyes water.'

Guenther looked unconvinced. 'You're always welcome to spend the night with me, you know, if you're feeling lonely,' he offered.

Libby smiled and wiped her wet cheeks. 'That's very kind of you, but I'll be fine. What do you call this peculiar thing?' The vegetable had purple stalks and a thick bulb.

'Kohlrabi,' Guenther said. 'Good source of minerals. Not so much vitamin C.' He showed her how to slice the fleshy part.

'How are your plans for Cuba?'

'Fine. No problem. You want to come?'

Libby laughed. 'Not this year. Berlin will do me for a while.'

The next day the smell of metallic chemicals permeated the Cartwrights' flat. Libby decided to take Kirkland junior for a walk rather than stay inside. 'Hi, Libby, great of you to come. I want you to meet Lindsay and Carolyn.'

Two young women, both with long wet hair, greeted Libby.

'The place smells like a beauty salon, all right,' Libby said.

'Kirkland's still asleep,' Ardena said. 'When he wakes up, he has four ounces of formula. It's all ready in the fridge, you just heat the bottle to about body temperature in this thing.'

'Fine. Is it okay if I take him out for a walk?'

'We don't have a pram yet. You mind taking him in the little carrier I use?'

'No, it looks great.'

'I'll show you how to put it on.' Ardena demonstrated the clasps on the sling.

'Good golly Miss Molly,' Carolyn complained, 'the knots in my hair.'

'What I can't stand about mine,' Lindsay said, 'is the way the colour's growing out at the roots. Maybe I should only get streaks, then the regrowth wouldn't show through the way it does.'

'What colour's that in your hair, Libby?'

'Libby's colour is natural,' Ardena said. 'Isn't she lucky? She thinks everyone should just wear their hair how it grows. She wanted me to try an Afro. Can you imagine?'

'Don would just up and leave me if I came home with an Afro,' Lindsay said. 'He'd think I'd turned into some kind of hippie or something.'

'Like you were about to go out and demonstrate with those college bums,' Carolyn said. 'Against the war. Jim thinks that anyone who burns the American flag ought to be deported. They can go and live in North Vietnam if they're so crazy about the communists.'

Libby picked up a copy of *Hair and Beauty* and tried to ignore the conversation. She studied diagrams for Six Feminine Ways to Get a New Look With Long Hair. So far as she could make out, the six ways all involved a ponytail or a chignon, with different types of clasp or ribbon. Was her hair long enough for a French twist? That looked quite good.

Kirkland junior's whimpers roused her from the realm of beauty hints. After giving him his bottle she was glad to get away from the house and its enveloping chemical smells. She felt the change in breathing and muscle response as Kirkland junior concluded that this new source of motion meant him no harm. She kept to the shadier footpaths to shield his eyes from the direct sun.

She looked down into the tender brown face and for a second she was overcome by an emotion she could not name. She might be able to call it tenderness if it were not for the streak of possessiveness that came with it. She'd heard of women getting clucky, but this was ridiculous. Weak at the knees, breathless. Was this the emotion that led childless women to kidnap babies? Kirkland widened his eyes and held out a hand with fingers outspread. Instinctively Libby responded by letting him grasp one of her fingers.

'The most beautiful in the whole world,' she murmured as her feet took her up the steps of the painting gallery at the Dahlem Museum. 'Come and I'll show you the Rembrandts,' she murmured. Stupid, she chided herself, as if he gave a hoot in hell about Rembrandt. What power this baby had, making a member of a revolutionary commune spout baby talk and rubbish.

Halfway through the gallery the self-portraits of a brash young man gave way to the face of an old man who had long since abandoned his swagger. Libby halted. She ran her eyes again and again over the sequence of pictures, from the certainties of youth to the yearning expression of age where only a shred of faith remains. A plaque on the wall made some points about the techniques of chiaroscuro, the dark backgrounds highlighting the pale flesh tones. While true, that was only an aspect of technique. Something more profound was here too, a message about not expecting the world to meet readymade formulas. Gazing into the sad, brown eyes of the final portrait, she thought involuntarily of Russell. Brown eyes always moved her more than blue ones. The baby kicked and shuddered in his sling, and she moved to reassure him with gentle pats and words. In the doorway she glanced back at the final portrait with a sudden knowledge that she was taking her leave of it, perhaps steeling herself to farewell the city.

In a hallway another painting made her stop still. A sensualist from the sixteenth century regarded her with a half-smile. The young man had long, straight hair; his dark woollen cap was placed at a dandy's angle; his clothes, of rich fabrics, were nonchalantly worn. It was a questioning, taunting face. The intelligent, large black eyes, the strong nose, the olive complexion, the ambiguity of the mouth: this was a man who would take his pleasure first and worry about the wages of sin later. And if he stepped out of the canvas towards Libby now, she would do all she could to seduce him. Why were patently unsuitable men so irresistible? She wondered if Harry Stonebridge once looked a little like the contemptuous young man in the portrait. The deliberate pause of someone sizing up an opponent before making a devastating comment. At least Russell's fieriness had nothing of this calculated self-satisfaction about it. Surely his passions were more genuine, less a series of power games?

Libby sighed. The baby brushed her chin with his fingertips. 'Kirkland junior, Kirkland junior,' Libby murmured in a singsong, rubbing his spine gently. 'We'll skip the Botticellis, they're not half as beautiful as you are.'

In the fume-filled flat, Ardena was blow-drying Lindsay's blonde mane, while Carolyn, in newly permed burgundy waves, looked on. Libby threw open the windows. 'Phew,' she said, 'that hairspray really hits you.'

'You-all have a nice walk?'

'Lovely. Just as well I had Kirkland junior with me or I might have run away with the man of my dreams.'

'Huh? You been out meeting strange men at this hour?'

'Not to worry, Ardena,' Libby said. 'I'm four hundred years too late for him.'

CHAPTER 13

'**F**orgive me, Libby.'

Russell was not only back, but apologising. He'd found her alone in the Breisacherstraβe apartment.

'So I'm not spying on you for the CIA all of a sudden?' she demanded.

'No. It was a stupid mistake. I'm sorry. Christ, what else do you expect me to say?' His voice had a strange sound in it, almost a quaver. Russell, vulnerable?

'Nothing.'

'You seem dubious.'

'Well, in my mind I'd kind of ruled a line under the whole episode.'

'Never say that.' He held out a hand to skim her hair, then drew it along her shoulder blades and arm. He grasped her hand. 'Ah, Lib.'

Libby pulled away. 'You just turned into this hostile stranger,' she said.

Russell's brown eyes had dark circles under them. His skin looked papery. 'So much has been happening,' he said. 'I was on edge. I thought someone had given us away just before some big breakthroughs.'

'Meaning me.'

'Look, Libby, I was wrong. Do I have to keep on saying it?'

'I guess not.' She stretched her mouth into a smile, turning towards him. Instantly she felt the rasp of Russell's red beard on her cheek, his arms around her, and one of his knees forcing hers apart as he pushed her towards the sofa.

Libby broke free. 'We'll have to go into one of our bedrooms. It's too public out here.'

'Yours or mine?'

'Yours.' She'd never been beyond the doorway of Russell's room. He slipped the bolt across the door once they were inside.

'Private enough for you now?' he asked. The walls were covered from floor to ceiling with black and white photographs. Scenes of mass demonstrations, portraits of old women in parks, people sitting on chairs in hospital waiting rooms, children at play in sandpits, teenage gang members smoking and scowling: four walls of social documentary. Libby traced around Russell's eyes with her fingertips. 'You look kind of worn out,' she said.

'Don't speak too soon.'

'I meant your eyes, not the rest of the physical evidence.' She moved a hand towards his crotch. 'I love the way even the hair on your stomach is red.'

'Do you, lass?'

'Yes, I . . . ' Libby began, but Russell thrust into her so swiftly that her sentence ended in a gasp. His rhythm was urgent and reckless. The tenderness of the night at Schlactensee was entirely absent. Libby felt that her individuality was being obliterated. They were not making love, they were having sex. Had sex, had sex, had sex . . . Her ears drummed to a two-beat tune. She closed her eyes and drew her ankles up, hoping to change the tempo. Russell appeared to take no notice. The urgency of their coupling made Libby feel faint, as close to pain as ecstasy. Suddenly her body rippled with involuntary sensations of release. A sharp pleasure, still not far from pain, shook her: her body was betraying her. Russell reached his climax almost immediately. Afterwards they lay silently next to one another, without caresses, stirred and taken aback.

At length Libby spoke. 'My body seems to want you even when I don't.'

'You've got a good body. You ought to trust it.'

Libby gave a rueful smile and nuzzled into the pillow. She closed her eyes, stretched out her toes, and exhaled long after each breath. She had a sudden flash of the petulant, ambivalent face of the sixteenth-century young man in the black hat. She glanced across at Russell. His eyelids were lowered, his dry skin was very white, and a scattering of microsopic light brown freckles could be seen on his arms and shoulders. He, too, was breathing deeply, but if he was disturbed by the animosity that had entered their passion, he gave no sign of it. He looked more like a scholar exhausted from sleepless nights deciphering manuscripts by an oil lamp than an inconsiderate lover prepared to take a woman by storm.

'I have to go and see that Australian military attaché tomorrow.'

'Oh, yeah? Well, tell him you live with very nice respectable people.'

'Of course.'

'Medical students and a kindergarten teacher. It might be best not to say anything at all about Akbar, and as little as you can about me.'

'Why would he care? He's just a bureaucrat.'

'Och, all these people talk to each other. You'll see.'

'Well, I suppose we all talk to each other if it comes to that. Romy and Akbar have been going out at all hours to meet people from other communes.'

'That's what I mean. That's the sort of thing we don't want any outsiders to know.'

'You can trust me.'

'Maybe I can, Lib, but you're so bloody sociable. You accept every damn invitation that's going.'

'And I fill in for you and Romy when you need a spare tutor or teacher.'

'True enough. I'm just saying you should take care.'

'I will, don't worry.'

The Australian military attaché's office was in the British sector to the north. The secretary in his outer office was a bilingual woman with shoulder-length hair and a mauve crocheted sweater which looked as if it might unravel at any moment. 'Mr Mackenzie won't be long,' she said. Libby glanced through the papers and magazines on the coffee table and picked up a copy of *Art in Australia*. She found herself hoping for shamelessly nostalgic landscapes: desert vistas, the harbour in the twilight, cattle knee-high in pasture. Instead she skimmed an article about silk-screening, illustrated by pictures of derelict buildings, tumbledown machinery and traffic jams.

A light flashed near the telephone. 'Mr Mackenzie will see you now.' The mauve crocheted breasts lurched to the right as the secretary nodded towards the door.

A dapper, shortish man was standing with his back to her, hands clasped behind him as he gazed out the window pretending to be unaware of her presence. In the distance, mounted troops were drilling on a parade ground.

'Mr Mackenzie?'

The man turned, feigning surprise. 'Ah, Miss Elizabeth Milroy . . .'

'Yes.'

'Do sit down. Sandy Mackenzie.'

'How do you do?' She was about to hold out her hand but Sandy Mackenzie had already settled himself behind the wide desk. He took a manila envelope out of a drawer.

'You didn't register with this office upon arriving in Berlin, Miss Milroy.'

'I'm not military personnel, Mr Mackenzie.'

'That's beside the point. Berlin is still, legally speaking, occupied by the four powers, and it is standard procedure for nationals of any of the three allied forces to register with us, purely as a formality you understand.'

'Really?'

'Yes, Miss Milroy—really. In addition, the local custom is to register with the police at your local police station, to confirm the identity of residents at every given address.'

'Bizarre.'

'Certainly it is not what you're used to at home, but may I remind you that we are not at home. We are guests in a unique city, one that offers much but imposes certain obligations and restrictions in return.'

I bet this guy was a house prefect, Libby was thinking. And an officer in the school cadets. She wondered how old he was. Thirty? Thirty-two at the outside.

'Where am I supposed to get the form to register with you?'

'From my secretary, Miss Erika Bittenbinder.'

'I see. And I was supposed to know this, by some process of intuition?'

'That tone is quite unnecessary. You would have received documents from immigration, like every new arrival in Berlin.' He shook the manila envelope and a navy blue passport landed on the desk. Opening it at the page with the stamp that marked her entry to Berlin, he extracted a small printed notice and handed it across the desk. In the fine print, Libby found instructions about registering with the appropriate authorities. Had he planted this slip of paper, or had it been there since the day of her arrival? She blushed.

'May I have my passport back please?'

'Certainly, if I can have your assurance that you're willing to comply with all the relevant authorities, complete the necessary documentation, and so forth.' He turned the passport over and over in his left hand as if about to shuffle a pack of cards. He had broad, almost hairless hands, a Seiko watch on a stainless steel band, and a well-cut navy wool jacket over a white shirt with a grey pinstripe. He had light brown hair and brown eyes, with too-prominent ears that prevented him from being handsome. If he'd grown two inches taller and had his ears fixed, Libby reflected as she sat opposite him, he mightn't have ended up such a pompous little shit.

'You're living with some interesting people, Elizabeth.'

'Yes, I've been lucky.'

'An unusual kind of luck. May I ask where you heard of this particular household?'

'Through a friend in London.'

'So your contact was with Russell Muir?'

'I had an introduction to him from some friends, yes.'

'Muir hasn't made himself a very popular person with the allied authorities, as you may be aware.'

'Does this have anything to do with my passport? I'd appreciate its return.'

'All in good time. Come now, my remark about the versatile Mr Muir can't be much of a surprise to you. You must know that he's made himself very unpopular with the Americans by shouting obscenities with electronic amplifiers. He's done his best to interrupt several parades, and he's deeply involved in the antiwar movement.'

Libby smoothed her fawn skirt over her knees. 'I'm sure the Australian government isn't opposed to free speech, Mr Mackenzie. Even at home these days there are a lot of young people involved in antiwar demonstrations.'

'Thank you—I do get the Australian papers.'

'I don't know how long it's been since you were in Australia? You might be surprised by—'

'Thank you for your concern, but none of us is away from Canberra for too long a stretch, precisely because of the need to keep in touch. My point is, what you blithely call free speech is one thing, and some of the things that are afoot in Europe at present are another. I have reason to believe that Rosemarie Limberger, Russell Muir and Mohammed Akbar Zahedi may have some very undesirable connections.'

Libby stayed silent. It was the first time she'd heard Romy or Akbar's full names.

'Limberger is a famous—or infamous—name, as you may be aware. This girl's late father was an SS officer. The mother, an heiress in her own right, lives in Spain.'

'Is there any law against that?'

'Not at all. You're quick to defend your friends, Elizabeth.'

'Are you taping this conversation?'

'Of course not.'

Libby looked around the room. In a Bond movie, the recorder would be behind a picture, or on the ceiling. The overhead fan was stationary.

'Where does this information come from? What's it got to do with you anyway? Australian military attaché! You play soldiers with the intelligence boys from the allied forces, I suppose.'

'There's no need to be insulting. I'm not military, as it happens, I'm from foreign affairs. But it's perfectly normal for allies to share information in the interests of common security.'

'And to intrude on peaceful students' lives? May I have my passport back please?' He was still absently turning it from end to end like a pack of cards.

'In a moment, Elizabeth. One moment. I have only one further question: Does the name Margaretha Neuboldt mean anything to you?'

Libby blushed. 'Nothing.'

'Better known as Gretta, I understand.'

'Never heard of her.'

'My duty as the representative of the Australian government, Elizabeth, is to advise you to register immediately with your local police station—Dahlem, of course—and to keep my office informed of your movements—when you intend to leave the city, for instance. You have a return ticket from London to Sydney, I understand?'

'Why bother asking when you've already checked?'

Sandy Mackenzie shook a crumpled aerogram out of the enveloped and smoothed it on his desktop. 'Because, my dear Miss Milroy, the welfare of our citizens is of the deepest concern to us. Furthermore, I have what might be called a personal interest in your case. The political police took possession of a particularly interesting letter from your sister, Sue. Now, as it happens, I am acquainted with Sue myself. My cousin Evelyn Rhys-Johns used to ride with her. Evelyn's family all think the world of her. So does Eve herself.'

'Your cousin's still knocking them dead at equestrian events in England, I suppose?'

'Actually, yes, she's been terrifically successful. She's teaching dressage in Gloucestershire between meets, and training horses for the Olympics. Your sister could have done just as well, you know. Not as competitive as my cousin, perhaps. It looked as if she was going to join the international circuit at one stage, when she was up at the Riverstone stud. But a wonderful girl. You're lucky to have her as a sister.'

'I know.'

'Well, Elizabeth—I see she calls you Libby, perhaps you prefer that?—it's patently clear that she's worried about you. And with good reason. My advice to you is to listen to her. If you won't go home to Australia, go back to London immediately, you'll be safer there. You are playing with fire with these radical associates of yours. Believe me. I care about freedom and free speech as much as you do, and you're entitled to your opinions about the war in Southeast Asia. But you are not entitled to take foolish risks in an occupied city where the best endeavours of the authorities may not be enough to save you from your own folly. Do I make myself clear?'

He pushed the passport and the letter across the desk. Libby snatched them up and zipped them into her handbag's inner compartment.

'Very clear.'

'So I'll be expecting a phone call to confirm your movements?'

'I'll regularise my status with the police, at any rate.'

The military attaché stood up. 'I'm sorry I didn't know of your arrival sooner,' he said. 'Who knows? Perhaps I could have squired you round some of the Berlin nightspots myself.'

Libby smiled involuntarily. It seemed that she'd missed her big chance to see the mud wrestling. She held out her hand. 'Goodbye, Mr Mackenzie. It's been most interesting.'

'Take care, Elizabeth, take care.' He sighed paternalistically. 'You young people don't know how much trouble you cause us, whether it's intentional or not.'

Libby had already reached the door; in seconds she was outside in the sunshine. She could hear the barking of a sergeant at arms and the drums and brass of a military band. She strode along like a kid on Anzac Day, swinging her arms in time with the music. Horse chestnuts, a gleaming shade of brown, had spilt from their prickly green seed pods and lay on the footpaths. Conkers! She'd met the word in old-fashioned English schoolboy fiction, but never understood it before. She picked a couple up: they were smooth to the touch and had a fragrance like newly varnished wood.

After a few blocks she slowed down. She was nearing a shopping centre. A teacher led a line of kindergarten children across the road, each of them clutching, with one hand, a section of the long rope that stretched from the head of the crocodile to the tail. Most of the children had fair hair and complexions; the blue-black hair and darker skins of a handful of the children gleamed like dates in a bowl of porridge. She watched as the teacher shepherded the group into a waiting tour bus.

When the bus pulled away, she noticed a small fountain with a statue of some deer at the entrance to a park. She took Sue's letter, tore it into tiny fragments, and held the fistful of torn paper under water until the letters became indistinct, then lifted off completely in small inky whorls of pattern, a waterborne batik. She tossed the blank soggy fragments of paper into a nearby bin.

In Dahlem, she went into the local police station, where she discovered that the procedure for registering her address was simpler than she'd imagined. German bureaucracy seemed a minor target for fury and indignation compared to Sandy Mackenzie's invasion of her privacy. She gave a tolerant smile as a uniformed woman, about her age, struggled with the Australian place names.

As she unlocked the door of the apartment, she heard shrill voices. Commune meetings were usually so courteous in Breisacherstraße. Who could be yelling like that? When she reached the living room, she saw to her astonishment that the half-hysterical, high-pitched voice belonged to Romy, who was pounding the table. Tears were flowing down her cheeks; her words were punctuated by sobs. At Libby's approach, Romy fell silent apart from gasping for air and blowing her nose on a succession of tissues. Russell, Bahman and Akbar were quiet too. The four looked at Libby. Like conspirators, she thought.

'Something wrong?' Libby asked.

'A personal matter,' Russell said. 'She's not up to discussing it at the moment. How did you get on, Lib?'

'It was pretty weird. He seemed to know a lot about us.'

'Like what?'

'Oh, your interruptions at allied marches, and our names and—oh, all sorts of things. He even vaguely knows my sister.

151

That was supposed to be a lever to bring me into line. As if I haven't spent my life seething over people who expect me to be a carbon copy of my marvellous sister. Anyhow, I got my passport back.'

Romy, drying her eyes, was beginning to regain her composure. Bahman and Akbar spoke quietly to one another in Persian. Russell stood up. 'Who's for coffee?'

Libby followed him into the kitchen. 'What the fuck is going on? What's Bahman doing here? How many secret meetings do you four have without the rest of us? And what's up with Romy?'

'Calm down, sweetheart.' He had never used that term before; his words had no calming effect on Libby. 'We agreed weeks back not to involve you, Hannelore or Guenther in anything you'd object to.'

'Which makes a separate meeting of you guys all the more disturbing. And what in hell has got into Romy?'

Russell sighed. 'It's her father.'

'The SS man? But he died when she was a baby.'

'Yes, but not in battle, the way Romy was led to believe by her mother. He was summarily executed in Russia for his part in atrocities in the Caucasus. Villagers rounded up and shot, old people and children included. Barbaric stuff.'

'So how has this been discovered all of a sudden?'

'We've talked about our friend in the east, Gretta.'

'Margaretha Neuboldt?'

'How did you know her surname? What is all this?'

'I'm asking you the same question. Anyway, how do you know this information is genuine?'

'We've got copies of the documents.'

'They could be faked.'

'They're genuine.' Russell filled the coffeepot while Libby counted out mugs. 'They came from dead-set reliable sources.'

'Poor Romy. Imagine having to come to terms with this

stuff when she never even knew her father. It's just appalling for her. No wonder she's in such a state.'

Russell gave a sardonic half-smile. 'A small drama compared to twenty million Russian war dead,' he said.

CHAPTER 14

Romy did not want coffee. She dragged the telephone on its long cord cord from the reading lamp into her bedroom and closed the door. The four round the table drank quickly, aware that conversation was needed if they were not to seem to be eavesdropping, but not sure what to say to one another. Russell announced that he was leaving for his studio.

'I'll come with you,' Libby offered.

'Not the best time. Long boring hours in the darkroom,' Russell said. He and Bahman left together, after Bahman had given Libby a slightly foppish wave and grin. Akbar knocked on the bedroom door and went inside to confer with Romy. Libby stood alone for a second, then dashed after Russell and Bahman, calling out as she stumbled down the stairs and into the street.

'Lib!' Russell turned back with a look of exasperation. Bahman, holding a leather document pouch in front of him, stood with his back to a nearby wall, a quizzical expression on his face. 'What in heaven's name is this? I'm simply going to the studio for a few hours.'

'You four are up to something you don't want to discuss. I should have left the commune before this. Hannelore and I both should have. Guenther doesn't count; he's almost oblivious to his environment.'

'This is no place for this discussion, and you're only embarrassing Bahman by bailing me up like this.'

'Bahman embarrassed me in the Grunewald. Why shouldn't it be a bit mutual? Isn't that what communes are supposed to be about? Sharing things?'

'Is this about sharing things, or trying to control me? Get a grip on yourself, Libby. I'll be back later tonight. Leave a light on for me. Come on, love, don't burst into tears for Christ's sake.'

Libby blinked. She swallowed rapidly and blew her nose. 'I'm sorry. This is idiotic, I know. Terribly immature. When can I expect you?'

'Tennish? Eleven? Before midnight. I'll see you then.' Russell gave her a quick peck on the cheek; she felt the texture of his beard as she twisted her neck to prolong the moment of closeness.

'Bye.'

Russell and Bahman turned and walked briskly towards the station, leaving Libby alone in the street. Yellowing leaves fluttered among the green in the afternoon sunshine. She returned to the apartment, turning on the radio in the kitchen. On Voice of America, a plangent southern female voice was bewailing her broken heart and the treachery of travelling men. It was a sad song, but when tears began welling up in her eyes, Libby accused herself of sentimentality.

She could hear the faint cries from Romy's room. At first she took them for another spell of sobbing, but after a couple of seconds she realised that Romy and Akbar were consoling each other with sex. She picked up a lightweight sweater and went outside. The downstairs tenants' window boxes were overflowing with pink and purple geraniums. In Europe, she thought, people really know how to celebrate summer. She remembered the passionfruit vines on the trellis near the back veranda at home. Each year she'd watched the small green fruit turn blotchily brown, then a sheeny purple, and gathered them without ceremony, taking them for granted. If left too long, they began to pucker, acquiring a special sweetness just before they went dry.

Her cheque from the Ivy League Institute was overdue, but there was nothing in the letterbox. She strolled towards the Cartwright's place. In the parks, people sat motionless, their backs to the sun, absorbing the season's warmth while they could. *'Guten Tag, meine Dame!'* a man shouted from a park bench. She glanced across and saw the old man with the moth-eaten poodle. Even the dog was lying drowsily in the sun. It took her a moment to realise she was the person he was addressing. *'Guten Tag, wie geht's?'* she called back.

Kirkland junior was crying loudly. Libby pressed the bell and waited. Ardena came to the door, flustered-looking, the squalling bundle of rage in her arms. 'I'm out of my mind here,' she said. 'Nothing will make this child contented.'

'I wondered if you'd like to come out and sit in a park for a while?'

'Can't do any harm. In fact a change of scenery might cheer him up. I'll just get our things.'

The baby's wailing stopped after a couple of blocks' walking. They headed for a sheltered park and sat on an iron bench under a wide-girthed beech tree. 'This was a good idea,' Ardena sighed. 'We really needed to get out.'

'Me too.'

'Yes, you seem a bit upset, Libby. Russell been treating you mean?'

'You could call it that. In fact I don't know what Russell's up to. He and these Iranian guys have got some secret. And Romy, she's this other girl in the commune. I'm left on the outer all the time, feeling like a twit.'

'A twit. I just love your British words.'

'You know what I mean? Like a dill, a drongo, a fall guy. A complete idiot.'

'He's not doing you much good, is he, Libby? Maybe you just need to leave.'

'That's what I tell myself. But it's such a nice room, and such a good location, and the rent is reasonable, and it's so clean and well organised compared to most of the shared places I've seen.'

'Oh, yeah, and Russell's sex appeal has nothing to do with it?'

'You've got it in one, Ardena. It's sensational with him, it really is. I'd do anything for him. It has to be love, doesn't it, when you feel that way? I mean, even you and Kirkland must quarrel sometimes.'

'Kirkland and me, we have some all-out brawls. Like, he doesn't like it if I buy a dress or a blouse that's the wrong colour?'

'He what?'

'You know, say I buy something red or bright pink. Kirkland's liable to go stir crazy and accuse me of looking real cheap, like some red-hot mama.'

'So what does he want you to wear?'

'Oh, real quiet colours, you know. White, grey, beige, navy blue.'

'I'd never even noticed you were avoiding hot colours. So the quiet ones must suit you.'

'There you go. But Kirkland once tore a satin blouse right off my back and ripped it into pieces in front of me. Oh, we were at home, he didn't do that in public. But I thought it was a real pretty blouse. It was a kind of watermelon pink.'

'I like that colour. We wear bright colours a lot in Australia. They don't seem to here.'

'No. Some of the stuff here is real old-lady looking. Those funny little hats with the feathers! But Kirkland has it in his head that quiet and ladylike are the same thing, so it saves trouble if I just go along with it.'

'But why should we—should women—just adapt themselves to what men think? You ought to know what suits you as well as he does.'

'Sure I do, Libby, but some things just ain't worth the trouble. Kirk's worth more to me than all that shit.'

Libby sighed. 'I get the feeling I haven't made up my mind yet how much shit Russell is worth.'

'One thing about Kirkland, he's real straightforward.'

'Yes. That's one thing I couldn't say with such confidence about Russell. He's fast-tempered, but that's not quite the same thing.'

'Can you come back and have some supper with us, Libby? It's only fried chicken.'

'I'd love to.'

Libby gave the baby a bottle while Ardena sprinkled flour and spices into paper bags. She shook each piece of chicken in the spiced mixture before dropping it in hot oil. By the time Kirkland arrived home in his uniform the small apartment was filled with the warm scent of oil, spice and golden-brown chicken. There were only two dining chairs, so Libby perched on a kitchen stool as they munched fried food and listened to Voice of America. Kirkland and Ardena had an easy, laughing relationship, often reaching out to touch each other, sometimes affectionately, sometimes in mock aggression. Kirkland junior slept soundly. By the time Libby left she was feeling a great deal more relaxed. She embraced Ardena gratefully in the doorway.

'Don't you take no more shit, now, you hear?' Ardena demanded.

'No, I won't. Thank you both so much.'

As she walked through the dark streets she heard swoops of sound overhead, a joyful liquid outpouring unlike any birdsong she'd heard before. Jeepers creepers, Libby thought, it must be a nightingale. *Hail to thee, blithe spirit, bird thou never wert* and all that. The trills and lilts continued in the absolute blackness above the tall trees. She made her way home in a cocoon of enchantment.

Hannelore was alone in the living room. 'How do you say nightingale in German?' Libby asked. 'There's one outside.'

'*Nachtigall*,' Hannelore said. 'I've heard it a couple of times.'

'Why didn't you tell me? It's magical.'

'You don't have them in Australia?'

'No. Cuckoos, owls, mopokes. Melancholy sounds. Nothing sublime like this.'

'They are famous for their beautiful song, yes.'

'Yes,' Libby agreed, smiling. She opened her bedroom window and could still hear, though faintly, notes falling like water in the forest.

Later, when Russell entered her room, Libby's mood of rare joy proved contagious. Russell lit a candle and turned out the light. He and Libby stood close together, naked, near the open window, breathing in the scented night air. He took pillows from the bed and placed them on the floor near the billowing curtain. They made love silently, limbs and faces barely visible in the flickering light, physical harmony making them feel like celestial beings. Libby had the sensation of ascending above her body, beyond mere needs and desires and physical release, to a new terrain entirely. Russell's power to move her had shed its puzzling, even frightening aspects. In the quiet semi-darkness, with the nightingale singing in the distance, they reached a plane where every breath, every touch, every gesture took them into a blissful exaltation.

They lay quietly elated for a long time, their hands lightly touching each other's shoulders.

Libby gave a sudden, involuntary shudder.

'What is it?' Russell asked.

'I don't know. It's like I was on this magic carpet ride, and all of a sudden a dark comet shot across my bows. A sort of cold terror. Death, disfigurement. Something like that.'

Russell gave her a reassuring pat. 'Get back on the magic

carpet, and steer it somewhere safe,' he said. 'Back to the land of the genie with the lamp.'

'I'll try.' She felt her pulse slowing as she lay in his arms, breathing deeply and willing away the panic. Relaxation came, then drowsiness, but the blissfulness did not return.

When she woke up, Russell was no longer beside her. She could hear noises in the corridor outside, as if someone were dragging a piece of furniture. Tossing her head to get rid of the vestiges of her dream, which had had something to do with a demonstration of medieval warfare back in her Armidale school hall, she pulled on a wrap and opened the door of her room. There was no one to be seen, but someone was using the shower. On the table in the living room she found a note from Romy announcing that she and Akbar had gone away for a few days. Hannelore came out of the bathroom, her hair in a turban. 'You've seen this?' Libby asked.

'Yes, though I'm not too clear what's going on. There's no problem with the rent; they paid up to the end of the month.'

'I wasn't thinking about the rent. I was thinking that none of us knows what's going on any more.'

'Even Russell? He doesn't talk to you?'

Libby blushed. 'Russell communicates, I'd have to admit. But no, he doesn't say much. When I ask questions he gets so indignant.'

'Who knows?' Hannelore shrugged. 'Frankly, who cares what they're all doing?'

'Less people to cook for, I guess. But I feel left out of things. Yesterday the four of them were having a meeting when I arrived and—'

'Four? Not Guenther, surely?'

'No, no. Bahman was here.'

Hannelore sat down. 'Oh my God. And we look the other way because the place is so nice.'

'Anyhow, whatever they're all doing, there's nothing we can do about it.'

'No. Nothing.'

Libby dressed in her fawn town clothes and set out for the Ivy League Institute, intending to confront Jeremy Moulder and demand payment for the classes she'd taught. She climbed the narrow stairs to the Institute's premises, only to find a sign tacked on one of the doors. Libby recognised the institute's banner-topped letterhead. SEASONAL RECESS. THE ILILI HAS SUSPENDED CLASSES FOR THE REMAINDER OF THE HOLIDAY SEASON. HAPPY HOLIDAYS TO ALL OUR STUDENTS. J.M.

The door to one of the laboratories was open: Libby could see cardboard crates on the floor. She knocked; a man looked up from emptying files.

'I'm looking for Professor Moulder.'

'Can't help you, I'm afraid. We're just moving in. No professors on our staff. We're insurance adjusters.'

'Have you got the whole suite? This room next door as well? There's a notice on the door here from the professor.'

'We figured we'd leave it up for a few days as a courtesy to the previous tenant.'

'But where can he have gone?'

'Don't ask me, madam.'

'No, of course not. Thanks anyway. *Tchuss.*'

Libby descended the staircase. I should have seen this coming, she thought. One prompt cheque, then nothing. Perhaps the professor was a fly-by-night who regularly set up shop in different premises, exploiting different tutors each year. For all he knew, she could be destitute.

She wondered what recourse she had under German labour laws. People ought to be warned about Jeremy Moulder. A letter to the editor? Spray-painted slogans? Or personal acts of revenge? She could find out where he lived, let down his tyres, glue up his letterbox, pour weed killer on his geraniums.

For the moment, she did none of those things. She went to the British Council, where she asked the librarian if she could put something on the noticeboard. 'What sort of thing did you have in mind?'

'I've been exploited by a con man operating a language school,' Libby said. 'I just want to get in touch with other people who might have had similar experiences.'

'I don't see why not. Don't put any wording up that could be libellous, that's all.'

Libby thought for a while and finally wrote IVY LEAGUE INTERNATIONAL LINGUISTIC INSTITUTE EMPLOYEES OF 'PROFESSOR' JEREMY MOULDER: IF YOUR CHEQUES ARE STILL IN THE MAIL TOO, CONTACT—and she added her address and telephone number.

'I'm not sure about these inverted commas,' the librarian said. 'Jeremy Moulder's one of the better-known expatriate entrepreneurs in this town. But he is—or was—a professor. An associate professor perhaps. But you should know. He comes from your part of the world.'

'You're telling me he's Australian?'

'I always thought so. But now that you query it, I'm not positive. Could be a New Zealander.'

'Some jumped-up ex-teachers' college, no doubt. Anyway, he insists on being called Professor, so I don't see anything wrong with the quotation marks.'

'All right then.' The librarian smiled conspiratorially and reached for some drawing pins. 'Good luck with it.'

'Thanks. I suspect I'll need it.'

She looked up Moulder in volume two of the Berlin phone book, but his private address was not listed. Nor, when she checked the business section, was the Ivy League Institute.

Back in Breisacherstraβe, Libby cut up onions and capsicums for spaghetti sauce. Hannelore arrived just as the onions were browning. 'I thought a nice bowl of pasta would cheer us up,' Libby said.

'Don't make too much,' Hannelore said. 'There's only you and me here. Wherever Romy and Akbar have gone, I'll bet you Russell's with them. And Guenther spoke to me at the clinic. He's moved out permanently. Says we can let his room.'

'He's been there day and night for months now.'

'I know. But he's got sudden misgivings about what's going on here.'

'Seditious spaghetti sauces!'

'Seriously, Libby. He thinks the others are getting into something major. Something dangerous.'

'What would count as something major?'

'I don't know, that's the trouble. But you remember the Grunewald.'

'Yes, but they were just playing guns like kids. You don't mean to tell me those amateurs see themselves as urban guerillas?'

'Who were the Red Army faction a few months ago? Students, journalists, mothers.'

'And a prisoner. And two arsonists. You have to credit Romy with more sense than that, at least. Except, she was kind of distraught last time I spoke to her.' Libby added tomato paste and black pepper to her sauce, covered it and turned down the heat. The telephone rang and Hannelore went to answer it.

'It's for you, Libby. Russell. Sounds like long distance.'

Libby's hands were wet from the kitchen tap. She dried them on a tea-towel as she went to the phone.

'Libby?'

'Yes.'

'Hello. Listen very carefully. It was great with you this afternoon.'

'It was what?'

'It was great with you this afternoon.'

'I had a shocking time, actually. That Jeremy Moulder turns out to be a crook, and to make matters worse, he might be Australian.'

'Listen to me. I can't talk for long. It was sensational in bed with you.'

'Yes, it was great for me too, Russell.'

Russell sounded impatient. 'This afternoon. It was great with you this afternoon.'

'You mean, you're asking me to—? Where are you, Russell? What's going on?'

'If you give a tinker's cuss for me, Libby, do try to understand.'

'I'm doing my best. Are you in trouble, Russell?'

'So far, so good. I have to go, Lib.'

'Russell, don't hang up. I'm terribly con—' Her word hung unfinished as the call was cut off, to be followed by an engaged signal.

Hannelore had brought water to the boil and was listening to the kitchen radio. Libby was about to ask Hannelore to help her decipher Russell's message when the news bulletin began. *Police have yet to apprehend the three accomplices of the gunman shot down today in an attempted robbery at the London Berlin trading bank in Westfalischestraβe. One man, believed to be an Iranian national, was shot dead in a gun battle with a security guard, who received wounds in the shoulder. The three accomplices escaped in a fawn and brown panel van, believed to be a rented vehicle. Police are investigating possible links between this crime and a recent spate of robberies by a terrorist gang which styles itself on the Red Army faction.*

Libby and Hannelore looked at one another. Hannelore dropped a spoon. It hit the kitchen floor with a clang.

'What do we do now?' Libby asked, collapsing on the kitchen chair with her head on the table.

Hannelore stroked the back of Libby's neck. 'What can we do? We eat spaghetti, and we wait. It will only be worse for us if we run away.'

'I've lost my appetite. I feel all peculiar. Oh, Jesus. We've had our heads in the sand, haven't we?'

Hannelore measured two small helpings of spaghetti strands. 'We'll need our strength tomorrow. No point wasting good food.'

Libby was shaking. 'I know this will sound terrible,' she said, 'but I hope to hell it was Bahman who was killed, not Akbar. Romy's got enough to worry about at the moment.'

'We've all got enough to worry about. But yes, I find myself wishing that too.'

'They'll come here for sure. Should we go and hide somewhere?'

'We're probably being watched already. Running would only make us all look guilty.'

Libby's head throbbed. An image flashed into her mind like a frame from a newsreel: the back of Hannelore's resolute shoulders after she stalked away from the misbegotten wilderness weekend. The sun showed highlights in Hannelore's long plait as every stride put distance between herself and the others. Inertia and lust had prevented Libby from following. Now there was nothing to be done.

'You're right, as usual,' she said.

CHAPTER 15

Sleep was out of the question. It was a night of waiting and talking, of anxious pacing, of crouching over the radio for every news bulletin. There was nothing new about the bank robbery or the whereabouts of the robbers. At Hannelore's suggestion, they left lights on all over the apartment. 'That way, they might actually knock, instead of battering the doors down,' she said.

Libby went over and over her telephone conversation with Russell, reconstructing it as exactly as she could.

'I doubt if there's any point trying to give him an alibi. There are cameras in all those banks, aren't there?'

'I guess they wore masks.'

'Yes, but the police seem to have so much information about us all already. I'll help him if I possibly can.'

'Do you imagine he'd help you?'

'Russell? You can't be serious. He may look uncaring, but he's the most passionate, incredible man.'

'He's treated you shockingly on occasion.'

'Yes. But it was so great last night. He's only asking me to move the time forward a little.'

'Please yourself, Libby, but I wouldn't tell any lies for him or any of them. Even telling the truth, this is going to be difficult enough.'

'Oh, Jesus. As long as the bloody bank guard doesn't die.'

'We should have done more for Romy,' Hannelore said. 'All of us should have helped her talk through the things she has discovered. Instead she has turned to Akbar, not just because he's her lover, but because he has a rage to match hers. And now our hesitation is punished.'

'I've always been a bit in awe of Romy, or something. The fact that she owns the place. That almost forbidding glamour she has. And her air of being better at anything you name than we could possibly be. Smarter, better looking, more committed politically, richer.'

'And more reckless,' Hannelore said. 'But perhaps we could have had more influence over her. We didn't care enough.'

'I cared. But I didn't want to say I knew how she must feel because she could just fling it back at me that I couldn't possibly know. How can someone from the other side of the world breeze in here and say she can just imagine how it must feel to discover your father is a Nazi war criminal?'

'We could have let her talk. That's what I mean.'

'You could be right. I wonder if I project some of my feelings about my older sister on to Romy. With my sister I always felt my best wasn't good enough, Sue had already scooped up all the prizes in everything.'

'So you pretend you do not take things too seriously.'

'Yes, that's one of the ways I react.'

'I too have my ways of turning away. Studying medicine, it is all too true that there's always work to be done. But it's an excuse all the same.'

'I know I should care more about Romy, but it's Russell who's on my mind.'

If you give a tinker's cuss for me, cuss for me . . . Russell's plea echoed and re-echoed in her mind. She imagined him in a telephone booth, glancing around to see if he was being followed. But where was he? Was he alone? Why in the hell hadn't he given her some idea of what was afoot?

The knocking came well before dawn. Hannelore opened the door. Police swarmed into the apartment, shouting. To Libby's ears they sounded like extras in a movie about German submarines, calling out to their commanding officer in urgent tones as they made their heavy-booted, uniformed way about. Libby stood trembling, face to the wall, as ordered by the first officers to reach her. One of her hands was spread out at beard level with the Lenin poster on the kitchen door. She half-hoped that a figure might materialise from behind the poster as he once had: enter Russell with a quip. But nothing of the kind happened. She waited with fear souring her saliva and her heart noisy in her chest. Hannelore had been immobilised in a similar pose nearer the front door. The police kicked open doors and cupboards and checked under beds, but eventually concluded that the two young women were the only occupants of the premises.

'Come with us to the metropolitan police station.' It was an order.

'Can I get my boots?'

'Quickly.'

Libby and Hannelore were marched to a police car, hands behind their backs. 'D'you have habeas corpus in Germany?' Libby asked, but Hannelore only shrugged. The car smelt of tobacco.

At the station they were taken to separate interview cells. Asked to prove her identity, Libby delved into her handbag for documents. She produced her bank book and her British Council library card. A female officer appeared with fingerprint gear and proceeded wordlessly to take prints from Libby's fingertips. 'Is this legal? I'm not charged with anything.'

'Routine procedure,' another officer assured her.

After the flurry of paperwork and fingerprinting, she was left alone. Minutes dragged like dull sermons. The black and white war film that had begun in her imagination at the time of the raid continued, but something had scrambled the soundtrack. The plot was indecipherable. What a hateful language German sounded, when only barked out monosyllables, *aus, raus, vorn, weg, schnell*, could be distinguished. Her cell was lit by ceiling lights, kept in place by wire-meshed glass. It was hard to retain a sense of time. She guessed that she was waiting for normal working hours, for senior officers and interpreters to report for duty.

And for Pillensbarger. She had known in her heart that it would not be long before she had to face the officer who'd been through her private papers. He stood in the doorway, tall and imperious in his flying boots officer insignia, good-looking too, if you liked dark hair, acne-scarred olive skin and Slavic cheekbones. Libby didn't.

'Well, well, Miss Elizabeth Milroy. I'm sorry we had to get you up so early, but your associates are involved in a very serious crime.'

'I can't imagine what you're talking about.'

'No? Come now, Miss Milroy, you have radio. You have television. You know about the bank robbery yesterday.'

'I heard something on the radio, but that's the limit of my knowledge.'

'Not quite the limit, Miss Milroy. I have my notes from our previous encounter. You told me on that occasion that only five of you were living in the Breisacherstraβe premises. Or commune, if that is the term you prefer.' Libby ignored the smirk that accompanied this heavy irony.

'You underestimated our sources, Elizabeth. We are well aware that Mohammed Akbar Zahedi has been living with your friend Rosemarie Limberger for some time. Now, is six the absolute total of residents of your commune?'

'Yes, only it's more like five. Guenther's been living at the clinic more than he's been home.'

'We'll be taking a statement from him, of course. Officers were despatched to the clinic at dawn. Now, what can you tell us of the masterplan for this robbery? What links does your group have to the Red Army faction? Is there a control in the east pulling strings or supplying money? What other groups send delegates to your meetings and vice versa?'

'What happened at the bank? Is Akbar all right?'

'He's far from all right. He's a sought-after criminal, a desperado, and should have been deported long since. We've been altogether too lax about so-called students in this city.'

'But he wasn't—?'

'Ah. I see. Well, of course, you couldn't have had much information. You may not yet have heard that Bahman Khalil Aref was shot after opening fire on a bank officer. And, I may say, on a filing cabinet, a chandelier, and a wooden counter.'

'Oh, God.'

'You knew him well?'

'I only met him a couple of times.'

'Did you discuss terrorism with him?'

'I didn't discuss anything with him. He was a friend of Akbar, that's all. They were living in the same dormitory, or something. You must know this already. How serious are the bank officer's injuries?'

'I haven't had a report on Mr Riegel's condition this morning, but he is not on the critical list. Last night he was serious but stable.'

'Thank God for that.'

'That sentiment does you some credit, at least. Now what can you tell me about Bahman Aref?'

'Next to nothing. He was very quiet. I only saw him once or twice. Never had a decent conversation with him. He struck me as a strange kind of guy. He had a private little smile all the time, even when nothing seemed at all funny. That's all I can tell you. I suppose his embassy will notify his family? Akbar's the only one of his friends that I can think of.'

'I'm sure all these things will be taken care of through the appropriate channels, yes. Now, how long has Akbar lived in the commune?'

'Just a few weeks less than me. He must have come in—oh, spring sometime.'

'Aha. Now was your commune ever the site for meetings of dissident Iranian students? Anti-Shah forces?'

'Never. We discussed the Middle East occasionally, but more the economics of the area. British and American oil companies, the exploitation of oil-producing nations by the multinationals. That sort of thing. All very theoretical.'

'And Bahman Aref was present?'

'No. Just Akbar. And he wasn't there because of his political views so much as a personal relationship.'

'He is the lover of Miss Limberger, yes?'

'Yes.'

'And apart from that has no political affiliations at all?'

'What would I know about his political affiliations? I'm just saying he's been living with us because of Romy, that's all, not because of anything political. Not because anything illegal was being planned.'

'You must have been aware that this hold-up had been planned.'

'I had no idea at all. I have absolutely no idea what the money might have been for, even if they'd succeeded in getting any.'

'And you, Elizabeth. What led you to this interesting household?'

'A friend in London. She gave me the address because she knew one of the people.'

'Russell Muir?'

'Yes. She knew Russell from London, and thought he might know of a room I could rent for a while. That's all there was to it. I just came on the off chance of a place to stay. Then I got to like the people, and Berlin, and . . . well that's it, really.'

'And when did you last see Russell Muir?'

'Yesterday afternoon.'

'Really? This is most interesting. Where would that have been?'

'At home. In my room.'

'You are lovers?'

'Yes.'

'Your loyalty is touching, Elizabeth, but you and I know that you were not with him yesterday. We have yet to trace your movements, but we have film and eyewitnesses to prove that Russell Muir was taking part in an armed hold-up.'

'No. He couldn't have been. You've made a mistake.' The threat of tears made her eyeballs itch; she blinked in a conscious effort to remain calm.

'So what is the extent of your relationship with Muir, apart from the sexual one? Do you perhaps assist him in his printing enterprises in Wedding?'

'He's a photographer, not a printer. But no, I've never been there. I've occasionally tutored a high school student for him, in Zehlendorf. That's all.'

'You've never been to his studio?'

'No.'

'And that doesn't seem somewhat strange, in itself?'

'Should it?'

Pillensbarger rose. 'I must ask you to wait a little while. I need to consult my colleagues. Perhaps it is time one of my assistants offered you a cup of coffee. Do you smoke?'

'No.'

'Well, then, just coffee. Until later.'

'Why do I have to stay here? I'm not charged with anything.'

'Patience, Elizabeth.' He left. The weighted door locked automatically behind him.

Alone, Libby allowed herself to cry. It was impossible to know whether she was being told a pack of lies, or whether some piece of evidence had already made nonsense of

Russell's alibi. She ought to ask for a lawyer, or an official representative, but the patronising Sandy Mackenzie was the last person she wanted to turn to. Without let or hindrance, she'd read in her passport. She'd wondered what the phrase meant, but it must include the interview rooms of metropolitan police stations, those with locks that operated only from the outside, at any rate. Where was Hannelore? She would know what to do. Perhaps she would summon a lawyer for both of them.

The woman who had fingerprinted her arrived with a cup of coffee and a wedge of unappetising pastry. Libby seized the chance to ask to go to the toilet, and was duly taken to the bathroom and back, under close supervision. Back in the small room, she found that the coffee had been sweetened already, with three or four spoons of sugar, judging by the taste. She drank it all the same.

Again time dragged. She was listening for any hint of Hannelore's voice, but could hear only the barked exchanges and guffaws of the police.

After a long interval Pillensbarger reappeared, imperious in his boots and shoulder badges.

'Elizabeth,' he announced, 'I've arranged a small excursion, just the three of us, you and me and Officer Schultz. I have the feeling you might find it enlightening. Don't be alarmed. If you are as uninvolved as you say, you have nothing to fear.' He led her along the corridor towards the front door. Libby tried unsuccessfully to see whether Hannelore was still in one of the other interview rooms.

'Where is my friend? Isn't she coming too?'

'Miss Buehler? She and the other medical student are talking to some of my colleagues.'

'Hannelore is absolutely innocent. She's one of the best people in the world.'

'How nice.'

'Don't be sarcastic about her. She really is.'

'Don't get upset, Elizabeth. Now if you'll just sit in the car, alongside Officer Schultz.' Libby sat handcuffed beside the solemn woman who had brought her the sugary coffee.

They drove out of the business area and into a tangle of warehouses, factories and cheap accommodation. Pillensbarger directed the driver to a small cul-de-sac behind a tyre repair shop. The hot, putrid fumes of tyre rubber floated through the open windows. The car came to a halt next to a big industrial waste bin. At an unmarked timber door, Pillensbarger nodded to his colleague, who inserted a key in the padlock. The police had obviously been here before. The door swung open.

Libby was propelled into the studio by Pillensbarger and his female colleague. The spacious studio was lit by dusty skylights. Posters and photographs took up nearly all the wall space, and cardboard cartons were stacked in rows three deep near a side bench. Tools, implements and metal gadgets were ranged on shelves. A silk-screen table, a printing press, two manual typewriters and canisters of ink stood towards the rear of the room. A screen door led to a small darkroom.

'Quite a nice little set-up,' Pillensbarger commented. 'And not cheap. Now I realise that some of the hippie communes of Berlin, including the one where you live, enjoy a very high standard of living. But the question of how all this is paid for is an intriguing one, is it not?'

Moving to the shelves he picked up a metal object consisting of chains and spikes. It resembled a prop from a Batman serial. 'This ingenious little invention,' Pillensbarger said, 'is obviously for throwing in the path of the police or anyone else who's in pursuit of a getaway car. These things just here are standard underground toys'—he indicated handcuffs, ropes and baseball bats—'but some of the gear has a touch of originality. A resourceful man, your friend Russell Muir. Shultz!'

The female officer put a glove on her right hand and went

up to what looked like a standard municipal rubbish bin. She pressed a lever, and within seconds a Glasgow accent filled the studio. 'One, two, three four: stop the fucking Vietnam war.' The message reverberated four times in the high-ceilinged room before the officer pushed the off button. Libby was feeling faint: Russell's voice added to her confusion as she tried to make sense of the deadly games the group had been playing.

The posters and photographs included illustrated quotations from Marx, Lenin and Marcuse, and a large batch of black and white posters promoting the Leipzig Quartet. A slim, blonde woman with an urchin haircut and a black sweater stood with three male musicians. 'You probably know who this is,' Pillensbarger said, indicating the woman.

'I've never seen her in my life,' Libby replied.

'No? But you've seen her photograph, perhaps, and had some idea of her importance to your friend?'

Libby was silent.

'The recent publications are quite elaborate,' Pillensbarger went on. 'Perhaps you've read this at Breisacherstraße?' He pulled up the flaps of a cardboard carton and extracted a booklet from the top of the pile. *The Urban Guerilla's Pocket Guide*, Libby read. *South American destabilisation techniques . . .*

She flipped to the index. The guide included instructions for surviving in the wilderness, map reading, changing identity, acquiring documents, making explosives and handling rifles and semi-automatics.

'Enlightening, yes?' Pillensbarger gloated.

Libby felt herself breaking into a sweat. 'I had no idea about any of this,' she said. 'Absolutely none.'

'You and Muir are lovers. Why would he not have brought you here? You look a useful kind of girl. You could have helped him in his various enterprises.'

'Once or twice I suggested coming here, but he always rejected the idea. I guess he didn't want me asking questions.'

'What sort of questions?'

'The ones you're asking. Who's funding all this, for starters.'

'Miss Milroy, I dare say you know that bungled bank robberies seldom attract the notice of the political police. It's usually a matter of stepping up security in nearby banks and waiting for the same petty thugs to try again. But this is no ordinary burglary. It has obvious links to international terrorism and we have reason to believe that a connection with the east has operated for some time.'

'You bug phone calls, I suppose?'

'We carry out a number of legitimate surveillance activities. We've had an eye on your colleagues for more than a year, and in recent weeks we've stepped up our monitoring of various indicators.'

Libby winced at the euphemisms. 'You've followed us?'

'Among other things, yes. And for that reason we are prepared to concede that we have no evidence at this point that you have been working out of this studio. Muir has kept his activities compartmentalised, it seems. So I must ask you to return to headquarters one more time while a colleague and I complete a formal interview. Then, who knows? You may be free to go.'

Libby looked around the interior of the studio, suddenly aware that something vital was missing. 'You've been here before, haven't you? Taken some things away?'

'A few weapons have been taken for fingerprinting and ballistic tests, yes.' When Libby inspected the benchtop, she saw little deposits of black dust where forensic officers had taken prints of Russell's hands. Suddenly something else caught her eye: a photograph of an absorbed young woman gazing into the eyes of a baby on the steps of the Dahlem Museum. She stared involuntarily: the picture had an intimacy and tenderness that a posed shot could never have achieved. But why had Russell been following her? What had he imagined she was doing? The photograph was even more unnerving than the multiple posters of Gretta.

'So what do you make of all that then?' Pillensbarger asked bluffly as they drove away.

Libby stared out the window without speaking, as if memorising the names of garage owners and shopkeepers might save her sanity.

'You're very thoughtful.'

'I've got a lot to think about.'

'Even so.'

She was trying to think of some childhood fable that should have forewarned her of all this. Not Beauty and the Beast, not Little Red Riding Hood. The one about the girl who married one of the robber barons might be closer to the mark. She'd discovered a tub of severed fingers or something horrific. Suddenly she had it: Bluebeard's Castle. She'd crossed the threshold of the forbidden room into the chamber of horrors. It was all there, the gory details, the obsessiveness, the double dealing, the other woman.

At the station she was given a barely warm hotdog with a long squiggle of mustard on it. She put it aside after a couple of bites. Pillensbarger had said something about waiting for a special investigator and an official interpreter. In the meantime she leafed through the proffered reading matter, a copy of *Petra*. This autumn the beauty news was a short bob with blonde highlights to pick up the sweep of the hair. Apart from the colouring, nearly all the models reminded her of Romy. Leather would be very popular this season. Black of course, and occasionally grey. Libby rested her head on the wall behind her and closed her eyes. Fatigue, panic, fear, and a shrill indignation at what felt like a betrayal by Russell jangled in her mind like synthesised percussion music.

CHAPTER 16

No one came. Libby was too demoralised to figure out what the delay might mean. Strung out, anxious and confused, she waited. And waited.

An unsettling emotion hovered in the further reaches of her consciousness like a chained animal in a darkened room. Rage. She was furious with Russell. How dare he get her into all this and then skip away, leaving her to parrot his unconvincing alibi?

At length a female officer looked in to offer her a toilet break. She shrugged when Libby asked her what was going on. The wait continued. She heard movement in an adjoining office as staff from the day shift cleared their desks for the night and said their goodbyes.

Libby was half-dozing when Pillensbarger and his two female associates finally appeared, laden with notebooks and tape-recorders. The interpreter, a thin woman with a high brown beehive and metal spectacles, spoke the meticulous, unaccented English of Zurich language institutes. She wore a cerise blouse, a colour Libby associated with the Anglican Bishop of Armidale's surplice.

'You were kind enough to offer us some documents to establish your identity,' Pillensbarger said. 'One of them, you recall, was a British Council library card. We've had an informative conversation with the librarian there. She not only saw you there yesterday afternoon, but you gave her a notice to pin up. I think we can take it that you won't continue with your previous claim that you spent an amorous afternoon with Russell Muir?'

The question was repeated in English by the woman in cerise.

'That's true. I was at the library. I'd just been to the Ivy League International Linguistic Institute—the owner owes me some money—and I went to the British Council after that. But I still had time to—'

'No, I assure you we checked the times. You didn't have time to meet your friend. He was otherwise engaged when you were at the library and he hasn't been home since.'

Had she somehow intended to sabotage Russell's alibi when she handed over her library card? Did her rage stem from the contents of the studio in Wedding or had it been there longer? These questions formed a self-interrogation that proceeded in tandem with the formal interview, which did not depart in essentials from the exchanges of earlier in the day. Pillensbarger framed his questions, Frau Cerise (Libby had already forgotten her real name) translated them, Libby replied as briefly and accurately as she could, and a uniformed man made tape-recordings. The only set of questions that had not been touched on earlier concerned what Pillensbarger called the Libyan connection.

'What Libyan connection?' Libby asked.

'You haven't heard your associates mention Libya? Moves by the government there to establish links with the radical left in Europe?'

'Never. The only connection in which I've ever heard Libya mentioned is the Second World War. My father was in the desert war there. Against Rommel.'

'Ah yes?'

'Yes. He said Rommel was just about the only German

officer of his generation you could respect. The allied soldiers apparently had a high regard for him.'

'Indeed? Well, this is interesting. My father said something very similar. But it is far from our purposes. You haven't heard anyone discussing funds from Libya or travel to Libya?'

'Not once.'

By the end of the interview, Libby was feeling exhausted, in part from the stress of her situation, in part from the effort of following proceedings in two languages after a sleepless night.

'Well, I don't think we need detain you further. You've been most co-operative. You're free to go.' Pillensbarger looked pleased with himself. Frau Cerise adjusted the hairpins at the back of her piled-up hair.

Libby's legs felt unsteady under her as she made her way along the institutional corridors towards the exit. She ran the fingers of one hand along the wall as if she were a blind person feeling her way. When they collided painfully with a portable fire extinguisher, she withdrew her hand to rub it.

Outside it was dark. At the nearest corner she hailed a taxi. It was as much as she could do to give the Breisacherstraße address.

She put her key in the lock of the commune's front door, but something was wrong. It did not slide properly, and it would not turn at all. She knocked. She rang the doorbell. No one came.

In a rising panic, she tried the key again. No doubt about it. The locks had been changed.

It was after eleven and she felt close to collapse. She made her way to the Cartwrights' place. It was cool in the streets, almost cold. She wished she had a jacket with her.

She rang the doorbell, which gave an incongruous Avon-calling chime. There was movement inside. 'Shit, girl, where did you put my pants?' she heard Kirkland ask. At length he opened the door, wearing a tracksuit. Ardena hovered behind him in a lacy robe.

'Libby! What you doin', this time of the night?'

'I'm sorry. I've come to ask you a favour. Would it be all right if I spent the night on your sofa? It's hard to explain, but I just can't sleep at our place tonight.'

Kirkland looked at his wife. 'You-all had a fight with Russell, I suppose?' Ardena asked.

'Something like that,' Libby said.

'Well, sure,' Ardena said. Her husband looked hesitant.

'Just one night,' Libby said. 'I'll get myself together in the morning. It's just that I'm terribly tired, for one reason and another.'

'You don't have to explain, Libby. I'll get you a pillow and a rug. The sofa's on the small side, but you're welcome to it. I'm just going to feed Kirk junior his night bottle and then we're off to bed.'

'This is terribly kind of you.' Libby wrapped herself in the acrylic tartan blanket and curled up on the two-seater sofa.

'You won't have a drink?'

'No, I'm really exhausted, I don't want anything.' Ardena carried the crib from the living room into her bedroom. Libby closed her eyes on the sounds of the Cartwright evening rituals, feeding the baby, settling him down, locking the door, and then watching television in bed. After a while the sound of television voices was replaced by scuffling, giggles and squeaking bedsprings. Finally, silence. Libby slept fitfully, dozing between nightmares. In these and in her wakeful periods she went over the day's events. Her mind kept adopting the insistent question-and-answer format of a police interview, mediated by the professional bystander's intonation of the interpreter.

She woke to bright sunshine and the sound of Elvis Presley singing 'All Shook Up'. Kirkland had already left; Ardena was up and dressed, and Kirkland junior lay propped in a plastic recliner, a bottle of juice in his hands. 'You sure must have been worn out,' Ardena said. 'You'll be wanting a shower.'

'What time is it?'

'Goin' on for nine. We didn't want to wake you.'

'Kirkland junior must have been very quiet.'

'We had him in with us, so we heard him as soon as he looked like he might start hollering.'

'He's an awfully good baby. I'm so grateful to you and Kirk, Ardena, that I could stay here last night. I'm going to have to leave Berlin, I'm afraid. Things have gone kind of sour at the commune.'

'Is Russell two-timing you or what?'

'That'd be the least of it. I can't really explain. It's just there are suddenly differences between us all that can't be put right.'

'You're just walking out on your job at that institute?'

'That's another thing that's gone wrong. The guy who owns the place has done a flit. I'm owed about five weeks' pay, and there's no sign of Jeremy Moulder.'

'It's not your week, Libby.'

'Say that again.'

Libby showered and washed her hair with some of Ardena's vast array of hair products. The herbal scent of the conditioner was so clean and tingly that the sour, soiled feeling began to evaporate. With the help of a heavy chrome blow-drier she styled and dried her hair. She had a glass of orange juice and a piece of toast before setting off for Breisacherstraβe, feeling that she could handle whatever the day had in store, even if she had to get her things with the help of a locksmith.

No locksmith was required. A chauffeur sat outside the building in a black limousine. When she rang the bell of the apartment, it was answered immediately by a short, formally dressed man with wavy black hair. 'I'm Libby Milroy,' she explained. 'I have to get my things.'

'One moment,' the man said. 'I don't speak German.'

'English?' Libby pleaded. 'I have to get my things.'

'Ah. Enter, please.'

He led the way along the corridor. As if he owned the place! Libby thought. Packing cases stood along one wall, and the Lenin poster had disappeared, leaving only a large faded rectangle on the kitchen door. She found herself facing a woman of perhaps fifty-five, whose silver hair was piled in an elaborate chignon and held with finely wrought silver clasps. 'Good morning, Miss Milroy. I'm Gisela Limberger.' Suntanned and expensively dressed, Romy's mother had the same chiselled features and cornflower blue eyes as her daughter. She sat on the arm of a chair with the air of someone posing a little coquettishly for a photographer. She was slim and brisk, neat ankles folded above black patent high heels. She held out a slim, suntanned hand, the wrist encircled with a heavy silver bracelet and the nails painted a magenta pink.

'How do you do?' Libby said, glad of her clean hair but wishing that she were dressed in something less crumpled than yesterday's shirt and jeans. Now she became aware of a third stranger, a heavyset man in a three-piece black suit.

'You met my accountant, Mr Sosimo Baca, at the door. This is my lawyer, Mr Werner Hauser.'

Libby murmured greetings. Her eyes travelled involuntarily back to the Romy-but-not-Romy features of the woman perched on the chair.

'I presume that if you had any idea of my daughter's whereabouts, you'd have told the police, and I'd be in possession of that knowledge already.'

'Of course. I have absolutely no idea where she is.'

'Daughters! A heartbreak. But that is no concern of yours. I must ask you to vacate your room at your earliest convenience. Do you need cartons? Or perhaps you—how do you say—travel light?'

'I guess so. Everything will fit in my suitcase, thanks.'

'Then I must request that you pack immediately.'

'My friend, Hannelore Buehler—have you seen her at all?'

'Not yet. If she doesn't arrive this morning, we'll have to pack her things up ourselves and leave them downstairs with one of the other tenants. I intend getting painters in here immediately so that Mr Hauser can make other arrangements for leasing it at the earliest opportunity. The owner of all the photographs is also missing, I gather. There aren't many personal things in his room; what there is may just as well be bundled off to a thrift shop.'

Libby glanced in the open door of Russell's room. The mosaic of photographs had been torn down; without them the room was impersonal, deserted. A black plastic garbage bag bulged on the bare mattress.

In her own room she opened her suitcase and transferred her belongings to it, drawer by drawer. There was something so surreal about the sudden materialisation of Gisela Limberger, the aristocratic languor of her gestures and the imperiousness of her commands, that Libby worked with the quiet, unthinking efficiency of someone in mild shock. All went well until she reached the top drawer where she kept her personal documents. With a kind of seasick deja vu, she realised that her passport was missing. Tears sprang into her eyes. 'It's beyond a joke,' she said aloud. 'Beyond a joke.' The strain of the past thirty-six hours caught up with her, and she sat on the bed, sobbing.

Gisela Limberger came into the room. 'My dear, this is a trial for us all.'

Libby looked at the carved, tanned features, the china-doll eyes, not ready to trust someone who swanned through life in limousines. 'My passport's gone,' she said, wiping her eyes.

'So, for this you blame my daughter also?'

'I don't know who to blame. It's just gone. Last time it was the cops, but this time I suspect it was someone from the group.'

'An inconvenience. I sympathise. But you will acquire another without difficulty, no?'

'I hope you're right.' She would be treated to more of Sandy Mackenzie's moral superiority.

'Perhaps you can tell me one thing. This—adventure—of Romy's and her friends. Was it planned over a long time or was it an impulse?' To Libby's surprise, Romy's mother sat down on the one wooden chair.

'They kept their plans from me, whatever they were. But something important happened the day before the robbery. Romy got some news—from the east—about the way her father died. She was distraught, quite unlike herself. I've never seen her so upset. I have no idea if what she was told was true, or whether it was planted in some way—you know—deliberately, to push her over the edge. Whatever the truth is, I believe they acted when they did because Romy was suddenly ready to take chances. Up to that point, she may have been more cautious.'

'I had a hysterical telephone call from her myself. She spoke of sending some document on to me. Perhaps she will. I'm afraid I'm impatient with the wish of so many of her generation to distort their personal history to match the worst of our national history. Some kind of collective guilt causes this overreaction. There are enough genuine horrors. Enough deaths. Enough violence. It is not what I wanted for my daughter. She never even knew her father; he was presumed dead by the time she was born. Why she has to shoulder this guilt is beyond me. I thought that in kindergarten work she had chosen something gentle.'

'Well, it's true. She's very good with the kids.'

'Was. She has closed the door on every sort of normal life. She has no concept yet what it will mean to be on the run. In exile.'

'You don't think she'll come back?'

'Not willingly. Not if I know Romy.'

The suntanned face looked more vulnerable now. Libby found herself wondering why Gisela Limberger herself had chosen exile. Too exotic a creature, perhaps, to spend her life among the desiccated, shabby widows of Berlin, or in this house with its prewar associations, whatever they were. The ice-queen poise of the mother might account in part for Romy's self-containment. Whatever their affinities, the two would now be kept apart by Romy's flight. Or did such people find ways to keep in touch, through the Sosimo Bacas and Werner Hausers of the world, through Swiss bank account numbers and untraceable couriers?

'If you're ready now, I can have you driven to your destination. I have a limousine downstairs. We'll be busy here for a little while yet.'

'I have to write a note for Hannelore. Please would you see that she gets it?' Libby flicked through the telephone book for the address and telephone number of the hotel she'd stayed in when she arrived. She did not know where else to go. There were limits to how far she could impose on the Cartwrights. She folded the note over and handed it to Frau Limberger, then said her farewells. The lawyer gave her a disdainful nod; the Spaniard volunteered to help her downstairs with her luggage. Something in Sosimo Baca's eagerness to help gave Libby a hint that he might be more to Gisela Limberger than a mere financial adviser.

Baca stowed her case in the trunk and held open the back door with what seemed to Libby almost a caricature of Latin courtesy. As the chauffeur guided the car along Bundes-Allee towards the city centre, Libby experienced a tingle at the back of her neck: a sense that she had abandoned her identity somewhere and was impersonating someone else. The feeling of unreality persisted as she registered at the hotel, asking for the cheapest room available. She was given the key to an attic cell in the corner of the building. After creaking up in the frail elevator in its wrought-iron enclosure, she locked her suitcase

186

and stowed it in a cupboard, then made her way to the post office. She wanted to make phone calls without the hotel surcharge or the risk of being intercepted.

First she made an appointment to see Sandy Mackenzie early the next morning. Then she took a fistful of coins and dialled the international code for London.

'Darling!' Jane Arnold drawled. 'Long time no hear. How is life in the cold war capital?'

'Rather strange. I'm about to leave, as soon as I can get some documents. Some bastard has stolen my passport.'

'What a bugger. You've told the police?'

'Not yet. The thing is, I think someone from the commune must have taken it.'

'Oh, Libby. The embassy people won't like that.'

'No, they won't. Do you know anyone at the London embassy, Jane?'

'Darling, we both do. Samantha Gerrett is there in some kind of junior capacity. And Neil Rennie—surely you remember him?'

'Only vaguely. He's one of a legion of people that my sister knew better than I did. My exemplary sister Sue who would never have got in a jam like this one.'

'Darling, come now, it's not your fault if someone nicks your passport. Do cheer up. I'd love you to come and stay here, the sooner the better. Can't you tell them you'll sort it all out when you get to London?'

'I'll try that, anyway. God, Jane, it's so good to hear your voice.'

'Yours too. Thought you'd disappeared behind the iron curtain or something.'

'Never.'

'I'm dying to hear about all the divine decadence of the life there. *I Am a Camera* and all that.'

'I think it's changed a bit since then.'

'Oh, don't be so modest and unromantic, Libby, I'm sure you've been having a madly exciting time.'

Libby smiled. 'Madly exciting,' she said. 'You've cheered me up enormously. It's been kind of tense here. I'll explain when I see you.'

'Oohh, mysteries! I can't wait. See you, darling!'

Libby drifted aimlessly for a few blocks, then took a bus to the National Gallery. The detritus of bombed buildings and barbed wire on either side of the Wall was clearly visible from the gallery steps. Inside she paced about, conscious that this was a farewell visit. She lingered at the series of paintings by Edvard Munch on the ground floor. The menacing mood captured on canvas stabbed at her like a dagger thrust. She gazed at *The Scream*, with the figure of the young woman on the bridge, all mouth, hollering in outrage to an unresponsive world.

The Munch women were studies in terror, frigidity, or an eerie seductiveness. Colours that would have seemed innocent in kindergarten fingerpaintings—bright reds, greens and purples—jostled against one another here. Despite their brightness they sang of death and decay.

In the foyer of the hotel a familiar figure was waiting. Hannelore wore a thick sweater over her jeans; her long plait hung forward over her left shoulder. She and Libby embraced.

'I just have to get something warm myself, then I'll come out with you.'

Hannelore accompanied Libby up in the clanging wire cage of an elevator. She held the controls of the inner door while Libby struggled with the wrought-iron outer one. 'These may be picturesque,' Libby commented, 'but they're a useless piece of design.'

'Easier to walk,' Hannelore said. After Libby picked up a cardigan, they made their way down the five flights of stairs to the narrow street.

'Romy's mother was incredibly hostile,' Hannelore said

when they reached a nearby cafe. 'She couldn't bear the sight of me for some reason. Perhaps it bugs her that Romy is in such deep shit and you and I had nothing to do with it. Or perhaps she thinks we dumped on Romy in our police interviews. I didn't, actually. I told them I didn't know what Romy and Akbar were up to.'

'Or Russell.'

'Yes. Or Russell. But this contessa-mother of Romy's looked at me as if I'd crawled out of a ditch. As if I were a cockroach or a sewer rat. Her actual words were civil enough, but there was such a coldness about her. Horrible.'

'She sort of loosened up with me in the end. Maybe because I was freaking out. One of the bastards has taken my passport.'

'Oh, no! You think that Russell—?'

'I don't know what I think. He or Romy or Akbar. One of our so-called comrades. Anyway I was falling apart a bit and she suddenly started talking. Even sent me into the city in the chauffeured limousine. That could have been to get rid of me all the quicker, of course, but she seemed a bit more human and vulnerable. She must be really shattered about Romy.'

'And she finds it unforgivable that the other two young women in the group managed to stay out of it. If Russell or Akbar was such a charismatic presence that none of us could resist him, Romy's involvement wouldn't look so bad. But you and I were critical enough for them not to involve us in the violence.'

'Maybe. I have to say that if Russell had actually begged me to do anything with him, I might have said yes. Especially after the other night. That's what's so extraordinary about this missing passport. That someone could be so loving and close and then so cold-blooded. I just don't get it.'

'I tried to warn you, Libby, that you were trusting him too much.'

'I know. And I got resentful every time. Thanks anyhow.'

'So you're leaving when you can get some papers?'

'Yes. What about you? Where are you moving to?'

'To a student residence near the clinic. Institutional, but I won't mind that for a while.'

'Write down the address for me. I'll miss you.'

'You too, Libbylein!'

They sat moist-eyed over their hot chocolates. Not far away, the bell of the Gedächniskirche began chiming.

CHAPTER 17

A not inconsiderable problem, Elizabeth.'

'Yes.' Libby fought to keep her voice level. She could not afford rudeness, no matter how pompous the man on the other side of the desk became.

Sandy Mackenzie toyed with a marble pen-holder. 'I'll have to notify the international authorities. They'll set up a watch on all ports. Of course, we may be too late. It's a pity you didn't notice the disappearance earlier.'

'I had no cause to look for it. Am I supposed to check my passport every morning or something?'

'If you were travelling, staying in hotels, you probably would.'

'But I wasn't.'

'No. But your associates in Dahlem were—well, my exasperation is understandable, Elizabeth. I did warn you. So did your sister.'

'Yep. So did my sister.'

'You don't seem to have given much thought to how all this might affect your family. How do you think your parents will feel when they find out you've been living with terrorists?'

'I haven't.'

'The authorities regard them as at least would-be terrorists.

I've been in this city longer than you have, Elizabeth. I know it better. Understand its dynamics better. It has a much lower flashpoint, politically, than ordinary European cities without occupying forces. You come here with your undergraduate expectations, fresh from whatever demonstration and sit-in you've been involved with in Sydney, and you think it's all simple fun here too.'

'It wasn't mere fun even in Australia.'

'Oh, forgive me. It was principles. Idealism. Are those the terms you prefer?'

'Without the sarcasm, yes.'

'I remind you, Elizabeth, you are in no position to be telling me whether sarcasm is called for. It is entirely up to me whether temporary papers are issued for your transfer to London, or whether I seek further instructions from Bonn or Canberra before taking a decision.'

Libby kept silent and watched the military attaché's clean fingernails as he twisted his desk ornament. She had never had much time for the slogan that you couldn't trust anyone over thirty, but Mackenzie's premature middle age made her reconsider. She hated being a supplicant.

'On the other hand, Elizabeth, perhaps the best course of action is to remove you at once from any undesirable associations you've acquired in Berlin.'

'I have someone to stay with in London. If I have to wait for documents from Canberra it'd be cheaper for me there.'

'That, also, is a consideration, I suppose.'

'It is. I haven't been paid for most of the tutoring I've been doing.'

'Indeed? I wasn't aware you had a work permit.'

Libby felt her cheeks getting hot. With an effort she continued gazing wordlessly at her clasped hands.

'You say you have friends in London?'

'Yes, my friend Jane Arnold's there. She's not a bit like my Berlin flatmates, if that's what you're worried about. She knows a couple of people at our embassy there. Neil Rennie, Samantha Gerrett—perhaps you know them?'

'I know Rennie of course. Can't say the girl's name rings a bell. Mmmhmm. Friend of Neil Rennie's, eh? Sounds suitable enough. Tell you what, Elizabeth, I'll speak to Canberra, and all being well, you can pick up a temporary pass from my secretary tomorrow afternoon. It will only be valid for Berlin to London. It's up to the embassy there to decide about issuing a replacement.'

'That's wonderful.'

'Best I can offer. Do keep out of trouble for a while, eh?'

'I'll do my best. Thank you very much.'

'You don't have your original birth certificate with you, Miss Milroy?'

'No. Am I supposed to travel with my birth certificate at the age of twenty-two?'

The embassy clerk cleared her throat. 'You're supposed to travel with your passport.'

'Touché.'

'Without other original documents, you'll be waiting close to a fortnight, I'm afraid.'

London in October was perpetually damp. Fine rain fell most days and mists hung around the spires of buildings in the early mornings and evenings of the few rainless days. Cool draughts sneaked through every crack in the walls and windows of the picturesque Victorian building where Jane Arnold lived. Libby's ankles felt cold even in her Oxford Street boots.

Jane left for her job on a magazine before eight every morning; she did not return until six. She would then shower, change into party clothes, and sip white wine while watching the news. After snatching a snack, she was ready for the evening's party, wherever it happened to be.

There was nearly always a party. Pleading fatigue, Libby turned down the first couple of invitations.

'You're pining for someone. Bet you quids it's Russell Muir.'

'What if it is?'

'Nothing at all, darling. Why didn't you bring him back with you? People think the world of him here.'

'It's a long story. He suddenly left Berlin.'

'He ditched you?'

'After a fashion.'

'None of the bastards is worth moping for, Libby love. Come out and meet someone else. Englishmen are much sexier than legend has it. They actually shower these days, too.'

'I've got nothing against Englishmen. It's not that. I'm just a bit worn out.' Instinct warned Libby not to tell Jane the details of the bank robbery; she did not want the story circulating in London while she waited for a replacement passport.

Jane switched on the television. The black and white footage showed Richard Nixon dodging missiles as he faced hostile students in San Jose. 'Bullseye!' Jane shouted in delight as egg yolk dribbled down the president's lapels. 'Come on, Lib, it's terrific, isn't it?'

'Is it?'

'We've got to stop the war somehow.'

'Sometimes I wonder if what we've been doing is having any effect on the war. That anti-Cambodia demo in Berlin was really terrifying. I'll never forget the way those horses looked and sounded. Protesters put their lives on the line. But you have to wonder what good it all does. People in both camps just seem to get dug deeper in. I mean, Nixon, a man like that, he's only going to get more convinced than ever that students are a different species, that they're just not what he defines as American.'

'You're very solemn all of a sudden.'

'Sorry. It's a terribly serious bunch you sent me to, you know. I told you I had to research deep political topics for commune meetings.'

'Yeah, what a hoot. Imagine Russell shacking up with weirdos like that. Must've been compensations. Nice house? Good-looking women?'

'Very nice house. Free-standing villa, high ceilings. The commune took up the whole of the second floor.'

'And women? Well, you're pretty good-looking yourself, Lib, when you care to be. Have you thought of getting something a bit more stylish done with your hair? No offence, but it's ever so slightly undergraduate.'

Libby laughed. 'You do me good, Jane, you really do. But one of my friends in Berlin is a hairdresser. If I'd wanted a drastic change, I had every opportunity.' She resolved to write to Ardena immediately and tell her everything. On second thoughts, she would write to Ardena and tell her just enough. Too frank a letter might find its way via Kirkland to American intelligence.

While Jane was at work, Libby wandered around London. She was watching her money and had to resist the allure of the shops, but the cool wind kept driving her indoors. She went into the Kensington library and read the newspapers at length. In the flat, she read Jane's copy of *The Female Eunuch*, the book everyone seemed to be talking about. Was Germaine Greer right—did women have no idea how much men hated them? Was that simple primitive emotion an explanation for Russell's behaviour? She thought not.

Jane had acquired some new habits of speech. She had taken to saying 'Yah, yah, yah,' with a strange intake of breath, like a Harley Street doctor's receptionist dealing with a patient's recitation of symptoms. This verbal tic, together with new intonation patterns that veered unpredictably from debutante to London shopgirl, warned Libby to keep her distance. Yet in practical ways Jane was extremely generous: Libby had her own key, could come and go as she liked. The divan bed was comfortable, and there were no rules about which brand or quantity of coffee to buy.

'What's happening with those bloody passport people?'

'They say I have to wait. It all seems pretty open-ended.'

'Did you insist on speaking to Neil?'

'No, I got stuck with someone at the desk.'

'Honestly, Libby, you're losing your grip. You mustn't let London *intimidate* you. I'd have thought Berlin would have toughened you up. You want me to ring Neil for you?'

'That'd be nice.'

'Elementary, my dear Milroy.'

'Thanks.'

That night, Jane pranced into the flat in triumph. 'One word from me, darling, and foreign affairs just *jumps* to it. Your passport will be there in forty-eight hours. I have to tell you this is going to cost me at least a lunch with Neil Rennie. Cheap pasta and a long spiel about how his wife doesn't understand him. Oh, God!'

'Jane, you work miracles.'

'The least you can do to show your gratitude is to come to this party with me tonight. It's in Islington. Terrific people. Jerry Stapanoff does artwork for record covers. And other art too. Posters, and stuff for galleries. All op art and pop art and psychedelic and whatnot. Brilliant chap.'

'Chap! How frightfully British.'

'Well, okay, these things are catching. What do they say in Berlin?'

'*Mensch.*'

'Okay, he's this brilliant *Mensch*. The place will be packed with musicians and artists and models and . . .'

'And groupies.'

'Sure. But you're coming, right?'

'Fine.'

'But at least do *something* with your hair. I've got this wonderful belt with temple bells on it that makes a great headband.'

'I'd look like I'd escaped from a seraglio. I'll find a scarf or something.'

Libby twisted a gold and bronze Indian scarf into a bandana and tied it round her head, the loose ends flowing over one shoulder. She put on a black sweater topped by every bead and chain she possessed, and outlined her eyes in kohl. Jane twirled her around under the pendant light in the hallway, causing metallic flashes in the oval mirror.

'You'll do,' Jane pronounced. 'A certain gypsyish charm.'

Jane wore tight black suede leggings with a fringed top. Her shoulder-length blonde hair was layered in loose waves around her face.

Music from the party flowed into the narrow street and all but deafened them as they ascended the narrow stairs. The lamps in the hall and bedrooms had been covered with purple cellophane, while in the living room a rotating disc emitted fractured, multicoloured beams of light over the op-art murals. The air was thick with tobacco and marijuana smoke.

'Great coat,' the host said, as Libby hung her Afghan garment on a hatstand in a bedroom. 'Where did you get it—Kabul? Morocco?'

'Berlin.'

'How amazing.'

'This is Jerry,' Jane said. 'Libby's been living in a truly bizarre commune in Berlin, with Russell Muir and a whole gang of people.'

'Really? What's become of Muir's photographs? I haven't seen one in the glossies for—oh, must be a year now.'

'He's—well—he's kind of diversified his interests,' Libby said. 'You know, posters and printing and stuff like that.'

'Pity, don't you think? The guy has a real eye.'

'I guess.'

'Olivia! Darling!' Jerry had drifted towards the door to greet some new arrivals.

Jane introduced Libby to a group of people near the drinks

table, then vanished to the dance floor with a small man who looked vaguely familiar. From television? Education tutorials? Libby had no idea. A dark, burly man handed her a champagne cocktail, which she drank rapidly.

'What's the music?' she asked, hearing a swirl of instruments and the word *trampoline*.

'You have to be joking. It's the Sergeant Pepper album.'

'Sorry, I've been in Berlin.'

'Surely they have Beatles records in Berlin.'

'Yes, of course, I just haven't been moving in party-going circles.'

'Better late than never. Didn't catch your name.'

'Libby.'

'Paul.'

'Hi.'

'Care to dance?'

'Love to.'

Libby had forgotten how much she liked to dance. She and Paul joined the couples under the circling rainbow lights. They danced without touching but with acute consciousness of each other's rhythms and movements.

'I've got some great grass,' Paul said, producing a matchbox. 'Or you could just eat the seeds before we light a joint. They're rather nice, I find.'

Libby crunched at the tiny white objects. 'I seem immune to them,' she said. 'No effect at all.'

'Give it time, sweetheart.'

Somebody put on a Joe Cocker record. Couples clasped each other tight and swayed like yachts at their moorings. Libby felt Paul's arms around her and his body pressed close to hers. He was crooning tunelessly in her ear, but that did not seem to diminish his physical appeal. He was well-built with a craggy profile.

'A drink!' he said, tugging her back towards the champagne bottles. 'Thirsty work, dancing.'

Libby smiled, but it occurred to her that the matinee idol looks did not have a high correlation with intelligence. She felt a pang for Russell's slenderness and sardonic turns of phrase.

'Too much!' Paul said. 'It's Annushka!'

Everyone turned to observe the entrance of a tall, thin blonde with cascading hair and a deep-cut leather vest.

'She's famous, I take it?'

'Come off it, sweetheart. You must see the occasional magazine, even if only at the hairdresser's. She's the highest paid model in the world, bar none.'

'She does look vaguely familiar, actually, but then so do several people here. That guy, for instance, do you know who he is?' She indicated Jane's partner.

'Guitarist with Lands End. Athol Constable.'

'Oh, of course.' Jane, feeling herself observed, looked up and grinned. In her boots she was taller than her partner; she compensated by dancing in a stooped-over fashion, her chin on his shoulder.

'What do you do, Paul?' Libby asked when the man with the craggy profile returned to the side of the room to refill their glasses.

'Me? I sell advertising space.'

'Oh yes? For a newspaper, or magazines or what?'

'Sweetheart, face it, the workaday world isn't really terribly fascinating, is it? Not the kind of thing to talk about at a party?'

Libby felt rebuffed. 'I didn't know there were rules about conversation these days. It sounds like one of those Edwardian manuals on manners. Topics to avoid. Trade, I suppose, would have been nearly as taboo as sex.'

Paul brightened. 'Sex was *fantastic* for the Edwardians. London was an absolute Mecca in those days. People talk about sexual freedom now, but from what I've read, the things that went on in the clubs and the backstreets then left the so-called swinging sixties absolutely for dead.'

'Fantastic for men. The women got VD, or had babies, and could never go home because they were regarded as soiled doves.'

'Crap. You can't tell me a woman of the world didn't know how to look after herself, even then.'

'A few, perhaps.'

'You know what would be really nice? A joint. Maybe we should find somewhere a bit quieter, and—'

'You go ahead, but I don't think I will. I'm getting a headache as it is. Sorry to be such a drag. I'll have to go home early, I'm afraid.'

'Darling, you could have come up with something a fraction more original than a headache.' He turned away, scanning the room for unattached females.

Libby made her way along the indigo corridor to find the room where she had put her coat. Through an open door she glimpsed five or six people writhing about, bare limbs in baroque combinations changing pattern like a kaleidoscope. In the next doorway she was relieved to see a familiar hatstand, the embroidery of her coat visible against its pale background in what seemed to be an empty room. As she stood pushing her arms into the sleeves, an interior door opened. A figure with cascading blonde hair was silhouetted against the pink tiles of the en suite bathroom, naked except for thigh-high boots. 'Ta-ran-ta-rah!' she said with a flourish. For a slim woman, she had surprisingly rounded breasts.

'I'm sorry,' Libby stammered.

'Oh shit!' cried the world's highest paid model. 'Where's Denis got to?'

'Can't help you, I'm afraid,' Libby said. Seconds later her foot collided with something heavy. She looked down and saw the semi-comatose form of a man lying on his side. 'Unless this is him over here.'

'Ah, Jesus,' the model lamented. 'Stoned again.'

Libby gave a sympathetic shrug.

'I don't know why we bother with them, I really don't,' Annushka said.

In the cab Libby looked out on a world of cascading lights, as shop neons, gaslights, headlights and the curtained squares of living rooms and bedrooms formed a glorious jumble of illumination. She felt exhilarated, exalted, punch drunk, an escapee, a speeding skater, a ski jumper, a balloonist. God, she thought, I'm high as a kite. I'm on a trampoline. I'm riding in a glass coach. Those things do have an effect after all. She saw the world through a zoom lens and then in long shot. Next, neon squiggles vibrated on a black background. It was glorious, it was bizarre, it was uplifting, it was banal. It was chemical. So far as she could remember, she had still been coherent when she gave the address.

She paid the driver and walked up the steps to Jane's front door, breathing in the cold air as she went in an effort to sober up. It was almost too successful. As she crossed the threshold she felt herself leaving the glass coach for a world of pumpkins and passports.

She made coffee and turned on the television. A reporter with an Australian accent was giving a gloomy assessment of the United States' Vietnamisation policy. In the background helicopters hovered over the jungle, with bursts of gunfire providing a soundtrack for a vista of napalm-blackened trees.

The day after tomorrow she would be free to travel. She had let things drift this year, as incapable of charting a new course as the warmongers she despised. There was no point hanging around in the northern hemisphere in the hope of resuming her affair with Russell. What she needed was a plan.

In February she would be appointed to a school somewhere where she would be able to get her life on course again. She counted the remaining weeks of the school year and decided there was little point trying to work as a casual teacher.

Besides, she felt a need to get away from cities for a while. Surely she could find a job as a governess or housekeeper on some property in the bush, not right in the middle of New England where she would have to sing Christmas carols with her parents, but somewhere well away from city lights.

It seemed extraordinary that the solution had not occurred to her before. Sue. After a good night's sleep she would get on the phone and make her peace with her sister Sue. With any luck, in not much more than a week's time, she would be grilling chops in a remote homestead on the Darling Downs.

CHAPTER 18

1990

The Lufthansa steward welcomed passengers aboard in English, then in German. Libby listened with slight alarm. She recognised the rhythms, but if she had not just heard the English equivalents, the words would have defeated her. Perhaps, on arrival, she would be tongue-tied.

A different language, a different hemisphere. But those were only the first of the differences. Was the young woman who had spent nearly a year in Berlin still the same in any significant ways, or had she changed completely? How many members of the commune would Hannelore succeed in locating? And what was the urgency? So far as she knew, there had been no word from Guenther, Romy or Akbar for twenty years. Or from Russell. Russell's silence had cut into her like acid at first; then anger had taken over. Finally she had decided to cultivate indifference. In time this turned into something close to genuine indifference; she succeeded in part in deadening her feeling for him. After she met Will, the memories of her intoxication with Russell receded, and for long stretches at a time she did not give him a thought.

She met Will in 1971 at the Come-by-Chance picnic races, to which she was invited by Pat Reeves, one of the teachers she shared a house with in Wilga Wilga. To Pat, who was engaged to a widower with three sons who lived on a sheep property, the Come-by-Chance picnics were the year's social highlight. She insisted that Libby buy a new outfit for the occasion, and that she take a pair of dancing shoes as well as the low heels she usually wore.

'None of your handcrafts of Asia tat,' Pat said. 'This is Come-by-Chance.'

'What did you have in mind? The sort of stitched-up linen suit my mother would wear?'

'Not some embroidered smock and sandals, anyway. I don't think you appreciate what a grand occasion this will be.'

Libby checked out the boutiques when she went to Sydney for a conference, and returned to Wilga Wilga with a long-sleeved green silk dress. 'The very thing,' Pat said.

'Handcrafts of Asia!'

'Okay, you win.' Pat's black and white spotted outfit had been made by a local dressmaker. All her accessories matched, down to black and white beads, and a black and white spotted handkerchief.

On the day of the picnics they bounced over the unsealed roads in Pat's old Falcon at a pace well above the speed limit. Red dust rose around them in clouds, covering the white car from bonnet to boot and forcing them to wind up the windows. Through the red-stained glass they saw a flat, endless landscape of yellow rape flowers under a sky of Nolan-painting blue. The plains stretched to the horizon in every direction with little evidence of human habitation apart from an occasional steel shed or lethargic windmill.

'This country is growing on me,' Libby said. 'When I got here in February I used to look over to the east to that blue ridge of mountains every morning, just to remind myself that the earth is not entirely flat. Now I'm starting to like the sense of disappearing in the middle of this vastness. And the primary colours are wonderful.'

'I like to see good grazing country more than this big expanse of nothing,' Pat said. 'Nice sheep or cattle, a few horses. I like the odd emu, though—you begin to get them this far west.' She turned on the radio, but the choice proved to be the Sydney racing guide or country and western music. She turned it off.

'I don't suppose anyone gives racing tips for Come-by-Chance,' Libby said.

'You don't need them. There are only three or four horses in most of the races. You can pick a winner either by going for the good jockeys, or by going down to the enclosure and seeing which horse looks fitter than the others.'

'My sister's the one with an eye for horses. Not surprising, I suppose. She's a vet.' Libby could now talk about Sue without hearing the tinge of younger-sister resentment in her voice. When Libby had returned from Berlin, Sue had found her a live-in job on a cattle station in southern Queensland. Through the long, slow summer she cooked and did housework in an old homestead with wide verandas. When the owners, the Treadwells, were at home, she also helped take care of their small children, but for much of the summer they were away at the coast. Libby's duties dwindled to feeding the household pets, turning on the sprinklers in the garden, cleaning out the pool, taking telephone messages, keeping the kitchen cupboards stocked, and providing a meal for the occasional cattle tick inspector. She smiled to herself as she scrubbed the baths and toilets to Breisacherstraße hygiene standards, thinking of Hannelore and her rosters. Hannelore wrote to her from time to time. She had no firm news of the whereabouts of the others, apart from Guenther, who was working in a hospital in Havana.

At weekends, Sue sometimes drove over to join her by the pool. They spoke very little of Berlin, or indeed of anywhere beyond the property gates. Like two laconic graziers, they confined themselves to brief, companionable observations about the heat, the rainfall, and the Treadwells' labradors. Slowly they were learning to trust and even like each other;

becoming, once again, the Milroy sisters. Libby no longer minded that people considered them two of a kind. One memorable afternoon they compared notes on their disastrous encounters with married men. Libby told Sue a little about her entanglement with the Stonebrooks, while Sue confessed to some of the difficulties which had occurred when she was working as a stable hand for a famous polo player. Her exit from the world of dressage and horse sports had less to do with Evelyn Rhys-Jones than Libby had always imagined. They discussed the dynamics of their parents' marriage, and tried to figure out why both of them had been drawn into three-cornered contests. It was the frankest they had ever been with one another.

Pat's car left the red dirt country and travelled through scrubby native pine forests and half-deserted logging camps. They passed a sign that promised a race track and finally reached a gate where a lone man in a Salvation Army uniform stood rattling a donation box as if it were a tambourine. Pat put fifty cents in the box and asked the way to the parking lot. Soon the Falcon had been stowed at the end of a line of jeeps, utility trucks and Rovers. It was only late morning, but already the air smelt of barbecue smoke, horse manure, sawdust and beer: a rustic but festive smell, the Easter Show minus the fairy floss.

They bought race books. Pat, who was looking around for her fiance's car, started greeting people. Not finding Joe, she suggested that they walk down to the enclosure to check out the horses for the first event. She found Joe and his mother leaning up on the post and rail fence, arguing about likely winners. There was a strong family likeness, sandy-haired, broad-shouldered and pink-complexioned. Five horses were parading around the small enclosure. 'Libby, I want you to meet Mrs Cameron, and this is my fiance, Joe.' Libby turned and murmured a few polite phrases, then turned her attention back to the horses, or to be more precise, to a tall man with green eyes and dark eyebrows whose handsomeness eclipsed the bay horse he was leading. As he came level with the small crowd of onlookers a nearby bugler played a fanfare. The horse, panicking at the unfamiliar sound, backed nervily out of the docile parade, pushing the man up close to the wooden fence. He staggered a little and readjusted his hold on the reins, but as he regained his balance his Akubra toppled over the fence, landing at Libby's feet. She stooped to pick up the hat and then, standing on the lower rung, handed it back to its owner. Pat Reeves obliged with more introductions: Libby Milroy, Will Dunbar. As Will's gaze met Libby's her fear that she might never meet anyone capable of dispelling Russell's power evaporated. In that instant she felt that her whole future flashed before her. In the more immediate future, she was glad that she had a pair of bronze dancing sandals in the back of Pat's car.

Libby married Will Dunbar that December, on the first Saturday of the Christmas holidays. They lived on Casuarina, his small farm on the river west of Wilga Wilga. She continued to teach at the school. By election day, 1972, which saw them working for rival parties at the Rowena Creek Community Centre—a corrugated iron hall twenty miles from any other booth—Libby was eight months pregnant. Like several of her fellow teachers, Libby was handing out how-to-votes for a high school teacher named Ted Hodges, the Labor candidate. Ted's chances of winning the Federal seat were never good, but he campaigned energetically, debating National Party members in remote community halls, and driving through the main streets of country towns on the back of a utility truck on Saturday mornings, accompanied by his kelpie, Mulga Bill. 'I'd just as soon vote for your dog,' drinkers would shout from the doorway of the Commercial or the Telegraph Hotel, as Ted called out to them through his loud-hailer.

That year the Labor campaign had more flair than usual: pop stars chorused a theme song, reinforcing the slogan, *It's time.* If the majority of voters in the federal seat of Crampton were unlikely ever to feel that it was time for a Labor government, they were aware from press reports that voters in the cities felt differently. Gough Whitlam's campaign had a gathering momentum which was felt even by candidates like Ted Hodges, who needed a swing of eighteen per cent in order to be elected. 'It's not impossible, never say die,' Ted insisted to his campaign workers.

The National Party incumbent, Denzil McCammon, was an oversized, genial campaigner who shook hands with everyone, called all women *dear*, and once safely elected, seldom rose to his feet in parliament. He contrived, in his debates with Ted, to associate the Labor party with the shearers' strikes of the 1950s and with taxes on petrol and farm machinery.

'Your bloke hasn't a hope in hell of winning,' Will told Libby.

'I know, but he's a decent sort of fellow. Truthful. Doesn't go round putting the fear of God into people.'

'Yeah, but what's the point of putting your energy into a lost cause?'

'More point than putting it into supporting a big, barrel-shaped hypocrite like McCammon.'

'He's the sitting member. That makes him a good contact for the Co-op, among other things.' Will had sown a couple of hundred acres of cotton, and was regarded as a promising grower by the marketing co-operative that operated the Wilga Wilga gin.

'Ted's a friend of the Co-op's too.'

'Ted's a nice fellow, sure, but he's not a politician's bootlace. I suppose you're going to bring poor little Marmaduke up to vote for schoolteachers, too.'

Libby patted her bulging smock. 'Whoever little Marmaduke turns out to be, I'll bring him or her up to understand the principle of the secret ballot.'

Will smiled. 'Fair enough. It's either that or schizophrenia.'

At the end of the day they went to a victory party given by McCammon's supporters on a wheat farm north of Wilga Wilga. As the night wore on and the extent of the Labor Party's federal win became clear, Libby was one of the few people rejoicing. 'Bloody schoolteachers, you're all closet radicals,' Gafford Maxwell teased Libby.

'You bet. We're single-handedly responsible for a huge nationwide swing.'

'All right. No need to gloat.'

The following month, after an eleven-hour labour in the new maternity wing of the Wilga Wilga Hospital, little Marmaduke metamorphosed into Evan William Dunbar, a robust baby with slate-blue eyes and sparse blond hair. As milk flowed into her breasts and unexpected after-pains made her uterus contract, Libby was catapulted into mood swings that veered from ecstatic protectiveness to sentimentality: to her amazement, her eyes would fill with tears at the dedications of Engelbert Humperdinck songs on the local radio. She enjoyed being at home with her baby, but when Evan was six months old, she found a babysitter and returned to teaching. Teachers had just received a good pay rise, while the farm income was risky. Her salary allowed them to ride out the bad times which farmers with small holdings inevitably faced. Once she came to trust the daycare mother, she liked being back at work: ten year olds were fun to teach, and Pat Reeves, now married also, was still on the staff.

Libby went through customs at Frankfurt and changed to a commuter plane for the final leg of her journey. From the air, Berlin did not look greatly changed, encircled by lakes and forests and studded with parks and squares. The late summer colours of green and yellow brightened the grimy greys of roads and buildings. A stewardess requested that everyone remain seated until the plane had come to a complete stop, but passengers started scrabbling in the overhead lockers immediately after touchdown. As she put her raincoat over her arm and hoisted her hand luggage over her shoulder, Libby felt a surge of nervous excitement.

Family groups were staging demonstrative reunions just beyond the exit doors. Libby walked forward alone, looking around for a familiar face. Suddenly her name was called by a figure on one of the nearby benches. She spun around to see an unmistakable silhouette: Hannelore was waving and smiling, hurrying forward with arms outstretched. Once Libby had taken in the gold-rimmed glasses and slight double chin, Hannelore looked much as she always had: a bustling, energetic woman, recognisably German. She now wore her plait pinned up behind her head. They hugged.

'You haven't changed a bit,' Hannelore said.

'Nor have you.'

They made their way out to the car park, dodging taxis and double-decker buses. 'I've got out of the way of looking to the right for oncoming traffic,' Libby said. Hannelore opened the boot of a blue Fiat.

'Funny,' Libby said, 'I was looking round for Romy's Renault.'

'Renault? Didn't she have a *hassliche Ente*? An ugly duckling?'

'No. Romy must have been the only left-wing student not to drive one of those two-horsepower Citroens, but I distinctly remember her Renault.'

'I must have mentally changed it into a 2-CV because everyone else drove them in those days. Premature senility! My memory's going.'

'Don't be silly, Hannelore.'

'Would you like to put your coat in the back seat? Here, I'll fold it for you.' Libby smiled, remembering rosters.

Hannelore turned on the ignition and they inched towards the exit of the parking station.

'It's so exciting to be here again,' Libby said.

'Libby, I'm so grateful you could come. There are decisions to be made. Something extraordinary has happened.'

'Your letters have been rather mysterious.'

'It's not safe to put things in letters, even now. Or to talk on the telephone unless you assume every word is overheard. I don't think you realise, Libby, how much suspicion we so-called "sympathisers" have had to contend with in Germany. There was a Radicals' Decree to keep us from full participation in society.'

'Sure, I knew it was pretty bad in the 1970s with all the murders and the reaction to them. You've given me a few hints in your letters, and I've read stuff here and there, but surely it's different now?'

'To an extent. But some things are still extremely sensitive. The whereabouts of our erstwhile commune members, for example.'

'It's Romy, isn't it? I'm sure it must be. There's no reason for any of the others to summon us to Berlin.'

They were driving along a six-lane road with the windows wound up, but still Hannelore glanced around before replying. 'Yes, it's Romy. She's going to give herself up. She's been here, in hiding, for several weeks. Some kind of plea bargain is being arranged.'

'But where's she been?'

'Where hasn't she been? East Berlin, Tripoli, Paris, America . . . "

'Really? But did you ever hear from her before?'

'No, never. Not until last month. Then I was contacted by a lawyer, and some rather strange interviews went on, until finally they arranged a meeting with Romy.'

'How is she? Is she all right?'

'She's right as rain, physically. Psychologically, she's concerned about her mother, who's gravely ill, and then there's the strain of coming back to life as Romy after living under a new identity for twenty years.'

'I suppose it would be peculiar.'

They were driving along Clay-Allee in an area that Libby recognised. 'Hey, we must be pretty close to Breisacherstraβe. Do you ever go past it, for old times' sake?'

'You'll have plenty of opportunity to visit Breisacherstraβe, never fear. That's partly what you're here for.'

'Hannelore, what is going on?'

'I'll explain properly if you give me a chance.' They stopped at a red light.

'What about the others—Guenther, Akbar, Russell? Have you ever heard anything about them? Are Romy and Akbar still together?'

'No, Romy and Akbar didn't stay together very long, I gather. She thinks he probably went back to Iran with the Ayatollah Khomeini a few years ago. I'm almost positive that Guenther is dead. He was working in Nicaragua, for the Sandinistas, about five years ago, in an area which was raided often by the Contras. He's simply disappeared. Missing in action, presumed dead.'

'Poor Guenther.'

'Yes, he was the most dedicated of all of us in the end. The only one who really put his beliefs into practice.'

'Unless Akbar?'

'That's true, we don't know exactly what Akbar's been doing in recent years.'

'I suppose Bahman was true to the end, by his own lights.'

'Bahman was a clown,' Hannelore said. 'I've been tainted my entire adult life for associating with people who could open fire in a bank, and all because that idiotic, immature little rat couldn't wait to start playing guns in the big league.'

'It's been terrible for you, then, Hannelore? Worse than you've said in your letters?'

'I've tried to tell you, Libby, letters and phone calls are not safe in this city. Or they weren't, while we had the Wall. Now they say there are thousands of spies and agents and detectives desperately trying to rescue their careers.'

'So what have they done to you, Hannelore? You've had your practice, haven't you? I had the impression it was going very well.'

'True. I have a very successful private practice. I am a highly regarded gerontologist. This year, for the first time in my life, I have been trusted to conduct an honours seminar in the subject at the medical school. Until then, although students have occasionally been sent out with me on placement, I've never been trusted in an official capacity such as a visiting professorship. Papers that I've written for journals have mysteriously been sent to two or three extra referees, every time. My requests for federal research funds have been turned down again and again. I won't bore you with the details of the phone taps or the interception of parcels, usually the most unremarkable medical supplies, but believe me, my caution in these matters is not a sign of paranoia. It stems from bitter experience. You've no idea what a frenzy of hate a mistrust the media whipped up here over terrorists and their supposed sympathisers. The authorities still interrogate graduates about their political views before they let them work in the public sector, or even in kindergartens.'

'I thought that the current crop of students was supposed to be terribly conservative. My son's friends certainly are.'

'Amazing, yes, Evan is now at the university! What does he study?'

'Agriculture.'

'Wonderful. A farmer like his father. But you are separated from Will, no?' Hannelore said *Vill*.

'Yes, sort of. It's not necessarily permanent. We've had a bit of strife. I'll explain it all later.'

'Yes, there is so much news all of a sudden. So much! Here we are then, at my little house. Welcome, I hope you will like it here.'

Hannelore swung the car into a garage adjoining a terrace house with a small front garden. It stood in a line of similar houses behind a neatly clipped hedge. Libby reached into the back seat for her trenchcoat, and managed to ask, face averted from Hannelore, 'And Russell? Do you know anything about what's happened to him?'

'I changed my mind, Libby, you aren't the same girl at all. It's taken you half an hour to get round to mentioning his name. Yes, that's one of the reasons I wanted you to come. Russell has turned up too. He's in Glasgow, but he says he can't travel. I was hoping you might be able to go and see him.'

Hannelore opened the boot; Libby dragged out her suitcase. She could feel her face burning despite her attempts to maintain her composure.

'See him?' she asked, unable to keep her voice from rising. 'What would you want me to see him about?'

CHAPTER 19

Stepping into Hannelore's neat townhouse, Libby felt a pang of nostalgia for the high ceilings, space and austerity of Breisacherstraße. Here everything was a fraction too cosy: beige walls and cinnamon carpet; fawn tweed chairs; undersized landscape paintings; peach silk scatter cushions that looked as if they were never used on the floor. Hannelore showed her to her room and demonstrated how to convert the futon sofa into a bed. 'You will be comfortable, I hope. I'll make tea. Ceylon or camomile?'

'Ceylon, please.' Libby wondered how many things Hannelore bought specially for visitors; herb teas were probably the norm here.

'Why would we need to talk to Russell?' She was still fighting to keep her voice from squeaking.

Hannelore sat behind the big china teapot, drinking the same tea as Libby.

'Romy has problems,' she said. 'Legal ones, personal ones, and some that involve all of us.'

'How's that? What could we do after all this time?'

'She's got a lawyer, Konstanze Anglin, who wants new depositions from all of us about Romy's role in preparations for the bank robbery. It's on the books as an unsolved act of terrorism, probably related to the Baader–Meinhof gang.'

'I wish I'd never heard of the Baader–Meinhof gang.'

Hannelore refilled the cups. 'You're not the only one. People here are insane about that whole episode. They see conspiracies in everything. And of course, after the kidnappings and murders of the late 1970s, then the bombs at military installations—well, it's no mystery why the public loathes the very name of the Red Army.'

'What can we possibly add to what we said before, that we weren't consulted about their plans? Quite frankly, I've got no desire to relive any of that insanity. The possibility that it was all going on under our noses while we refused to see it gives me nightmares. And it's had repercussions for me, too.'

'No doubt. We've all had nightmares. I've certainly thought I was a fool not to leave the commune entirely that day Bahman brought his guns to the Grunewald. But the fact is, we didn't. We liked them, and—'

'And it was a very nice place to live.'

'Precisely. Wonderful location, lovely big bedrooms, good organisation.'

'Rosters for everything, rigorously observed,' Libby teased.

'Well, yes. A well-run household. It is funny, when I read other people's accounts of how radical students lived in the 1970s. They say we thought we had a divinely sanctioned lawlessness.'

'While in fact we had rules about every damn thing. The kind of coffee to buy, even.'

'Okay, I was obnoxious sometimes. We were young. It must all have seemed very strange to you. And not easy, perhaps, to win the approval of the whole group while you became so fixated on Russell.'

'God, how transparent I must have been.'

'But we think you are the one who might be able to persuade Russell to co-operate. You see, Romy has . . .'

'Why can't he come here himself?'

'I believe his health is not good. He's a wanted criminal here still, don't forget. He'd risk being arrested, and sent to prison. He's already served a jail term, apparently, in Morocco.'

'Jesus. For how long?'

'I don't know. I know very little. Konstanze only just succeeded in finding where he's living, and we know only fragments about what's happened to him.'

'So what do you want him to do?'

'All of us. You, me, Russell. It relates to Romy's plans. It will be best if Romy and Konstanze explain. I have arranged that we see them tomorrow, after you have a chance to rest.'

'I'll be awake all night, with all this stuff going on. Did you say you know where Akbar is?'

'Probably in Teheran, but we haven't been in touch with him. Romy apparently had a falling out with him some time ago.'

'So why can't we see Romy now?'

'It's not so simple. She's here incognito. Only a handful of people know what is going on. The terms for her surrender are still being worked out. You met her mother, didn't you?'

'Briefly.'

'Well, she's not expected to live long. She's in a hospice in Switzerland. Romy has had a few secret meetings with her. Part of the drama that's going on has to do with Romy's inheritance. She can't take possession of her Berlin property, including Breisacherstraβe, while she's a wanted criminal. Oh, she's not top priority on the most-wanted lists or anything, the whole thing's died down to an extent. But she's still something of a star catch for the law enforcers.'

'Catch my foot. She's turning herself in.'

'Yes, but they'll extract the maximum publicity value from it; it will have to look as if it reflects their investigative brilliance.'

'And what does Romy get in return? A reduced sentence?'

'That's what they're bargaining for. But you can't be sure here. If the publicity backfires and the antiterrorist hysteria starts again, she can't be sure of that.'

'So where's she been all this time?'

A jumble of vowels and *k* sounds came from Hannelore.

'Where did you say?'

'I'll say it slowly. Al-bu-quer-que, New Mexico. Oh, she was other places before that, lots of places, but she's been there about fifteen years. She's got an American husband who's only ever known her as Lisa.'

'What's she been doing there?'

'Running a kindergarten. Very successfully, of course.'

'Trust Romy.'

'So what do you want to do? Go out for dinner, or have a quiet meal here?'

'First of all I want to go for a walk and get my bearings. I can't believe I'm back here. Then let's just stay here quietly tonight. Maybe I can buy pizza or something?'

'No need, I have soup and salad ready.'

'Great.'

Hannelore's townhouse was in Schlactensee, not far from the Lindenthaler Allee railway station. Libby walked a few blocks east in the late afternoon sunshine. It was an attractive part of the city with well-kept villas and apartment blocks set behind avenues of tall trees. A turn to the right led to the waterfront: the Schlactensee curved serenely to the north and south with a park jutting out into its centre. A group of boys was trying to extricate a kite from the high branches of a tree; families were feeding swans, and as she watched, a couple of windsurfers rounded a bend, scudding over the surface at a surprising clip. She gazed across the water towards the forested shore where she had first made love to Russell. From the perspective of this suburban park it scarcely seemed possible that they could have felt, that night, such a distance between themselves and the rest of Berlin. Perhaps lust had blinded them; perhaps the forest was thicker twenty years ago. For a moment it seemed that time had tricked her into standing on the middle-aged, carefully landscaped side of the water, while in reality she still belonged on the impulsive shore of youth.

'*Hallo!*' Someone shouted a warning. She ducked her head just in time to avoid a soccer ball. Two boys dashed after it, followed by their out-of-breath and apologetic father.

'It's quite all right,' Libby assured him, but she moved towards the water and sat on a bench overlooking the light-splashed water. She had a sudden physical longing for Evan, for a younger, less independent Evan who glanced towards her between his rare moments of contact with the ball when he first started playing soccer. A tender, grey-eyed boy, he had veered quickly from confidence to vulnerability, just as she had felt alternating impulses to protect him and to thrust him into the world. The passions and irritations of the love between mother and son were etched into them both. She had never been the kind of mother who interfered with his friend-ships or social life. As Evan reached his middle teens she made conscious efforts to grant him more independence. It had not always been easy, because she left her teaching job in his third year of high school. While she was teaching, she never made sandwiches for his lunch, but working at home as bookkeeper for Casuarina's increasingly successful cotton production, she had to struggle against a belated urge to make peanut butter sandwiches and buy muesli bars.

The Dunbars had been lucky as farmers. Partly because Libby's salary provided a backstop, they were able to borrow finance for hundreds of high-yield acres near the river in the years before interest rates peaked. By the time the rural crisis of the late 1980s began hurting farmers who could not meet their repayments, the Dunbars had repaid their loans and were enjoying good cotton prices. Libby did the accounts by computer, using software her father had recommended. She made some minor changes to the spreadsheets to tailor them for primary production.

The Camerons of Come-by-Chance were less fortunate. Pat appeared on Libby's doorstep one day, in tears. She was desperate, she said. On her worst days she was afraid that Joe might kill himself. They had borrowed huge sums at their bank manager's insistence, but the farm was not making enough money to cover even the interest payments, despite the fact that Joe and his eldest son were working as hard as they ever had, if not harder. Dry seasons followed by lower than expected wool prices had them all but bankrupt. 'They're talking about foreclosure, Libby,' Pat sobbed.

Summoning tact she did not know she possessed, Libby persuaded Joe Cameron to show her his books and the incomplete forms from the bank. Using her software, she developed a number of scenarios from selling out completely to repaying the loan over longer time spans. 'I don't think it's as desperate as your bank manager does,' she told him. 'Maybe if I can come with you both next time you talk to him, and bring this paperwork, we can negotiate better terms. There are grants you should be applying for, too.'

'I'm a farmer, not a bloody bureaucrat.'

'Well, as an ex-teacher, I'm not bad at filling out forms. I got us the first Aboriginal teachers' aides in the north-west. Primary production grants ought to be child's play. There's hope, there really is.'

The bank manager wore a short-sleeved yellow shirt, a brown and orange tie and a service club tiepin. He acted as if Libby and Pat were invisible, giving his entire attention to Joe. After about thirty minutes of being ignored, Libby strode towards the desk, brandishing her spreadsheets as if they were a twelve-bore rifle. The astonished bank manager found himself dealing with an effective advocate who could counter all his routine objections. The Camerons left the bank with a better than even chance of staying on the land.

That day marked the beginning of Libby's second career: gradually more and more farm families who need help with their forward planning or loan negotiations sought her out. In time she became a respected rural counsellor, with more work than she could handle. She addressed meetings of rural women, trainee accountants and even country bank managers. When she and Will separated in April 1990, she rented a cottage in Wilga Wilga, partly because she had grown to like the area, but chiefly because she did not want to lose her clientele.

She smiled to herself on her park bench, remembering the confrontation with that first bank manager. Surging adrenalin and barely controlled rage had made her almost as loose a cannon as Bahman in the London-Berlin trading bank. Fortunately the bank's security system was not activated by flapping computer printouts.

Romy was a blonde. There were half a dozen people in the room, but Libby's eyes kept returning to Romy's familiar chiselled features, framed in an unfamiliar platinum blonde urchin cut. Her eyebrows were different too, bleached or plucked, but to someone who had not known her Snow White brunette beauty, she would still have appeared an attractive and youthful woman. How old was she in fact? Forty-five at least. She wore a tiered denim skirt, white T-shirt and turquoise beads.

'Libby!'

'Romy!'

Not an embrace, please, Libby thought, stretching her hand out in the European fashion. Romy shook it.

'Libby Milroy from Australia,' Romy explained to the others in an American accent.

'Dunbar,' Libby said.

'This is Konstanze Anglin, my lawyer, and her assistant Rolf. And this is my husband, Gary Lucero.'

'Hi, Gary.'

'Good to meet you, Libby.'

Libby and Hannelore sat down. The silence made Libby nervous. 'This is like some parents' discussion group or something. Group therapy?' she joked. Gary gave a brief smile, but the lawyers looked disapproving.

'This is a most difficult and risky situation for all of us,' Konstanze said. 'I think you are aware already that Romy intends to give herself up shortly. We have been attempting a plea bargain for a reduced sentence, for a number of reasons. The fact that she's come forward voluntarily would be a strong factor in her favour in normal circumstances, but in the wake of the terrorism of the 1970s nothing is ever exactly normal. There may be attempts in the media to link your commune with more radical groups to which you were entirely unrelated. The fact that Romy can expect to be fairly well-off after her mother's death could be misconstrued by hostile forces. One way of strengthening her case immeasurably would be for others from the Breisacherstraße group to testify that she did not mastermind the robbery. The fact that Romy intends using the Breisacherstraße building for charitable purposes should help reinforce our argument that she has put the past behind her and now wants to contribute to society. Gary, too, has evidence from the States of her community work over the past fifteen years.'

'Lisa ran a preschool in the south valley of Albuquerque,' Gary explained. 'It's a poor area. She's tremendously respected for her work with Hispanic kids.'

'I've been Lisa for twenty years,' Romy said.

'So what are you asking us to do?' Libby asked.

'Do you think you could give a new deposition to me and Rolf about the inner workings of the group?' Konstanze asked. 'You wouldn't have to testify in court. It would be one strand of our case that Romy was never a terrorist or a terrorist sympathiser, but a good-hearted person who was led astray by others with stronger personalities at a time when she learned about her father's war crimes. Then we'd have the story of her really excellent work in early childhood education in the last few years, and—'

Libby broke in angrily.

'So I suppose you will tell us who we'll name in these depositions as the so-called mastermind too?'

'No, no, it will be your own deposition,' Konstanze assured her, 'but of course if you could confirm that Bahman introduced the idea of armed resistance to a formerly peaceful group, it would be helpful.'

'I'm sure,' Libby said. 'I'm damned sure it'd be helpful, but why should I feel like helping? What have Romy or Akbar or Russell done to help Hannelore or me for the past twenty years while we've been branded as terrorist sympathisers? The stupid thing is, in a way we were. We loved these people and they betrayed us. I agree that Bahman was the idiot who first showed up with guns, but was he the only one who imagined the urban guerilla was somehow heroic? I doubt it. Russell certainly was spouting that stuff, and Romy must have agreed or she wouldn't have become part of the inner circle while the robbery was being planned.'

'How dare you speak for me?' Romy demanded.

'How dare you tell me what to put in a sworn statement?' Libby countered.

'Libby,' Hannelore began, 'there are plans for the Breisacherstraße house. Generous, constructive plans.'

'Oh, yes, she'll donate it to Mother Teresa, I suppose.'

'Calm *down*, Libby,' Hannelore begged.

Libby took a breath. 'Okay, I may be jumping to conclusions. I'll try to be more reasonable. But have you considered how this will look in the media and in the court? Poor little rich girl repents just in time to inherit? Dying mother brings her out of the woodwork? All of a sudden we're told she's been doing saintly work with children for fifteen years. It's a bit much, don't you agree?'

Gary Lucero leant forward. He was an olive-skinned man with brown eyes and a slightly drooping moustache. 'This is all so weird to me,' he said. 'I mean, the very idea of Lisa getting involved in something illegal. I tell you, she's just the gentlest, most inspiring person in the world. She's . . .'

'I spoke too soon,' Libby said. 'It's actually Romy herself who's Mother Teresa.'

'*Libby!*' Hannelore said.

'This is ironic, Libby,' Romy said. 'I don't remember you as an aggressive person at all. Hannelore was always much quicker to judge than you were. But now you want to think the worst of me before I can even put my case.'

'Okay, okay, I'll try to listen.'

'You see, Libby,' Romy went on, 'there are decisions to be made about quite a bit of property in Berlin. My mother isn't expected to live more than a year, if that. Obviously, to take charge of anything here I have to assume my real identity again, though I have to tell you I don't regard my life in the States as a false one. I've become Lisa Lucero, I really have. I've worked hard for fifteen years, and I've seen children learn and thrive because of my efforts. I've made a life with Gary. We have a child.'

'A child?'

'Yes, we have a daughter Debra, back in New Mexico with Gary's mother. She's twelve. She's only known me as Lisa. Her parents are Gary and Lisa, it's as simple as that. But my conscience wouldn't let me ignore the past forever.'

'Your conscience or your inheritance? Couldn't your Swiss bank have laundered it for you somehow?'

'Believe it or not, my conscience does trouble me. I've had bouts of depression. You probably don't know what that's like, you look like someone who's floated through life. But I've suffered nightmares, conflicts, black moods, despite my family and my work. Then of course, I've only had the barest contact with my mother, and always through other people. It has been just so marvellous to be able to put my arms around her again, before it's too late.'

'This is all heart-rending, Romy, but why have I been dragged halfway around the world for it?'

'Because, Libby, you were there. You know what Breisacherstraße was like, that we weren't a bunch of gun-toting madmen.'

'No. We just knew a couple and some of you went into banks with them.'

'Okay, Libby. I don't know what's happened with you. Maybe you've been put through hell because of your connection with us; I don't know what this is about. But surely it's not unreasonable to ask you to expand on your original deposition, to mention Bahman's guns, and to point out that I was non-violent?'

'I think this is reasonable, Libby,' Hannelore said. 'Romy—Lisa—has suffered too. It is true that Bahman was the one to bring the guns . . .'

'You didn't see Russell's crappy publications. The idea of going round shooting selected targets was given this crazy heroism.'

'The shooting—Bahman's behaviour—was crazy,' Romy said. 'I don't deny that. But I'm asking you to help put it into perspective. I'm sure the prosecution will have copies of whatever publications you're referring to. But I didn't see them, believe me. I was just swayed by Bahman and Akbar's vehemence against the Shah, and by extension, against all authority and capitalist symbols.'

'Jesus, Romy, you weren't the passive, easily swayed type.'

'You think so? How do you explain your own passivity? Being so much under Russell's thumb?'

'I was never so much under Russell's thumb that he imagined I'd go out robbing banks with him.'

'Perhaps. But you accepted many of his ideas against your own better judgment.'

Libby's forehead felt hot. She wiped it with a tissue. 'I'm not saying I wasn't pretty stupid myself,' she said.

The lawyer intervened. 'Mrs Lucero's very generous proposal for the use of the real estate is that the Breisacherstraße villa be used for charitable purposes for the next ten years, while the Wedding properties would be sold and the proceeds used to establish a kind of community chest.'

'What Wedding properties?' Libby asked.

'I have the addresses here,' Konstanze said. 'They were originally zoned light industrial, but with the increase in population now that the Wall's down, the area is in high demand for residential properties. We expect the group of warehouses and former factories to bring a very good price, none of which would be used for Mrs Lucero's personal benefit.'

'Do you have a list of the addresses?'

Rolf, the junior lawyer, thumbed through some papers and handed a typed page to Libby. 'I knew it!' she said, as she scanned the list. Her pulse throbbed. Her jaw was tight as she spoke: 'One question, Romy. Did you use my passport to leave Germany?'

'Actually, no. Akbar and I had our own aliases. I had genuine papers from a child named Lisa Schaaf who'd died at the age of two. It was Russell who took your passport, in case Gretta needed it at any stage. I don't know why he bothered: she had access to marvellous forgers in Leipzig.'

Everyone waited for another furious response from Libby, but she sat with her head in her hands, unable to speak.

'I just couldn't handle it, I'm sorry.' Libby was back at Hannelore's.

'You got so enraged, Libby. It wasn't like you.'

'You scarcely know me, Hannelore. We haven't seen each other for twenty years. I just got so furious when they started handing me these lines about what I thought about the commune. And what can I say about the bloody robbery? They were careful to keep you and me in the dark.'

'Well, we can say that.'

'We said that before.'

'It is true that the only guns we saw belonged to Bahman.'

'Yes. But why are you so keen for me to do this?'

'Libby, it's such a great building. I could get the use of it for ten years, for patients who need a bit of rest and pampering without being nursed.'

'Is that what you had in mind?'

'Yes. You know I'm interested in the health of old people. Well, one of the things I've got involved in since the Wall came down is the health of people from Southeast Asia. Hundreds of people who were guest workers in the East have moved over here, and brought their wives and parents from Vietnam to join them. Among the older people especially, there is a problem with tuberculosis—it's on the rise again, internationally, as you may know. My dream is to have a kind of hostel where people could eat well and rest while their lungs recover. No rosters, Libby, I promise. They would run their own affairs. There's nowhere suitable at present. Hospitals can't afford long-term care, and the refugee quarters are hardly a stress-free environment.'

'So what are the good citizens of Dahlem going to think about a household of consumptive old Vietnamese in their nice street?'

'I don't suppose they'll be thrilled, but they'll find them quiet and unobjectionable. For anyone who's been around for a while, it might be preferable to living next to a commune of bank robbers.'

Libby smiled. 'You've got your heart set on this, haven't you? Have you got any aspirin, Hannelore? Making scenes gives me a headache.'

'Of course.'

'Look, I'll talk to one of the lawyers when no one else is

there, and I'll try and say something helpful, if I can do that without distorting my view of things. I might even be able to stomach Romy again, too, but not with a room full of supporters.'

'Gary's very sweet.'

'Gary may be an angel for all I care, but I've got used to life in Wilga Wilga. Men up there don't go round giving testimonials to their wives' saintliness. It's too much for me.'

'But he is devoted to her. It's an extraordinary experience for him, watching his wife shed her whole identity.'

'Like those babushka dolls from Russia. Unscrew one layer and there's another one inside.'

'If you like. But he'll have the responsibility for Debra while Romy's in jail.'

'How long is she expected to get?'

'If anyone knows, they haven't told me. Isn't it up to the judge?'

'Well, they're trying to do some deal to reward her for turning herself in. It all makes me ill.'

'Libby, none of this is what's eating you. It's Russell, really, isn't it?'

Libby blew her nose, then looked up to meet Hannelore's gaze. 'That bloody studio he had in Wedding—the building belongs to Romy's mother, and half the street it's in. Must be worth a fortune now. But it makes me realise how little I ever understood. He treated me so appallingly, Hannelore. This thing with Gretta was going on all the time—I was just a pawn. Of course it's eating me. What did you expect? I'm not sure I'm the right person to be an envoy to Glasgow.'

'He may feel bad about it himself. Konstanze says he really isn't at all well. You might have a better chance of putting it all behind you if you do go and talk to him.'

'Jeepers creepers. Just let me get rid of this headache first.'

CHAPTER 20

McVicar's Guesthouse was a warren of rooms with undulating floors. Three adjoining Victorian terraces had been linked by a series of passages and staircases to form one snug, architecturally bizarre establishment. Taken to her room by the desk clerk on arrival, Libby took several wrong turnings before retracing her steps to the lobby. She liked the Glasgow streetscapes, the way the roads curved to accommodate the river, the hills provided vantage points, and the spruce and the sleazy stood companionably together. She liked the Glasgow accent, its suggestion of both toughness and tenderness. Orange double-decker buses sped through most of the streets, but a few had been kept as pedestrian malls. The city gave the impression that its residents were proud of it.

The first time she tried Russell's number, there was no answer. When she rang again in the mid-afternoon, a woman answered. 'Oh, aye, Russell's expecting to hear from you. Can I tell him where he can contact you?'

Libby gave her number and asked when Russell was expected.

'Oh, about six as a rule.'

'Fine. Thanks.'

City map in hand, Libby set off for the art gallery in

Kelvingrove Park. Her pocket guide mentioned that the high-ceilinged entrance hall was often used for organ recitals and special exhibitions, but on this occasion it was dotted with blankets and plastic torsos. Two dozen schoolgirls in black watch skirts knelt beside the legless teaching aids while first-aid experts from St John's ambulance brigade demonstrated mouth-to-mouth resuscitation techniques. Libby had always hated the synthetic hair of the mock victims, and the dreadful angle at which their heads were tilted back. She dashed up a staircase and was instantly folded into a group tour. A slightly deaf volunteer was explaining to two American college girls, 'This blank space here belongs to what was always thought to be a Giorgione. It went to Italy as a Giorgione but chances are it will come back as a Titian. It's a calamity. A Titian's nothing to a Giorgione. Giorgione lived to thirty-three and there are only about ten known paintings in existence, while Titian lived to ninety.'

Libby smiled. Will would be amused by that instance of the power of market forces. She reminded herself that amusing Will was no longer supposed to be any business of hers. When she had first left Casuarina she was delighted to be free of the farm routines: dogs and poultry to feed, telephones to answer, books to keep, outdoor chores to help with, cotton chippers to hire and supervise, and trees to prune. Being away from Will was more complicated. During their years together, they had developed a set of shorthand references and family jokes; they had been aware of minor mood changes and at times felt capable of reading each other's minds. Will was heavier than when she'd met him, and his hair was receding a little at the temples, but he remained an extremely attractive man. Before they split up, Libby had never worried greatly over his appeal to other women, but an uncomfortable feeling gnawed at her when she thought of him alone and unattached in Wilga Wilga. But there was no logic in jealousy, when she had been the one to leave.

The elderly volunteer was telling the college girls how the Trojan War started; they seemed fascinated by his monologue, but Libby was wondering when she could escape without being too rude. A middle-aged black couple in denim jackets approached the guide, who asked where they were from. 'Nigeria,' they replied.

'Ah yes, West Africa,' the guide said. 'Plenty of strife in your part of the world. Wars all over the world, mind you.'

'Not in Nigeria,' the couple insisted.

'Not in Nigeria? But I always say, man is a fighting animal. No peace anywhere.'

Raising his voice in the manner of a cartoon Englishman speaking loudly for foreigners, the black man asked, 'Could you tell us something about Mary Queen of Scots please, a bit about her background?'

'No peace at all,' the guide muttered.

Libby also began speaking loudly and articulating one syllable at a time. 'This gentleman was asking about Mary Queen of Scots. *Mary—Queen—of Scots.*'

The guide smiled. 'Aye, there's a picture of her in the next room,' he said, heading towards an archway. Libby seized the chance to slip away down the stairs. Dodging the first-aid trainees, she picked out some postcards in the gallery shop and took them to the counter. As the assistant came towards her, reality somersaulted. The young man was slim with a red beard. Trembling, she paid and went out into the high-domed vestibule again. Of course he wasn't Russell. Russell would be twenty years older by now.

Her momentary sense of recognition was a deluded trip on a time machine, with the rise and fall of Glasgow accents providing psychedelic background music. Suddenly, just in front of her, a schoolgirl tossed a head and torso towards one of her friends. It curved leglessly through the air with synthetic blond hair streaming out beneath it like a macabre shampoo commmercial. Libby, winded, staggered and fell forward, clinging to a stone pillar.

'Are you feeling all right, madam?' The solicitous man in the St Johns ambulance uniform put his arm around her shoulders. 'You look a little pale and unsteady. You might like to sit down with your head between your knees.'

Libby let herself be led to a chair. Obediently she bent forward, her head down at knee level, and breathed in-two-three, out-two-three-four to a pace dictated by the first-aid officer. After a minute or so she felt much better. 'I'm fine, really,' she said, sitting up. A circle of uniformed schoolgirls gathered around to watch, delighted by the unexpected real-life emergency.

'You see what your silliness has done?' the man demanded. 'You start skylarking round and it gives this poor lady a panic attack. How would you like to have a legless monster tossed in front of you like that? I'll thank you all to be more considerate of the people's feelings in the future. In the case of a minor fainting fit, for future reference, you should sit the patient down with her head between her knees until blood-flow and breathing patterns return to normal. Now I want the silly asses who were using the doll as a basketball to go and get this lady a cup of hot tea. Right away, noo! Quick!'

'Thank you,' Libby said. 'You're very kind. But it wasn't really the girls' fault. I'm a bit tense at the moment. It's a reaction to all the Scots accents as much as anything else.'

'Aye, I've heard complaints about Glasgow accents before, but never that they cause fainting fits.'

'It's a long story,' Libby said.

'Aye, love, you just relax. Have you had a panic attack before?'

'Never.'

'Chances are ye'll be fit as a fiddle after a cuppa, but if it happens again, you should get a medical check-up.'

'I'm sure I'll be fine.' A schoolgirl handed her a cup of sweet black tea.

'We're ever so sorry, miss.'

'It's not your fault. Thanks for the tea. I chose a good time and place to faint, anyway. Expert help all around. Thank you.'

The incident left Libby drained but light-headed: she had no energy left for anxiety, and when the telephone rang in her bedroom that night, she was almost calm.

'Libby?'

Russell's voice was not as she remembered it.

'Russell?'

'Aye. What is this cloak and dagger stuff? Hannelore says you've got a message for me.'

'I do. You might ask how I am.'

'How are you, Libby?'

'I'm okay, Russell. How are you?'

'Not the best, lass. Now, when did you want to meet?'

'You're very curt.'

'Just brief. How about tomorrow afternoon?'

'Fine.'

'Right then. Let's say two thirty. I'll tell you where to come. You know the People's Palace?'

'No. I only just got here.'

'Well, it's not difficult. It's a big red brick Victorian structure in Glasgow Green: that's a park about half a mile west of George's Square. You go through the arch at the front, past the museum entrances, and the winter garden is out the back. There's a kind of cafeteria. You'll find it. I'll be expecting you.'

'You sound different, Russell.'

'We are different, Libby. You're coming alone, aren't you? This isn't a set-up?'

'What do you take me for?'

'Just checking. Still got that shoulder-length hair?'

'Yes.'

233

'Aye, well, it won't be hard to recognise you. Half past two then.'

'See you then. Bye.'

It was true. The People's Palace was easy to find. Libby took the 18A bus and arrived early after a short walk from the bus stop. It was only just after two fifteen, so she filled in time by looking at an exhibit of the city's history, reading of the eighteenth-century tobacco and cotton lords and their trade with Virginia, and the dips in their fortunes caused by the American Revolution and the civil war. She liked the the way the mercantile buildings were designed, with an arch for horse and carriage in the front, an interior courtyard surrounded by warehouse space, and upper floors devoted to commerce and living quarters.

Half past two. She went through a sealed door into the winter garden, and found herself in a warmer climate, almost a hothouse. In the foreground, row upon row of small cactus plants were laid out for a horticultural contest; in the background there were tropical palms and the squawks of parrots. She went to the counter of the cafeteria section, ordered a coffee and looked around. Not far away, a silver-haired man in a wheelchair was bending low to pick up a piece of cake with his mouth. She glanced away instinctively, remembering childhood injunctions not to stare at the disabled.

She took the coffee to a cast-iron table and looked around. Russell should have told her what he'd be wearing, or arranged to carry a copy of the *Times* and a furled umbrella or something. However, there were not many people about, and she would have a good view from here of anyone who came through the heavy door. It was a fine space; a pity that prickly cactus had pride of place this week. Orchids would have been more exciting.

The sense that she was being stared at made her swivel once more towards the man in the wheelchair. Slowly chewing the remains of his cake, he was looking fixedly towards her, his eyes steady as his jaws moved up and down. A blush spread up over her neck and both ears tingled as she finally met the man's eyes. Thick tortoiseshell spectacles with thick lenses did not obscure the brown eyes. Russell's eyes. Libby got to her feet, determined not to make a spectacle of herself as she had the day before. 'Russell!' she said with a slightly cracked note of bonhomie as she made her way to his table, her coffee cup clinking in its saucer. 'I didn't realise it was you.'

'Well, Libby.' He was enjoying her discomfort. His Adam's apple bulged as he swallowed the last fragment. 'A bit of a surprise, eh?'

She sat down, placing her hand briefly on his slightly contorted one. 'Yes,' she admitted. 'But Hannelore said you hadn't been well. What's the matter with you?'

'Always direct. Just as I remember. It's MS. Multiple sclerosis. Bugger of a thing. Progressive.'

'When did it start?'

'In jail, as luck would have it. I was in jail in Morocco. Not to be recommended, I assure you. Locked up in a stone cell with twenty other men, most of them speaking Arabic and all of them moody and territorial. Privacy didn't exist; hygiene was primitive. Food was the kind of stuff that keeps you alive, that's all. I got early symptoms there, muscle weakness, pins and needles, the occasional spasm in a muscle. The guards took a long time to believe it wasn't just malingering. I mean, this place was a nightmare. Enough to make anyone go weak in the legs. Exercise was a joke, a few rounds of a little courtyard, jostling against other people. I won't describe the sanitary arrangements. One tap for all our bathing and cooking. We had no visitors, no letters, no faith in the courts. We were jammed in that confined space with each others' stink and moans and groans and no reprieve, day and night.'

'It sounds like hell on earth.'

'Pretty close. I used to remind myself that German prisons

were worse, how they drove the Red Army people to suicide. I'd have gone berserk if I hadn't picked up a knack of thinking myself somewhere else entirely. I used to pick a place—this room was one of them, the studio in Wedding was another—and mentally picture it object by object until I had the sense of actually being there. That was a lifesaver.'

'So what got you in the jail in the first place? And how did you get out?'

'I was in Majorca, living with some people, oh—international crowd, very late seventies. Hippies, you could say. We didn't have a bad scene there, nice climate, good food. But we needed to sustain it with some cash, so—'

'You dashed into the occasional bank with a semi-automatic.'

'Christ, Libby, give me a break. I'm trying to tell you this story.'

'Gretta was with you in Majorca?'

'No, she left me in Tripoli, very early on. Do you want to hear about the jail sentence or not?'

'I guess so, but then you'd better start again with what happened after Berlin.'

'Okay. Well, this was 1978. I'd been in Majorca for years, trading produce in a small way, and making periodic treks over to Africa for hashish to sell in Barcelona.'

'Oh, yes. Was Romy in all this?'

'No. Romy and Akbar took off after Tripoli too. Anyhow, to cut a long story short, I was in Morocco with this English guy in a decrepit truck with a load full of hashish and he panicked and gave the wrong answers at a checkpoint. We were supposed to have given a sweetener to the right local cops, but something went terribly wrong, either because of John's panic or some local doublecross, it was never really clear. The next thing we knew, the truck was impounded, we were in custody, and it was impossible to get decent information about how the local legal system worked or anything.

We were thrown into cells, and we could hear people being interrogated under torture.'

'Jesus.'

'Well, I'll spare you the sordid details. As I say, Germany could have been worse. We were sentenced separately, to five years each, and bugger-all in the way of remissions and parole.'

'But then you got sick.'

'Not immediately. I'd been there nearly eighteen months when the symptoms began.'

'How is it transmitted?'

'Big scientific mystery. They don't know if we nearly all carry the potential for the disease around with us, or what. Anyhow, whatever activates it, it grabbed hold of me. It's a bit suspicious, if you're looking for psychological causes, that it happened when it did, when I had plenty of time to look back on the farce of my years as a self-styled revolutionary. I'd ended up, stranded politically and every other way, a captive in this hell hole.'

'So they released you when you got sick?'

'Not exactly. I had an appeal pending—I had to bribe fellow prisoners to help me write my case in French—and when they finally had a doctor diagnose what all my symptoms meant, they moved the case up the list somehow.'

'And you came back to Scotland under your own name?'

'Let's just say that I came back to Scotland, then I assumed my own name again.'

'Romy's been going round as Lisa Lucero for fifteen years. In Albuquerque!'

'So tell me what's going on with her. Hannelore has only trusted me with hints.'

'No, you tell me what happened to you after you stole my passport.'

'I did regret that, Lib. It seemed necessary at the time. I suppose it caused a few problems?'

'Christ, Russell, you couldn't begin to guess the problems it caused. But get on with your story.'

'Okay. We went into the bank because Gretta and the rest of us wanted some cash to take to Tripoli. We'd heard that Gaddafi was interested in sponsoring anarchists and urban guerillas in capitalist countries.'

'Terrorists.'

'That's not my term. Anyway, we didn't have a track record for that sort of thing, we were just a kind of bourgeois discussion group when you get right down to it. So we got the idea of establishing our credibility through a successful bank robbery, going to Tripoli for more guerilla training, and going back to Europe to destabilise the militaristic establishment.'

'Modest, weren't you?'

'Okay, it was naive. And when Bahman started spraying bullets around out of pure bravado or loss of nerve, we were goners. We left without a cent, not knowing if the guy he wounded was dead or alive, or how much the security cameras had picked up.'

'Gretta wasn't with you?'

'No. We met her in East Berlin that night. She was pretty pissed off that the big robbery we'd planned had been such a flop, but we all had false papers and just enough money for tickets to Beirut. Eventually, through various connections, we made it to Tripoli, but we never got to square one with the Colonel. Never met him. We were more of a laughing stock than credible potential agents.'

'Surprise, surprise.'

'So Gretta wired whoever her superiors were—she was always more a puppet than I'd realised—and took off back to East Germany, just dumping me. Romy and Akbar decided to head for Paris, where various Iranian dissidents had a kind of government-in-exile. I bummed around North Africa for a while, taught English in Morocco, got stoned too often. You know the sort of thing. Then I got in with this crowd with John and his friends and went to live on a kind of rural commune in Majorca. We'd been back to Africa without any problems half a dozen times before the time we were pinched.'

'And after that, the loving arms of Thatcher's Britain.'

'Don't smile when you say that name. It's blasphemy in this town. But yes, the health service hasn't been totally dismantled yet, so I'm better off here than I would be most places. You can be sure the German police wouldn't get much joy out of charging me with the 1970 fiasco if it meant taking on my medical bills while I did time. So I've been left alone, not because Interpol doesn't know about me, but because nobody cares much any more.'

'Hannelore and Romy do. It's all high drama still in Berlin.'

'Dear Hannelore! How is she?'

'Much the same. Busy. Successful in her work. Somewhat bitter about the price she's paid for being considered a sympathiser. You know, legal barriers to public sector jobs, and all that. She's stayed in Berlin, concentrating on old people's health problems. She has a scheme to turn Breisacherstraβe into a sanitorium for tubercular Vietnamese.'

Russell laughed. 'You're kidding.'

'You know Hannelore. She's not one for jokes. It's perfectly true, Romy intends to turn the building over for charitable purposes before she goes to trial. She's putting in some kind of plea bargain, in the hope of a short sentence. The whole scene is pretty weird. There's an American husband who's always called her Lisa, and a daughter back in New Mexico with his parents.'

'What's she been doing in New Mexico?'

'Running a preschool for poor Hispanics, what else? Santa Lisa of the Rio Grande.'

'You've always been hard on Romy, but she's good with kids. Even in Berlin, she worked in that kindergarten.'

'And you and Hannelore have always stuck up for her. She

makes a really brassy blonde; it's a pity you haven't seen her recently. I just find it a bit too convenient, turning herself in when her mother's close to death, so she can get her hands on the cash, even if she does donate some of it for good works.'

'Her mother owned quite a few buildings in Berlin.'

'Yes, including your bloody studio. No wonder you're grateful to Romy. She subsidised all your little war games.'

'You went there?'

'The political police took me there, yes.'

'So what's Romy want us to do now?'

'Oh, they want new depositions, to the effect that Romy never had so much as a single violent thought, that you were all influenced by the Iranians.'

'That's true, to a point. There was Gretta, too, in my case.'

'I can't bear to hear that woman's name.'

'Libby, I never pretended she didn't exist. You even saw the photographs. You came on to me all lit up like the Queen Mary. What was I supposed to do? It doesn't mean I didn't care at all for you.'

'You treated me like the complete patsy, and then expected me to provide an alibi. It didn't stand up ten minutes, because you'd all been such amateur criminals. I was besotted with you, and you treated me like shit.'

'I know. It's pretty embarrassing in retrospect.'

'Embarrassing! It's just about ruined my life, and you talk about embarrassment.'

'What's this? I know nothing about your life. From the look of you I'd say you've had a pretty easy time. Only a line or two on your face, no grey hair, fit as a flea. Unlike me.'

'Russell, I'm devastated about the MS, but that doesn't stop me being angry about the way I was treated.' This time she allowed herself to close her fingers momentarily around his twisted ones.

A waitress in a white apron came to the table. 'Can I bring you anything to eat or drink?'

'No thanks,' they said in unison. From the back of the room came the high-pitched ruckus of tropical birds quarrelling.

'Those are cockatoos,' Libby said. 'We have them at home on the farm, in the hundreds. I can't bear the thought of them being in cages.'

'It's warm enough outside,' Russell said. 'It might be a good idea to go and sit out in the park.'

'If you say so. You'll have to tell me how to push this thing.'

'It's motorised. Just stand by to do a bit of steering in doorways.'

The wheelchair jolted down the flagstone steps, with Libby holding it at a tilt from behind. She pushed it towards a wooden seat under a yellowing elm. 'Is there a brake?' she asked.

'Aye. I'll look after that. You just sit down.'

'I gather you're living with someone,' Libby said.

'Yes. Ruth's a joy. I met her when I was making radio programs on self-help for the disabled.'

'You mean she's . . .'

'No—she's not in a wheelchair, if that's what you mean.'

'I apologise for jumping to vulgar conclusions. An old failing.'

'You'll only laugh if I tell you what group she does belong to.'

'Never.'

'All right then. She's into self-help for people with bipolar mood disorders.'

Libby threw her head back and howled with laughter.

'I knew it. You haven't changed a scrap.'

'I suppose life together has its ups and downs?' she asked, dabbing her eyes. 'Smooth sailing as long as you all take your lithium? Sorry, I can't help myself sometimes.'

'Okay, even I can see the ridiculous side, and actually Ruth can too. She's quite a wit. Not as good-looking as you, maybe, but—well, she's just a sweetie.'

'You're happy.'

'In a manner of speaking, aye. We do a lot of political work together. We're both very involved with Scottish nationalism. It's becoming a real force again here.'

'Twenty years ago you'd have found that a really bourgeois thing to be into.'

'Aye, Libby, but we change, all of us.'

'I suppose women materialised to look after you all through the 1970s, too, in Majorca and everywhere?'

'I've been pretty lucky, in that way. But what about you, Libby? I know nothing about your life at all.'

'Me? I'm a rural counsellor in Wilga Wilga.'

'Where in the name of fortune is Wilga Wilga? What's a rural counsellor?'

'A rural counsellor is someone who can weigh up the viability of farms and the value of land and livestock, and who can deal with all the people involved—farmers and their families, and bank managers, mainly.'

'And you like it, obviously.'

'Yes, it's fascinating. Tragic now and then, when a family has to leave the land, but more often very rewarding. People gain confidence; they learn new skills; they communicate better. Too many men have shut their wives out of financial decisions until things are desperate. I have to find ways of helping them to share information.'

'Regular marriage counsellor too, by the sound of it.'

'It feels that way at times, yes.'

'And you're married?'

'In a manner of speaking.'

'Children?'

'Just one. Evan's eighteen. He's at university in Sydney now, quite independent. Actually I've been living on my own too. Will and I had a bit of a falling out.'

'You did? What do people fall out over in far-off Wilga Wilga? Sex? Drugs? Money? Careers?'

'Berlin, actually.'

'Sounds pretty weird.'

Libby sighed. 'Isn't there an expression in Scotland—a lad of parts? A local boy who makes good through talent and hard work? Well, Will is the Wilga Wilga equivalent. His father had a very small sheep farm. Will's taken it over, expanded it, irrigated it, and turned it into a profitable cotton farm. Perhaps I should have mentioned he's good-looking and funny and smart, too. Well, up our way, everyone except me and a few other eccentrics votes for the National Party. Our local member, Denzil McCammon, who's been almost mute in parliament, finally announced that he wouldn't recontest the seat at the 1987 election. The party machine people and the district power brokers started casting around for a successor. Various names started being mentioned, including—'

'Your Will.'

'Yes. Will. And he was terribly flattered. He started looking into whether he could still run the farm if he was off in Canberra for six or seven months a year, and counting up how much support he had in various branches. It didn't look bad, but he wasn't McCammon's first choice because he wasn't a real party insider. And of course there were rival candidates.'

'Inevitably.'

'No doubt. Well, one of them was a man named Gafford Maxwell. He was a bit older than Will, and by his own lights he'd paid his dues in the party longer. Never mind that Will looked better and sounded better and had more to offer, this guy wanted the seat and was prepared to do just about anything to get it. So he looked around for ways to smear Will.'

'I'm beginning to get the drift of this.'

'There weren't any sex scandals because our marriage has

been pretty good. No money scandals, because we've been able to pay our way. But then Maxwell got talking to a friend of his in Brisbane who was an organiser with the party up there, and who used to be a junior diplomat.'

'Not that guy . . . ?'

'Precisely. None other than Sandy Mackenzie, the former attaché in Berlin. I'd been pretty tactless in the way I'd treated him, and there's no question all the Breisacherstraße mess was a diplomatic headache. He knew I'd taken no part in the robbery, but he also knew that my old associations could be used to damage Will. In small towns, you don't realise how many enemies you have until something like this gathers momentum. People came out of the woodwork with claims that I wore Labor Party badges in the classroom, though I never did, and that Will would only be a stooge for the Labor Party, because he would enter parliament as a National Party member but take his orders from me. And to cap it all, of course, they got hold of this story that I was a member of the Baader–Meinhof gang, a terrorist, a wild woman out to destabilise democracy, no less.'

'Jesus, Libby. But he didn't believe it?'

'No, he didn't. But he spent more time listening to it and asking me about it than I could forgive. And of course it was no help that I couldn't go to preselection meetings looking like a dewy-eyed conservative who'd been home baking pumpkin scones for years. So Maxwell went into parliament, but by a much smaller majority than you'd have expected in a safe seat. There are a lot of small splinter parties and strange one-issue movements around just now. There was a very strong anti-uranium group; there were Greens; there were all sorts of conservative groups. Well, being in rural counselling, I'd seen the inside stories of a lot of rural heartache. The federal government's aid schemes were some help, but not all that much. The Labor Party doesn't get many votes from farmers, and it's never done much for them. Anyway, things seemed to settle down. I imagined that Will had got over his disappointment at not getting preselection. I was furious with bloody Sandy Mackenzie, who was always a little turd, but I got over it too, more or less. I realised I was still bloody unhappy about you and Romy and Akbar and Bahman for getting us into such an ambiguous situation in the first place. I'd never properly come to terms with all that confusion and anger. Still haven't, I realised when I met Romy the other day. But things seemed to be all right between Will and me. We both ignored the extent to which we'd buried a lot of anger.'

'And it all blew up again?'

'Yes. Round Christmas, one of the minor parties approached Will. He went to some of their meetings. There were a lot of disillusioned farmers who wanted a new sort of representation, outside the existing parties and farmers' federations. Called themselves the Rural Renaissance. They had an RR symbol, a bit like Rolls Royce. Anyway, Will was one of the brighter people they attracted. They asked him if he'd stand for the election in March this year.'

'And your Berlin days became an issue again.'

'Not exactly. It didn't get to that point. I did a bit of research on Rural Renaissance. There was a kind of whiff about them that made me suspicious. Then I read some of their newsletters. They were full of rhetoric about United Nations conspiracies to undermine the family, and socialist agendas in schools. That was enough for me. I did a bit more digging, and discovered a link to one of the most notoriously racist conservative organisations in Australia.'

'So Will changed his mind?'

'That's just the trouble. He couldn't see it. These were country people, they talked his language, they seemed perfectly decent to him. We had some unbelievable quarrels. I said if he stood I wouldn't appear at a single election event with him. I went further than that. I said I'd issue press statements denouncing Rural Renaissance as a neo-fascist front.'

'And you did?'

'No. I got sick of all the quarrels and misunderstandings, and it occurred to me that I could ruin his chances very simply just by leaving. You know how the ideal candidate has a smiling wife, 2.3 children and a border collie. He'd be left without any of that. The gossip is phenomenal in country towns. Nowhere more global than a village, as one of our poets paraphrased McLuhan.'

'So you left?'

'Yes. I rented a place in town, and it had pretty much the result I expected. Will gave up any thought of being a Rural Renaissance candidate.'

'He was bitter?'

'Not exactly. More like a cold rage. I kept wanting him to snap out of it and admit I was right.'

'And he hasn't?'

'No. It's been months now. I'm sure if he wanted to, he could get hold of enough evidence that Rural Renaissance is a front for the rabid right, but he just doesn't want to see it. It's incredible how obtuse he's been.'

'So the marriage is over?'

'I don't know. Maybe it can be salvaged, if we take the time to listen to each other and sort out some of the misunder-standings and hurts. God knows there's a financial incentive for a reconciliation; after all the years I worked I'd be entitled to a hefty share of the acreage. So I guess it's a question of which of us is prepared to swallow our pride and suggest it.'

'It's not something that comes naturally to you, swallowing your pride.'

'No. And not to him either.'

'You sound well-matched.'

'I always thought so.'

'You might have to do it, Libby.'

'Swallow my pride?'

'Sounds like it. Libby, I'm expecting Ruth to come by with the van in a few minutes. Do you think we could make our way over towards the road?'

'Sure.'

'But there's something I want to give you first. Fish around in that pack on the back of the chair, you should find a manila envelope with your name on it.'

Libby located the unsealed stiff envelope. Slowly she extracted a black and white photograph from the cardboard covering.

A young woman with wavy light hair spilling over her shoulders stood on the steps of the Dahlem Museum. Her face was lowered as she murmured to the baby in her arms. The photograph captured an intimate smile meant only for Kirkland junior.

'How could I involve you in a bank robbery, or even tell you about one in advance, when I'd seen you like that?' Russell asked. 'Obviously you belonged somewhere else, way beyond Berlin. Babies, cockatoos—another world!'

'I can keep this?'

'Aye, I said so.'

Libby put the picture back in the envelope and slipped it in the front compartment of her carryall. She brushed at her eyelashes and blinked. Russell released the brake and they began their progress towards the road, imprinting the carpet of yellow leaves with two narrow lines of tyre marks.

CHAPTER 21

On the flight back to Berlin Libby flipped through the magazine rack and discovered a familiar face on the cover of *Stern*. 'The repentant terrorist', Romy was called. In the cover photograph she was a brunette again; a small inset picture showed her as the blonde Lisa Lucero. The story included pictures of Gary, Romy and Debra in the garden of their small adobe cottage in Albuquerque, Romy/Lisa reading stories to a group of Hispanic children, and a fuzzy 1970 black and white shot of Bahman, who was portrayed as the mastermind of the robbery at the London-Berlin Trading Bank.

Libby did not know the current mood of Germans well enough to judge whether or not Romy's story would be found forgivable. Gary was quoted with a formula about forgiveness which Libby considered sentimental New Age claptrap. Hannelore made a plea for understanding based on Romy's emotional turmoil on discovering her father's part in wartime killings of Russian villagers. The magazine article speculated that Romy would go to jail for about a year, or as little as six months with remissions. If the security officer had died, she could have faced a life sentence. Fortunately for Romy, he had survived. Bernd Riegel was pictured in retirement in Essen, sitting in his garden in a pose not unlike the one the Lucero family had adopted.

At the end of the article came a section entitled 'Where are they now?' Most of the Baader–Meinhof gang were dead: Ulrike Meinhof had suicided in May 1976; her colleagues had killed themselves in prison after the failure of the terrorist hijack in Mogadishu in 1977. Some radicals from the early 1970s were still in prison; a handful were in other countries, Cuba and eastern Europe. A number of prominent left-wingers who had not taken part in violent activities had survived the reprisals against sympathisers and made careers for themselves as writers, lawyers and teachers.

This time Libby was not to stay with Hannelore in Schlactensee. 'I hope you won't mind, Libby,' Hannelore apologised, 'but my lover, Dr Kim Duoc Ng, will be staying, and it might be easiest if you stayed in a hotel.' Libby said that she did not mind in the least. With the school year beginning in America, beds were again available in the crowded city. She booked into an old hotel with high ceilings and turn-of-the century decor: the bedspreads and pillowslips were hand-embroidered with white flowers. Inviting as the bed looked, there was something she had to do before she could sleep. She lifted the handset of the old black telephone. 'I want to make an international call please, collect.'

Will sounded half-asleep. 'Christ, Libby, it's four in the morning.'

'What kind of a greeting is that?'

'I can think of one or two people who'd call at this hour, and one or two who'd call collect, but you're the only one who's capable of the double.'

'Sorry. Was I forgetting summertime or something?'

'Or something. You're okay?'

'Yes, fine. You?'

'Can't complain.'

Libby could hear the conversation sliding into grazier-speak. She took a breath.

'Look, Will, I was wondering if you'd like to come over here?'

'Just like that? Just pack my bags for Europe?'

'For Berlin, yes. It's exhilarating here at the moment, really it is, with the cold war over. There's a kind of perpetual street party going on.'

'What's all that got to do with me? It's your scene, Europe.'

'It's funny about Europe, Will. All my life I've been searching for some kind of depth that I've thought of as European. History, you might say, but it's not so simple. In Glasgow I was raving on to someone when I heard these squawking birds in the background. Cockatoos. Don't ask me how they got there, but they did. Just like the ones at Casuarina. They've got a really Australian accent, you know, cockatoos? Sort of raucous and unfinished.'

'So you rang me up about cockatoos.'

'No. Look, I really am sorry I woke you. I rang because we do need to talk to each other, and it occurred to me we could talk to each other better away from all the district gossips. If you're ever going to understand about my time in Berlin, this might be your only chance to meet some of the people I knew here.'

'Libby, about Rural Renaissance. I've been talking to some people from the Liberal Party. It looks as if you could have been right about the links between Rural Renaissance and some right-wing mob in Melbourne.'

'As I told you a dozen times.'

'Well, don't rub it in, Lib. I just couldn't see it at the time. Give me a chance. They got a lot of things right, or it seemed to me at the time that they did. How was I to know the whole story?'

'Precisely what I could ask about the whole Breisacherstraße affair.'

'There could be parallels, Libby, I guess. I wonder whether I could get a discount on the ticket.'

'You'll never know if you don't ring the travel agent's. Will, it would be terrific to see you, it really would. I miss you terribly.'

'Yeah, well, I miss you too, I guess. Now and then.'

'That's what I love about cotton farmers. They're so eloquent.'

Hannelore and Libby picked their way through the hordes of young tourists from every country on earth who were crammed into the Zoo station. They were sitting around talking, lying on groundsheets, and standing in slow-moving queues. The two women made their way to the S-Bahn. With no inspection of documents at the former checkpoint, they were soon strolling from the Alexanderplatz station towards the city square and Unter den Linden. On the sidewalks people were selling electrical goods from the eastern bloc, Russian military hats, and wrapped sweets. Begonias were blooming in neat rows in concrete trays, their petals an anachronistic bright red.

As they neared the Brandenburg Gate it seemed that a huge folk carnival was in progress. A few bulwarks of the Wall still stood, chipped by pickaxe blows and covered with graffiti, a jumble of obscenities, initials and dates. Bratwurst grilling on braziers and a multitude of ice-creams gave the air a scent in which vanilla mingled with barbecue sauce.

'Do you want a souvenir? Genuine bit of the Wall?' Hannelore asked.

Fragments of cement had been fashioned into novelty pins and hair clips; larger chunks were going for higher prices.

'I don't think so. Will might want one—but he'll just have to buy one himself, in that case.'

'When does he get here?'

'Thursday.'

'And he'll stay at your hotel?'

'Yes, of course.'

Libby looked around the makeshift marketplace which now surrounded the Brandenburg Gate, once a forlorn landmark beside the tank traps and concrete. The gate itself was obscured by scaffolding; notices announced that it was being restored in readiness for Germany's reunification celebrations. Brass medals and badges glittered on table after table of Russian hats, the symbols of an armed border now just another item of commerce. Old women in shabby skirts that could only have been made in the east, Scandinavian students with backpacks and peeling noses, lovers, vendors, tourists, and Berliners swirled around in a dance that was no less celebratory for lacking a choreographer.

'Berlin seems at peace with itself at last,' Hannelore said. 'If it were not for the occasional swastika with a sign saying "Foreigners out, Germany for the Germans", I'd be really optimistic about our future.'

'I can't resist those ice-creams,' Libby said. 'Will you have one?'

'No, but you go ahead.'

They sat down, making a bench of a horizontal tree root, as Libby did her best to lick up the soft ice before it melted down the sides of the cone.

Wordlessly, a small gypsy girl, perhaps four years old, came up beside her and made imploring gestures, miming licks with her tongue. Libby handed over the half-eaten cone. The child glanced around to make sure that she was unobserved by her brothers and sisters, then plopped down behind a rack of second-hand Russian greatcoats.

Libby and Hannelore walked on towards the green spaces of the Tiergarten. Behind them, the gypsy child polished off the ice-cream at top speed.